PENGUIN CLASSICS

THE SHOOTING PARTY

ANTON PAVLOVICH CHEKHOV, the son of a former serf, was born in 1860 in Taganrog, a port on the Sea of Azov. He received a classical education at the Taganrog Gymnasium, then in 1879 he went to Moscow, where he entered the medical faculty of the university, graduating in 1884. During his university years he supported his family by contributing humorous stories and sketches to magazines. He published his first volume of stories, *Motley Stories*, in 1886 and a year later his second volume, *In the Twilight*, for which he was awarded the Pushkin Prize. His most famous stories were written after his return from the convict island of Sakhalin, which he visited in 1890. For five years he lived on his small country estate near Moscow, but when his health began to fail he moved to the Crimea. After 1900, the rest of his life was spent at Yalta, where he met Tolstoy and Gorky. He wrote very few stories during the last years of his life, devoting most of his time to a thorough revision of his stories, of which the first comprehensive edition was published in 1899–1901, and to the writing of his great plays. In 1901 Chekhov married Olga Knipper, an actress of the Moscow Art Theatre. He died of consumption in 1904.

RONALD WILKS studied Russian language and literature at Trinity College, Cambridge, after training as a Naval interpreter, and later Russian literature at London University, where he received his Ph.D. in 1972. Among his translations for Penguin Classics are *My Childhood, My Apprenticeship* and *My Universities* by Gorky, *Diary of a Madman* by Gogol, filmed for Irish Television, *The Golovlyov Family* by Saltykov-Shchedrin, *How Much Land Does a Man Need?* by Tolstoy, *Tales of Belkin and Other Prose Writings* by Pushkin, and six other volumes of stories by Chekhov: *The Party and Other Stories, The Kiss and Other Stories, The Fiancée and Other Stories*, *The Duel and Other Stories*, *The Steppe and Other Stories* and *Ward No. 6 and Other Stories*. He has also translated *The Little Demon* by Sologub for Penguin.

JOHN SUTHERLAND has edited Wilkie Collins's *Armadale*, William Thackeray's *The History of Henry Esmond* and Anthony Trollope's *The Eustace Diamonds*, *Phineas Finn* and *Rachel Ray* for Penguin Classics. He is now Lord Northcliffe Professor of Modern English at University College London. His other publications include *The Longman Companion to English Literature*, *Mrs Humphry Ward* and *Is Heathcliff a Murderer?*, a collection of puzzle-pieces on Victorian fiction.

ANTON CHEKHOV

The Shooting Party

Translated with Notes by RONALD WILKS
With an Introduction by JOHN SUTHERLAND

PENGUIN BOOKS

PENGUIN BOOKS

Published by the Penguin Group
Penguin Books Ltd, 80 Strand, London WC2R 0RL, England
Penguin Group (USA) Inc., 375 Hudson Street, New York, New York 10014, USA
Penguin Books Australia Ltd, 250 Camberwell Road, Camberwell, Victoria 3124, Australia
Penguin Books Canada Ltd, 10 Alcorn Avenue, Toronto, Ontario, Canada M4V 3B2
Penguin Books India (P) Ltd, 11, Community Centre, Panchsheel Park, New Delhi – 110 017, India
Penguin Group (NZ), cnr Airborne and Rosedale Roads, Albany, Auckland 1310, New Zealand
Penguin Books (South Africa) (Pty) Ltd, 24 Sturdee Avenue, Rosebank 2196, South Africa

Penguin Books Ltd, Registered Offices: 80 Strand, London WC2R 0RL, England

www.penguin.com

First published 2004
3

Set in 10.25/12.25 pt PostScript Adobe Sabon
Typeset by Rowland Phototypesetting Ltd, Bury St Edmunds, Suffolk
Printed in England by Clays Ltd, St Ives plc

Contents

Chronology

1836 Gogol's *The Government Inspector*

1852 Turgenev's *Sketches from a Hunter's Album*

1860 Dostoyevsky's *Notes From the House of the Dead* (1860–61)
Anton Pavlovich Chekhov born on 17 January at Taganrog, a port on the Sea of Azov, the third son of Pavel Yegorovich Chekhov, a grocer, and Yevgeniya Yakovlevna, née Morozova

1861 Emancipation of the serfs by Alexander II. Formation of revolutionary Land and Liberty Movement

1862 Turgenev's *Fathers and Sons*

1863–4 Polish revolt. Commencement of intensive industrialization; spread of the railways; banks established; factories built. Elective District Councils (*zemstvos*) set up; judicial reform
Tolstoy's *The Cossacks* (1863)

1865 *Lady Macbeth of Mtsensk* (1864) by Leskov, a writer much admired by Chekhov

1866 Attempted assassination of Alexander II by Karakozov
Dostoyevsky's *Crime and Punishment*

1867 Emile Zola's *Thérèse Raquin*

1868 Dostoyevsky's *The Idiot*
Chekhov begins to attend Taganrog Gymnasium after wasted year at a Greek school

1869 Tolstoy's *War and Peace*

1870 Municipal government reform

1870–71 Franco-Prussian War

1873 Tolstoy's *Anna Karenina* (1873–7)
Chekhov sees local productions of *Hamlet* and Gogol's *The Government Inspector*

1875 Chekhov writes and produces humorous magazine for his brothers in Moscow, *The Stammerer*, containing sketches of life in Taganrog

1876 Chekhov's father declared bankrupt and flees to Moscow, followed by family except Chekhov, who is left in Taganrog to complete schooling. Reads Buckle, Hugo and Schopenhauer

1877–8 War with Turkey

1877 Chekhov's first visit to Moscow; his family living in great hardship

1878 Chekhov writes dramatic juvenilia: full-length drama *Fatherlessness* (MS destroyed), comedy *Diamond Cut Diamond* and vaudeville *Why Hens Cluck* (none published)

1879 Dostoyevsky's *The Brothers Karamazov* (1879–80)
Tolstoy's *Confession* (1879–82)
Chekhov matriculates from Gymnasium with good grades. Wins scholarship to Moscow University to study medicine
Makes regular contributions to humorous magazine *Alarm Clock*

1880 General Loris-Melikov organizes struggle against terrorism
Guy de Maupassant's *Boule de Suif*
Chekhov introduced by artist brother Nikolay to landscape painter Levitan with whom has lifelong friendship
First short story, 'A Letter from the Don Landowner Vladimirovich N to His Learned Neighbour', published in humorous magazine *Dragonfly*. More stories published in *Dragonfly* under pseudonyms, chiefly Antosha Chekhonte

1881 Assassination of Alexander II; reactionary, stifling regime of Alexander III begins
Sarah Bernhardt visits Moscow (Chekhov calls her acting 'superficial')
Chekhov continues to write very large numbers of humorous sketches for weekly magazines (until 1883). Becomes regular contributor to Nikolay Leykin's *Fragments*, a St Petersburg weekly humorous magazine. Writes (1881–2) play now usually known as *Platonov* (discovered 1923), rejected by Maly Theatre; tries to destroy manuscript

1882 Student riots at St Petersburg and Kazan universities. More discrimination against Jews

Chekhov is able to support the family with scholarship money and earnings from contributions to humorous weeklies

1883 Tolstoy's *What I Believe*

Chekhov gains practical experience at Chikino Rural Hospital

1884 Henrik Ibsen's *The Wild Duck*. J.-K. Huysmans' *À Rebours*

Chekhov graduates and becomes practising physician at Chikino. First signs of his tuberculosis in December

Six stories about the theatre published as *Fairy-Tales of Melpomene*. His crime novel, *The Shooting Party*, serialized in *News of the Day*

1885–6 Tolstoy's *The Death of Ivan Ilyich* (1886)

On first visit to St Petersburg, Chekhov begins friendship with very influential Aleksey Suvorin (1834–1912), editor of the highly regarded daily newspaper *New Times*. Chekhov has love affairs with Dunya Efros and Natalya Golden (later his sister-in-law). His TB is now unmistakable

Publishes more than 100 short stories. 'The Requiem' is the first story to appear under own name and his first in *New Times* (February 1886). First collection, *Motley Stories*

1887 Five students hanged for attempted assassination of Tsar; one is Lenin's brother

Tolstoy's drama *Power of Darkness* (first performed in Paris), for which he was called nihilist and blasphemer by Alexander III

Chekhov elected member of Literary Fund. Makes trip to Taganrog and Don steppes

Second book of collected short stories *In the Twilight*. *Ivanov* produced – a disaster

1888 Chekhov meets Stanislavsky. Attends many performances at Maly and Korsh theatres and becomes widely acquainted with actors, stage managers, etc. Meets Tchaikovsky

Completes 'The Steppe', which marks his 'entry' into serious literature. Wins Pushkin Prize for 'the best literary production distinguished by high artistic value' for *In the Twilight*, presented by literary division of Academy of Sciences. His one-act farces *The Bear* (highly praised by Tolstoy) and *The Proposal* extremely successful. Begins work on *The Wood Demon* (later *Uncle Vanya*). Radically revises *Ivanov* for St Petersburg performance

1889 Tolstoy's *The Kreutzer Sonata* (at first highly praised by Chekhov)

Chekhov meets Lidiya Avilova, who later claims love affair with him. Tolstoy begins to take an interest in Chekhov, who is elected to Society of Lovers of Russian Literature

'A Dreary Story'. *The Wood Demon* a resounding failure

1890 World weary, Chekhov travels across Siberia by carriage and river boat to Sakhalin to investigate conditions at the penal colony (recorded in *The Island of Sakhalin*). After seven months returns to Moscow (via Hong Kong, Singapore and Ceylon (Sri Lanka))

Collection *Gloomy People* (dedicated to Tchaikovsky). Only two stories published – 'Gusev' and 'Thieves'. Immense amount of preparatory reading for *The Island of Sakhalin*

1891 Severe famine in Volga basin (Chekhov organizes relief)

Chekhov undertakes six-week tour of Western Europe with Suvorin. Intense affair with Lika Mizinova

Works on *The Island of Sakhalin*. 'The Duel' published serially. Works on 'The Grasshopper'

1892 Chekhov buys small estate at Melikhovo, near Moscow; parents and sister live there with him. Gives free medical aid to peasants. Re-reads Turgenev; regards him as inferior to Tolstoy and very critical of his heroines

'Ward No. 6' and 'An Anonymous Story'

1893 *The Island of Sakhalin* completed and published serially

1894 Death of Alexander III; accession of Nicholas II; 1,000 trampled to death at Khodynka Field during coronation celebrations. Strikes in St Petersburg

Chekhov makes another trip to Western Europe

'The Student', 'Teacher of Literature', 'At a Country House' and 'The Black Monk'

1895 'Three Years'. Writes 'Ariadna', 'Murder' and 'Anna Round the Neck'. First draft of *The Seagull*

1896 Chekhov agitates personally for projects in rural education and transport; helps in building of village school at Talezh; makes large donation of books to Taganrog Public Library

'My Life' published in instalments. *The Seagull* meets with hostile reception at Aleksandrinsky Theatre

1897 Chekhov works for national census; builds second rural school. Crisis in health with lung haemorrhage; convalesces in Nice

'Peasants' is strongly attacked by reactionary critics and mutilated by censors. Publishes *Uncle Vanya*, but refuses to allow performance (until 1899)

1898 Formation of Social Democrat Party. Dreyfus affair

Stanislavsky founds Moscow Art Theatre with Nemirovich-Danchenko

Chekhov very indignant over Dreyfus affair and supports Zola; conflict with anti-Semitic Suvorin over this. His father dies. Travels to Yalta, where he buys land. Friendly with Gorky and Bunin (both of whom left interesting memoirs of Chekhov). Attracted to Olga Knipper at Moscow Art Theatre rehearsal of *The Seagull*, but leaves almost immediately for Yalta. Correspondence with Gorky

Trilogy 'Man in a Case', 'Gooseberries' and 'About Love'. 'Ionych'. *The Seagull* has first performance at Moscow Art Theatre and Chekhov is established as a playwright

1899 Widespread student riots

Tolstoy's *Resurrection* serialized

Chekhov has rift with Suvorin over student riots. Olga Knipper visits Melikhovo. He sells Melikhovo in June and moves with mother and sister to Yalta. Awarded Order of St Stanislav for educational work

'Darling', 'New Country Villa' and 'On Official Duty'. Signs highly unfavourable contract with A. F. Marks for complete edition of his works. Taxing and time-consuming work of compiling first two volumes. Moderate success of *Uncle Vanya* at Moscow Art Theatre. Publishes one of finest stories, 'The Lady with the Little Dog'. Completes 'In the Ravine'. Begins serious work on *Three Sisters*; goes to Nice to revise last two acts

1900 Chekhov settles in the house built by him in Yalta. Actors from the Moscow Art Theatre visit Sevastopol and Yalta at his request. Low opinion of Ibsen

Sees *Uncle Vanya* for first time

1901 Formation of Socialist Revolutionary Party. Tolstoy excommunicated by Russian Orthodox Church
Chekhov marries Olga Knipper
Première of *Three Sisters* at Moscow Art Theatre, with Olga Knipper as Masha. Works on 'The Bishop'

1902 Sipyagin, Minister of Interior, assassinated. Gorky excluded from Academy of Sciences by Nicholas II
Gorky's *The Lower Depths* produced at Moscow Art Theatre
Chekhov resigns from Academy of Sciences together with Korolenko in protest at exclusion of Gorky. Awarded Griboyedov Prize by Society of Dramatic Writers and Opera Composers for *Three Sisters*
Completes 'The Bishop'. Begins 'The Bride', his last story. Begins *The Cherry Orchard*

1903 Completion of Trans-Siberian Railway. Massacre of Jews at Kishinev pogrom
Chekhov elected provisional president of Society of Lovers of Russian Literature
Completes 'The Bride' and the first draft of *The Cherry Orchard*. Arrives in Moscow for Art Theatre rehearsal of *The Cherry Orchard*; strong disagreement with Stanislavsky over its interpretation

1904 Assassination of Plehve, Minister of Interior, by Socialist revolutionaries. War with Japan
Chekhov dies of TB on 15 July at Badenweiler in the Black Forest (Germany)
Première of *The Cherry Orchard* at Moscow Art Theatre

Introduction

Say '*The Shooting Party* is a detective story, first published in 1885' and most readers of Penguin Classics will adjust their sets accordingly. The publication date locates Chekhov's novel (his first and only full-length one) plumb in the centre of the genre's cradle – at the point at which a clever plot gimmick, plausibly invented by Edgar Allan Poe, with his *The Murders in the Rue Morgue* (1841), was growing into one of the five big categories of popular fiction (Poe, coincidentally, can take credit for a couple of the others – Gothic/Horror and SF).

Francophiles, however, claim priority in the invention of the *roman policier*, with François-Eugène Vidocq's *Memoirs* (1828), the autobiography of a celebrated chief of the Paris secret police. Vidocq's book laid out the ground rules of the sleuthing genre. A mysterious and sensational crime is committed which must be solved by the skilled interpretation of certain 'clues'. The baffled reader, meanwhile, is challenged to match his or her wits with those of the criminal – or sometimes the author. Of all the literary genres, detective fiction ('mysteries', as they are aptly called) is the most gamesome.

The setting up of organized police forces, with detective bureaux in London (Scotland Yard) and Paris (the Sûreté) in the 1830s was a necessary precondition to the genre's emergence. First came the detective service, then the detective novel. The genre as we know it took a distinctive turn in the English-speaking world with Dickens's Inspector Bucket (based on the Yard's best-known thief-taker, Inspector Field) in *Bleak House* (1852–3). Dickens's favourite protégé, Wilkie Collins, patented what would become central conventions of the genre with his

1860s whodunits, *The Woman in White* (who murdered Laura Glyde, and was she in fact murdered?) and *The Moonstone* (who stole the most precious gem in England? Sergeant Cuff of Scotland Yard will investigate). Then, in the mid 1880s, appeared the writer who would elevate the detective novel to a level of popularity it has never since lost – Arthur Conan Doyle, with his Sherlock Holmes stories.

Like other Russian writers of the period, Chekhov was clearly more alert to French literary influence than English although, as chauvinists will approvingly note, there are numerous allusions to Shakespeare in *The Shooting Party*. The most direct foreign source for the novel would seem to be Emile Gaboriau, whose series hero, Inspector Lecoq, was introduced in *L'Affaire Lerouge* (1865–6), a pioneering story of murder and criminal impersonation super-ingeniously solved. Chekhov refers frequently throughout his novel to Gaboriau (one of Chekhov's hero's nicknames is 'Lecoq').

There is – following Poe – a strong American input into early detective fiction. Many historians of the genre, for example, would see Anna Katherine Green's *The Leavenworth Case* (1878) (with its series hero, Ebenezer Gryce) as one of the great progenitors and also a forecast of the strong presence which women writers will have in the field. In 1886, a few months after the publication of *The Shooting Party*, there appeared *The Mystery of a Hansom Cab* by an obscure young New Zealander named Fergus Hume. It sold a quarter of a million copies in a year (Chekhov should have been envious), widening the appeal for the genre and creating its mass-reader base.

Members of the twenty-first-century reader base have become accustomed to a dash of internationalism in their favourite reading matter (Peter Hoeg, Umberto Eco, Henning Mankell and a mountain of Maigret are all to be found on the shelves of most high-street bookshops), but they should prepare themselves for two surprises in *The Shooting Party*. The first is where the book comes from. The otherwise majestic Russian novel – if we discount *Crime and Punishment* – has never been a strong presence in detective fiction. Even more surprising, perhaps, is the author himself. Chekhov is as internationally renowned as any of his compatriots – but he is known for his drama and his short stories. Neither the achievement represented by *The Cherry Orchard* (1904), nor 'The Lady with the Little Dog' (1899), can prepare us for *The Shooting Party*. This is, of course, an early work (juvenilia almost) dating from a period when Chekhov was 'feeling his way to a method', Thomas Hardy's description of his own early foray into crime fiction.[1] It was published between August 1884 and April 1885, when the author was still in his early twenties. He was also writing for a living: as a newly qualified doctor he had to support his family by writing for pulp magazines. Chekhov's apprenticeship, like that of many writers, was served in the depths of the book world, inhabited by hacks, bloodsucking editors and uncultivated readers. *The Shooting Party* was consciously designed as a feuilleton – or serial – for a low-grade (and spectacularly low-paying) journal.

The detective novel would, as we now know, prove a dead end for Chekhov, but his exploration of it remains fascinating nonetheless. As Chekhov's most recent biographer, Donald Rayfield, observes, '*The Shooting Party* is unjustly ignored'.[2]

It is tempting to suggest a link between the young Chekhov and his exact contemporary, Conan Doyle, who brought out the first of the Sherlock Holmes novels, *A Study in Scarlet*, in 1887. Neither, of course, can have read the other's work (*The Shooting Party* had not yet been published in English), but there are piquant points of contact. Both authors were newly trained doctors. The link between the physician, diagnosing a disease from inscrutable 'symptoms', and the detective, cracking a case by close examination of mysterious 'clues', is a standard observation in the history of the genre. (Whether Chekhov was influenced by a mentor like Doyle's Joseph Bell, the original of Holmes, is not known.)

For most readers of *The Shooting Party* it is not so much the similarities with our familiar classics of the genre than strange dissimilarities which will be most striking. In one of Ray Bradbury's *Martian Chronicles* (1950), Mars is described as being just like earth for its colonizing earthlings except that the sandwiches have an odd tendency to turn blue. Readers steeped in an Anglo-Saxon, American or French tradition of detective fiction will experience the same disconcerting feeling in *The Shooting Party*.

The action of the story is set in a mythic southern Russia countryside in the 1870s. There is a strange, at times allegorical, feel to the landscape – thunderstorms are apocalyptically loud, forests impenetrably dense, the atmosphere unnaturally sultry. There is lively dispute among Chekhovian experts about the tone of the work, as there almost always is with this author. Is it 'Parodic'? 'Sensational'? 'Hyper-realistic'? It opens with the ominous shriek: 'A husband murdered his wife!' It is, we discover, not a bulletin from some crime scene, but the hero's parrot. It is indeed hard to take seriously a narrative which begins with a prophetic parrot call. Is the author pulling our leg? With Chekhov we can never be entirely sure.

The narrative of *The Shooting Party* is elaborately and ironically framed. An unknown writer (with a mysterious badge in his hat) deposits a manuscript with a publisher. The unsolicited package is, the stranger says, the record of a 'true event'. Ivan Petrovich Kamyshev's physiognomy would seem to confirm his bona fides – or does it? As the Editor notes:

> His entire face simply radiated ingenuousness, an expansive, simple character, truth. If it isn't a lie that the face is the mirror of the soul, I could have sworn from the very first day of my meeting with the gentleman with the badge that he was incapable of lying. I might even have laid a bet on it. Whether I would have lost or won, the reader will discover later [p. 4].

'There's no art', as Chekhov's beloved Shakespeare would say, 'to find the mind's construction in the face'. Unless, of course, you are a Holmes, a Lecoq or an Ebenezer Gryce. The editor also has a detective's instincts. Kamyshev claims he is broke, and has written his 'From the Memoirs of an Investigating Magistrate' (also known as *The Shooting Party*) for a quick rouble. But the diamond ring on his finger 'didn't tally at all with having to write for a living'. The game, we apprehend, is afoot.

The Editor puts off reading *The Shooting Party* for a couple of months, until he has some leisure time at his summer villa. It is, he discovers, that most valued thing among connoisseurs of the genre, a 'page-turner'. It costs the Editor a night's sleep, so unputdownable is the story. But, gripping as it is, it is no masterpiece. Chekhov (typically) offers – via the Editor's judicious verdict – his own self-deprecating evaluation of the detective fiction of Anton Pavlovich Chekhov:

> It's really a very ordinary story, containing many longueurs and in places the style is very uneven. The author has a weakness for striking effects and resounding phrases. Obviously he's writing for the very first time, with an inexperienced, untrained hand. For all that, his story makes for easy reading. There's a plot, it makes sense and – most important of all – it's original, with a very distinctive character – it's what one would call *sui generis*. And it does have *some* literary merit [p. 8].

Indeed it does.

The narrative which follows is an autobiographical account – written as a kind of pseudo-journal at the same time as the events it describes – by an investigating magistrate. The Russian legal system at this period resembled that of the French. When a notifiable crime was committed, evidence was first collected and evaluated by an investigating magistrate who combined the role of detective and Director of Prosecution. This functionary had the privilege of having all the evidence made immediately available to him, while it was still warm. He did not have to hunt it down (the police had already done that for him); he did not have to work outside the law – unlike Sherlock Holmes, for example, who can only trespass on the crime scene by permission of the bone-headed Inspector Le Strade (Conan Doyle's little Anglo-Saxon sarcasm against his rival's Inspector Lecoq).

From the point of view of the writer of detective fiction, the investigating magistrate has advantages over some of the traditional types of detective in the Anglo-Saxon literary traditions. Those who spring immediately to mind are the amateur sleuth (Hercule Poirot), the private eye (Philip Marlowe), the spinster detective (Miss Marple), the flatfoot (Inspector Morse) and the defence-lawyer detective (Perry Mason). The nearest equivalent to the investigating magistrate in current bestsellers in the genre would be a chief medical examiner, such as Patricia Cornwell's Kay Scarpetta.

The Shooting Party is arranged around three major narrative events: an orgy, a wedding and a murder. The crime is held off until very late (chapter xx) and – in a brilliantly conceived deception on the reader – seems destined to remain, if not forever unsolved, at least inadequately explained.

As we first encounter him, the hero, investigating magistrate Sergey Petrovich Zinovyev, is wallowing in that state of ennui which afflicts many of Chekhov's characters (most eloquently, the drunken Chebutykin in *Three Sisters*). It is a cosmically dissatisfied condition relished by the great Russian writers – melancholy, morbid, self-hating and yet strangely excited. Sergey describes it with eloquent disgust:

> The man who, under the influence of mental pain or plagued with unbearable suffering, puts a bullet in his brains is called a suicide. But for those who give full rein to their pathetic, spiritually debasing passions during the sacred days of their youth there is no name in the language of man. Bullets are followed by the peace of the grave, ruined youth is followed by years of grief and agonizing memories. Anyone who has profaned his youth will understand my present state of mind. I'm not old yet, I'm not grey, but I'm no longer alive [p. 41]

How, precisely, has the hero 'profaned' his youth – exterminated all possibility of joy in life? We never find out.

Sergey's jurisdiction is a sleepy town, Tenevo, without much for an investigating magistrate to investigate. It is a comfortable berth, but he has no career prospects. It is summer – traditionally the holiday season, the time for relaxed attention to business. But Sergey is still chained to his desk, carrying out his insignificant duties. He is nagged, censoriously, by his servant Polikarp, a liberated serf we apprehend, who is both servile and uppity, in the way of slaves who know that their masters belong to them as much as they to their masters. He won't have any fornication in 'his' house, Polikarp later informs the raffish Sergey; on the other hand he would not complain, one guesses, if his master took a whip to his shoulders.

Sergey is jolted out of his torpor by an unexpected invitation. His extravagantly dissolute friend Count Karneyev has returned from his travels to his country estate. The Count is degenerate – the last in the line of Karneyevs, we deduce. His estate, although still magnificent, is in an irrecoverable state of decay. In describing it, Chekhov forecasts – as he often does – the revolutionary cataclysm to come, forty years on:

> Only the spiritually blind or poor could fail to see on every grey marble slab, in every painting, in every dark corner of the Count's garden, the sweat, tears and calloused hands of the people whose children now sheltered in those miserable little huts in the Count's wretched village [p. 90].

A reckoning, well beyond the time frame of the novel, is anticipated when those children will come of age and rise up against their careless oppressor. We sense it in the distance. 'Bad omens' surround Sergey's ride to the estate. His horse stumbles. He 'detests' his aristocratic friend, he thinks. Why, then, is he going? Boredom, presumably. The Count is found in the company of a mysterious, taciturn Pole, Pshekhotsky, and his elderly, prim estate manager, Pyotr Yegorych Urbenin. The Count's doctors have sternly forbidden him to drink. His liver is wrecked. Another debauch could kill him. He will, of course, follow their instructions, he sighs; but – as he goes on to say – he will do so 'gradually'. Sobriety can wait a little longer.

'Let's have a real orgy' the Count proposes, as blithely as Algernon might say 'another cucumber sandwich, Jack?' in Oscar Wilde's *The Importance of Being Earnest* (1895). Sergey, like the Count, has sworn off drink 'for ages' as he piously says. But he has no apparent difficulty in falling (hurling himself, in fact) off the wagon with the prospect of a real (three-day, that is) orgy before him.

Once the Count has started the ball rolling by broaching the champagne, there is no holding Sergey: 'without further hesitation I filled five glasses and, one after the other, poured their contents down my throat. That was the only way I knew how to drink.' After which Sergey and the Count, who has himself already tossed back five glasses, set to work on the sucking-pig. Then the brandy, then the vodka, then the ten-year-old liqueurs. Then the gipsies, summoned, surreally, from the nearby town by telegram. Then the balalaikas and wild dancing. Then the girls. Sergey enjoys a beautiful gipsy, Tina, first – luxuriously – on an ottoman, then vertiginously on a garden swing. Tina turns somewhat savage when – for his third bout – Sergey transfers his favours to 'a fair-haired girl with a sharp little nose, the eyes of a child and a very slender waist'. But he returns to his dark-haired beauty, we apprehend, for a fourth engagement. Russian orgies are full-blooded things. Blood, in fact, runs as freely as the vodka in drunken brawls and homicidal assaults, mainly against the servant class – who cannot, of course, resist or complain; it has always been thus. The sober-sided Urbenin joins in the general riot. Only the sinister Pole holds aloof. Why? we wonder.

From this point on the narrative is marinaded in booze. All the principal characters descend into what we (but not they, apparently) would see as chronic, self-destructive alcoholism. Among its other many parts, *The Shooting Party* could serve as an abstinence tract. Borne up on a mounting tide of strong liquor, the narrative moves to its strange and homicidal climax.

Sexual passion plays its part, in deadly combination with the vodka. Each of the three principal characters – the Count, the magistrate and the estate manager – becomes infatuated with 'a girl in red' whom they encounter during an excursion in the forest where they also encounter a snake in their path, another grim omen. The girl – Olga (Olenka to her friends, Olya to her lovers) – is part child sprite, part adult coquette; and complete trouble:

> a girl of about nineteen, with beautiful fair hair, kind blue eyes and long curls. She was dressed in a bright red frock, halfway between a child's and a young girl's. Her little legs, as straight as

> needles in their red stockings, reposed in tiny, almost childish shoes [pp. 28–9].

'Chekhov', Janet Malcolm notes, was 'acutely sensitive to the appearance of women.'[3] He was also acutely aware of what attracted men in their appearance. The Count is principally drawn to her 'development' (her breasts, that is), Sergey to her white teeth, Urbenin to her radiant youth.

The hero, the Count and the manager (who alone of the three is prepared to offer marriage) are entranced with this child of the forest – intoxicated, one might say, were that word not reserved for their other main activity in life. Innocent as she is, Olga is sufficiently feminine to play her admirers off against each other. She gives her body to each of them in turn, until the bloody – and enigmatic – climax.

The Shooting Party is a richly melodramatic tale – so much so that it was adapted into *The Summer Storm*, a film directed by Douglas Sirk in 1944. Sirk, the master of full-blown big-screen romance, stressed in his adaptation the passion in the *crime passionel* provoked by the incendiary 'girl in red'. But there is much that does not easily translate. The class structures in the world that Chekhov describes will be, one suspects, inscrutable to the English or American reader. Take, for instance, the cats-cradle of social relationships in the description of the wedding ceremony of Urbenin and Olenka:

> Vain Olenka must have been in her seventh heaven. From the nuptial lectern, right up to the main doors, stretched two rows of female representatives from our local 'flower-garden' [i.e. attractive womanhood]. The lady guests were dressed as they would have been if the Count himself were getting married – one couldn't have wished for more elegant outfits. The majority of these ladies were aristocrats – not one priest's wife, not one shopkeeper's wife. There were ladies to whom Olenka had never before thought that she even had the right to curtsy. Olenka's groom was an estate manager, merely a privileged servant, but that could not have wounded her vanity. He was of the gentry and owned a mortgaged estate in the neighbouring district. His father had been

> district marshal of the nobility and he himself had already been a JP for nine years in his native district. What more could an ambitious daughter of a personal nobleman have wanted? [p. 86].

Let alone a penniless child of a woodcutter.

One thinks of the Inuit, and the forty words they have for snow. Our crude class lexicon (upper, middle, lower) is far too blunt an instrument for the social stratifications and blurred lines of Chekhov's world. It is a cosmos formed by residual feudal fragments, new upwardly mobile elements rapidly acquiring the property and wealth of the neutered aristocrats, and an unregenerate and surly peasantry. One recalls the author's own complicated pedigree: the grandchild of a serf, the son of a failed merchant (and subsequently a failed shopkeeper), a newly qualified – but not yet solvent – professional man, keeping body and soul together by writing for pulp magazines. Where, in the chaotic yet intricate society of the new Russia, was Anton Chekhov? Rising? Falling? Stuck? He could not know, of course, while writing *The Shooting Party*, that he was destined for immortality. To have thought so would have made him seem more vain even than Olenka.

Notoriously, Russian fiction of the late tsarist era was censored by the state. But what will strike those who know the Anglo-American tradition, particularly the prudish nineteenth-century detective novel, is the astonishing sexual frankness of *The Shooting Party*. On his arrival at his estate the first thing the Count ('a depraved animal') does is to ask his factotum, Urbenin, and his odious one-eyed servant Kuzma, 'Are there any . . . nice new girls around'. 'There's all kinds, Your Excellency, for every taste', replies Kuzma. 'Dark ones, fair ones . . . all sorts.' All of them, he adds lubriciously, 'well oiled'. In nine months' time, we apprehend, there will be a new crop of well-provided-for bastards on the estate to go with the no-longer new girls. Serfdom may have been abolished fifteen years prior to the time of the story, but old seigneurial habits die hard.

Equally frank, and equally repulsive in his sexual appetite, is Sergey Petrovich Zinovyev. As best man at Urbenin's marriage to Olenka he seduces the bride, in a convenient grotto, some quarter of an hour after the ceremony, while she is still attired in her virginal white. She had wanted to marry him all along, Olya confesses – not that 'old' man, her newly acquired husband, who is waiting, expectantly, with the other wedding guests, a few yards away. Chekhov's description is breathtakingly explicit:

> 'That's enough, Olya,' I said, taking her hand. 'Now, wipe your little eyes and let's go back. They're waiting for us. Come on, enough of those tears, enough!' I kissed her hand. 'Now, that's enough, little girl! You did something silly and now you must pay for it. It's your own fault . . . Come on, that's enough . . . calm down.'
>
> 'But you do love me, don't you? You're so big, so handsome! You do love me, don't you?'
>
> 'It's time to go, my dear,' I said, noticing to my great horror that I was kissing her forehead, putting my arm around her waist, that she was scorching me with her hot breath, and hanging on my neck.
>
> 'That's enough!' I muttered. 'Enough of this!'
>
> . . .
>
> Five minutes later, when I had carried her out of the grotto in my arms, and wearied by new sensations, had set her down, I spotted Pshekhotsky almost at the entrance. He was standing there maliciously eyeing me and silently applauding [pp. 94–5].

No need to ask what the sarcastic Pole implies by his applause. Happy the bride who loses her maidenhood between the church altar and the wedding bed. It may be worth noting that Chekhov was not temperamentally romantic, or inclined towards conventional ideas about the permanence of love. As Donald Rayfield puts it: 'Zoologists might compare Anton's sexuality with that of the cheetah, which can only mate with a stranger.'[4] But even a cheetah might find the defloration of Olga, in the intervals of her wedding, somewhat perfunctory and irregular.

Judged less as an open window on the last years of tsarist Russia than as an early example of detective fiction, *The Shooting Party* is fiendishly well plotted, so much so that Agatha

Christie is, plausibly, supposed to have drawn on it for one of her first great popular successes. To say more would be to give the game away, but readers of an investigatory persuasion can follow up the clue that the first translation of *The Shooting Party* came out in England in 1926. Enough said.

Another master of the crime novel, Ellery Queen, listed twenty 'classic' sub-varieties of detective fiction. *The Shooting Party* can be classified under five of Queen's categories: the third (the 'Crime Passionel'), the fourth (the 'Perfect Crime'), the sixth (the 'Psychiatric'), the seventh (the 'Deductive') and the eighth (the 'Trick Ending'). One may also note, while in technical mode, how skilfully Chekhov uses the machinery of the writer for serial publication – principally his skilful attention to Wilkie Collins's imperative: 'Make 'em laugh, make 'em cry, make 'em wait.' The observant reader will also note the 'curtain lines' at the end of the chapter instalments, and the tactful résumé at strategic points, reminding the reader of what happened earlier and may, with the original passage of weeks between instalments, have been forgotten.

The Shooting Party is, most will agree, something more than the juvenilia of a writer already showing signs of literary genius. It is an accomplished crime novel in its own right. Like the Editor in the story's framing introduction, few who start reading the work will be tempted to lay it down. Why, then, did Chekhov not reprint *The Shooting Party* during his subsequent years of fame, his failure to do so effectively dooming the work to posthumous neglect? Why, even more curiously, having displayed such precocious skill in the genre, did he not write more detective fiction?

There are no obvious answers. There is a dearth of correspondence surviving from this early period of Chekhov's life and his motives are typically obscure, even to his many biographers. But a couple of reasons plausibly suggest themselves. He did not, as his later development testifies, like novel-length narrative. Indeed, at times *The Shooting Party* seems to want to disassemble itself into independent set-pieces; the above orgy, for example, could stand by itself as an early Chekhov story, as could the narrator's perverse courtship and neglect of

Nadezhda. It is likely too that Chekhov associated *The Shooting Party* with the early low point of his career that he would rather forget. He was paid abysmally for his novel and not always with money (on one bizarre occasion, as A Note on the Text points out, with 'a pair of new trousers'). It was, he may have thought, hack work. His career took a distinctive turn three years later in 1888, when his long short story, 'The Steppe', was published in a literary journal, the *Northern Herald*, rather than a newspaper. He ceased being simply a writer earning a copeck per line and became an author. In his mature years Chekhov had higher aspirations than he had in 1884, and those aspirations drove him away from the formulae and clichés of genre fiction into powerfully elliptical realism. It was detective fiction's loss.

We tend, as the British theatre critic Kenneth Tynan said, 'to make Chekhov in our image just as drastically as the Germans have made *Hamlet* in theirs'.[5] Our Chekhovian cobwebs, Tynan went on to say, having just seen a Moscow Art Theatre performance of *The Cherry Orchard*, must be 'blown away'. There is no better way to begin that hygienic operation on the author's fiction than by reading *The Shooting Party*.

NOTES

1. See Hardy's late-life introduction to his 1871 debut novel, *Desperate Remedies*.
2. Donald Rayfield, *Anton Chekhov: A Life* (New York, 1998), p. 107.
3. Janet Malcolm, *Reading Chekhov: A Critical Journey* (London, 2003), p. 109.
4. Rayfield, p. 8.
5. Kenneth Tynan, *Tynan on Theatre* (London, 1964), p. 267

Further Reading

Callow, Philip, *Chekhov: The Hidden Ground* (London, Constable & Robinson, 1998).

Gilles, Daniel, *Chekhov: Observer Without Illusion* (New York, 1967, Funk & Wagnalls, 1968).

Hagan, John, '"The Shooting Party", Cexov's Early Novel: Its Place in His Development', *Slavic and East European Journal*, 9, (1965), pp. 123–40.

Jackson, Robert L. (ed.), *Reading Chekhov's Text*, Evanston: Ill., Northwestern University Press, 1993).

Karlinsky, Simon, and Heim, Michael H., *Anton Chekhov's Life and Thought: Selected Letters and Commentary* (Evanston: Ill., Northwestern University Press, 1973).

Magarshack, David, *Chekhov: A Life* (London, Faber & Faber, 1952).

Malcolm, Janet, *Reading Chekhov: A Critical Journey* (London, Granta Books, 2003).

Matlaw, Ralph, 'Chekhov and the Novel', in Eekman, Thomas (ed.), *Anton Cechov, 1860–1960: Some Essays* (Leiden, E. J. Brill, 1960).

Nabokov, Vladimir, 'Anton Chekhov', in *Lectures on Russian Literature* (1981, repr. London, 2002).

Pritchett, V. S., *Chekhov: A Spirit Set Free* (London, Hodder & Stoughton, 1988).

Rayfield, Donald, *Anton Chekhov: A Life* (New York, Henry Holt, 1998).

— *Understanding Chekhov: A Critical Study of Chekhov's Prose and Drama* (Bristol Classical Press, 1999).

Troyat, Henri, *Chekhov* (London, Macmillan, 1987).

A Note on the Text

The Shooting Party was published in the popular Moscow daily, *News of the Day*, from August 1884 to April 1885, in thirty-two instalments, under the pen-name Chekhov used at this time – Antosha Chekhonte. By far the longest story Chekhov wrote, this novel has an unusual publishing history, since after its publication he never returned to it and it was never included by him in the Marks complete edition. Strangely, he appears to have thought more highly of the inferior detective novel, *The Safety Match* (1884),[1] included in both *Motley Stories* (1886) and in the complete edition of 1899–1901. Very rarely does he refer to *The Shooting Party* in his letters and in fact there is scant information about the history of its composition and few comments on Chekhov's part.

The Shooting Party was actually completed before its serialization in *News of the Day*, in which Chekhov had begun to publish in 1883. In 1915 S. N. Alekseyev, the editor and publisher of the magazine *The Theatre*, recalled: 'Antosha Chekhonte . . . rather shy, but so charming. Already a writer with a reputation, showing great promise, although he was very often compelled to write for the "cheap press" at a maximum of five copecks a line. A. P. contracted to sell his story *The Shooting Party* "wholesale" to *News of the Day*. A. P. handed over almost the whole of his bulky manuscript, written in a fine, elaborate hand, emphasizing that in the event of cuts by the censors he had sufficient "replacement stock". At that time I was working on the editorial staff of that newspaper and that's where I first met A. P.' (*The Theatre*, 1915, no. 1702). Therefore the novel was not written in instalments, separately for each issue, but basically completed before serialization.

On 27 June 1883 Chekhov wrote to Leykin: 'Received an invitation from *News of the Day*. What kind of paper this is I don't know, but it's a new one. It appears to be authorized by the censors. All I'll have to do is make the typesetters and the censor laugh, but hide from the readers behind the censor's "red crosses".' Payment for *The Shooting Party* was terribly protracted, as Mikhail Chekhov amusingly recalls: 'For his novel *The Shooting Party* . . . my brother Anton should have been paid three roubles a week. I would go to the editorial office and wait for ages until the proprietor came up with some money:

"What are you waiting for?" the editor[2] would finally say.

"For three roubles."

"I don't have them. Perhaps you'd like a theatre ticket – or a pair of new trousers, in which case go to Arontricher the tailor and get yourself some on my account"' (M. P. Chekhov, *Around Chekhov*, M.-L., 1933).

And in an undated letter of 1885 Mikhail wrote to his brother: 'Yesterday I dropped in on Lipskerov. He tried to stall me. I told him that I was about to leave for Voskresensk, that you needed the money and that I'd come back around the 26th. He made a big effort and gave me three roubles.' Chekhov similarly complains in a letter of 15 September 1884 to Leykin, stating that Lipskerov had paid him seven roubles for about four months' work. And later, writing to his brother Aleksandr (22/23 February 1887), Chekhov recalls Mikhail having to chase payment for *The Shooting Party* over several years and being paid in miserly sums, commenting that 'since Lipskerov has been jailed for six months to whom will Misha go now to collect what is owed me?'

In the 1870s and 1880s, detective and adventure novels were immensely popular in Russia, both in translation and by Russian authors. Chekhov followed the trend in his early work, being a great admirer of the French crime novelist Gaboriau,[3] whose detective Lecoq was a forerunner of Sherlock Holmes, and tried his hand at the genre in *The Safety Match* (1884), partly a parody. The market was simply flooded with detective novels and crude novels of adventure, and in the literary section of *News of the Day* the following were published contemporaneously with *The Shooting Party* – their very titles give a good indication of their contents: *The Parricide*, by V. A. Prokhorov[4] *The Black Band*, by Labourier; *Blood for Blood: A Tale from the Criminal Archives*, by A. Chumak; *The Fratricide*, signed Marquis Toujours Partout (A. L. Gillin); *The Woman of Wax: From a Detective's Memoirs* (unsigned) and so on. Chekhov was extremely scathing about this cheap 'boulevard' literature and in the satirical fortnightly sketches, *Fragments of Moscow Life*, that he contributed anonymously to Leykin's *Fragments*, from 1883 to 1885, he writes: 'Our newspapers are divided into two camps: one of them scares the public with "advanced" articles, the other with novels. Terrible things have existed in this world and still exist, beginning with Polyphemus and ending with rural liberals, but such horrors (I'm referring to the novels with which our Muscovite paper devourers such as Evil Spirit and Dominoes[5] of all colours regale our public) have never existed before. Just read them and your flesh will creep. You feel terrified at the thought that there exist such appalling minds out of which these terrible "Parricides" and "Dramas" can crawl. Murders, cannibalism, million-rouble losses, apparitions, false counts, ruined castles, owls, skeletons, sleepwalkers and . . . the devil only knows what you don't find in these hysterical displays of captive, drunken thought![6] With one author, for no earthly reason the hero bashes his father in the face (evidently for dramatic effect), another describes a lake in the suburbs of Moscow, with mosquitoes, albatrosses, frenzied horsemen and tropical heat [interestingly, there are a lake, a frenzied horseman, mosquitoes and tropical heat in *The Shooting Party*]; with another the hero takes hot baths of innocent maidens' blood in the mornings, but later turns over a new leaf and marries a girl without any dowry . . . The plots, characters, logic and syntax are terrible – but most terrible of all is their knowledge of life . . . district police officers swear in French at magistrates, majors discuss the 1868 war, stationmasters make arrests, pickpockets are sent to Siberia, and so on. Psychology takes pride of place – our novelists are experts at it. Their heroes even spit with trembling in their voices and clench their "throbbing" temples. The public's hair stands on end, their stomachs turn, but for all that they devour and they praise . . . they *like* our scribblers! *Suum cuique*.' (*Fragments of Moscow Life*, no. 35, 24 November 1884.)

At this stage in his development, Chekhov appears to be experimenting with longer narrative forms. In his memoirs (*Around Chekhov*) his brother Mikhail writes: 'The big novel *The Shooting Party* was not Anton Chekhov's first. Even earlier, in the *Alarm Clock*, there was printed his novel *An Unnecessary Victory* (1882), which came about entirely by chance. My brother argued with A. D. Kurenin, editor of the *Alarm Clock*, that he could write a novel about foreign life no worse than those appearing abroad and being translated into Russian. Kurenin disputed this. So they decided that my brother Anton would start writing such a novel – Kurenin would reserve the right to stop the printing at any moment. But the novel turned out so interesting that it was completed.' *An Unnecessary Victory* (about eighty pages long) was apparently an imitation of the sensational adventure novels of the Hungarian writer Mor Jokay, whose works were extremely popular in Russia at the time. Chekhov's short novel was so well written that it was taken to be an actual translation from the Hungarian.

NOTES

1. In a letter to Leykin of 19 September 1883 Chekhov writes: '. . . I've become an expert and written the most enormous story . . . it's going to turn out very well . . . its name is *The Safety Match* and is essentially a parody of detective novels . . .' Chekhov's detective Dyukovsky shows exceptional ingenuity in following up clues: here the 'murder victim' is found to be alive and well. In this respect, critics are divided over whether *The Shooting Party* was wholly intended as a parody. Perhaps it may best be called 'part parody'.
2. Abram Yakovlevich Lipskerov (1851–1910), editor of the popular Moscow daily, *News of the Day*, from 1883 to 1894, and *Russian Satirical Leaflet* (1882–4; 1886–9). In his memoirs,

Around Chekhov, Mikhail Chekhov records that *News of the Day* had very humble beginnings in a one-room office in Tversky Street in Moscow. The newspaper prospered (as did Lipskerov), printing cheap novels – and even forecasting winners at the races. Chekhov echoes his brother's remarks in his uninhibitedly satirical *Fragments of Moscow Life*, stating: 'since he [Lipskerov] started publishing his *News of the Day* [elsewhere Chekhov called it *Filth of the Day*] he wears double-soled shoes, drinks tea with sugar and goes to the Gentlemen's Baths'. And in a letter of 8 March 1896 to his brother Aleksandr, Chekhov later writes: 'Lipskerov is no longer a Yid but an English gentleman and lives near the Red Gates in a luxurious palazzo, like a duke. *Tempora mutantur* – and no one supposed such a genius would emerge from a latrine.' (The six months of imprisonment mentioned were imposed because Lipskerov, in a feuilleton in *News of the Day*, accused a choirmaster, N. P. Bystrov, of not paying his choristers. Although this was true, Lipskerov was nonetheless sent to prison.) That Lipskerov was a journalistic shark, quite unprincipled and exploitative, can be seen in his treatment of Chekhov regarding payment for *The Shooting Party*. Lipskerov also printed some stories of Chekhov's under his full name – not with the pseudonym 'Antosha Chekhonte' that he used at this time, but without the author's permission and obviously to win more readers.

3. For Gaboriau, see note 3 in Notes.
4. V. A. Prokhorov (1858?–97) also wrote under the pseudonym Voldemar Valentinochkin. His *Parricide*, printed in *News of the Day* (1884), includes chapters entitled *Vampires*, *The Bloody Eye* and so on!
5. 'Evil Spirit' – a pseudonym of V. A. Prokhorov. 'Dominoes' alludes to Blue Domino, the pen-name of A. I. Sokolova (1836–1914), authoress of detective novels. The 'Dramas' mentioned below refer to her *Contemporary Drama*, published in *News of the Day* (1884).
6. Reference to Lermontov's *Trust Not Thyself* (1839).

The Shooting Party

THE SHOOTING PARTY

(A True Event)

One April afternoon in 1880 Andrey the janitor came into my room and announced in hushed tones that a certain gentleman had turned up at the editorial offices and was persistently requesting an interview with the Editor.

'A civil servant, by the look of him, sir,' added Andrey, 'with a badge in his cap.'

'Ask him to call some other time,' I said. 'I'm really tied up today. Tell him that the Editor sees visitors on Saturdays only.'

'But he came asking for you the day before yesterday too. It's most important, he says. Keeps on and on, he does, and he's close to tears! Says he's not free on Saturdays. Shall I ask him to come in?'

I sighed, put down my pen and settled myself to wait for the gentleman with the badge. Writers who are mere beginners, and everyone, in fact, who hasn't yet been initiated into the secrets of publishing and who is overcome with fear and trembling at the words 'Editor's Office', keep you waiting for ages. After the Editor's 'show him in', they're inclined to cough and blow their noses interminably, after which they slowly open the door and enter even more slowly, consequently wasting a lot of your time. But this gentleman with the badge didn't keep me waiting. Hardly had the door closed behind Andrey than I saw in my office a tall, broad-shouldered man with a bundle of papers in one hand and a cap with a badge in the other.

This gentleman, who had thus managed to grab an interview with me, plays a leading part in my story, so I must describe his appearance.

As I have said already, he was tall, broad-shouldered, and as solidly built as a handsome carthorse. His whole body radiated health and strength. His face was rosy, his hands large, his chest broad and muscular, his hair as thick and curly as a young healthy boy's. He was about forty, tastefully dressed in the latest fashion, in a tweed suit fresh from the tailor's. Across his chest was a large gold chain with charms dangling from it; a diamond ring sparkled with tiny flashing stars on his little finger. And – what is essential, what is most important of all for the hero of any novel or short story who is in the slightest degree respectable – he was extraordinarily handsome. I am neither woman nor artist, I don't have much idea about male beauty, but the appearance of that gentleman with the badge in his cap really impressed me. His large, muscular face has remained forever engraved on my memory. In that face you could see a truly Grecian, slightly hooked nose, fine lips and handsome blue eyes that glowed with kindness – and with something else for which it is hard to find a suitable name. This 'something' is noticeable in the eyes of small animals when they are miserable or feeling pain – it is something imploring, childlike, silently suffering. Cunning and very clever people don't have such eyes.

His entire face simply radiated ingenuousness, an expansive, simple character, truth. If it isn't a lie that the face is the mirror of the soul, I could have sworn from the very first day of my meeting with the gentleman with the badge that he was incapable of lying. I might even have laid a bet on it. Whether I would have lost or won the reader will discover later.

His chestnut hair and beard were thick and as soft as silk. They say that soft hair is a sign of a gentle, sensitive, 'meek and mild' soul: criminals and evil desperadoes tend to have wiry hair. Whether that's true or not the reader will in any event find out later. But neither his facial expression nor his beard – nothing about that gentleman with the badge was so gentle and delicate as the movements of his huge, heavy body. In those movements you could detect good breeding, ease, grace and even – forgive the expression – a certain effeminacy. It would have cost my hero only a slight effort to bend a horseshoe or crush a sardine tin in his fist. However, not one movement revealed any sign of physical strength. He grasped the door handle or his cap as if they were butterflies – delicately, carefully, barely touching them with his fingers. His steps were noiseless, his handshake feeble. Looking at him you forgot he was as strong as Goliath and that with one hand he could lift what five editorial Andreys could never have budged. As I watched his delicate movements it was hard to believe that he was so strong and heavily built. Spencer[1] would have hailed him as the very model of grace.

When he entered my office he became confused. Most likely my sullen, disgruntled look came as a shock to his gentle, sensitive nature.

'Heavens, I'm sorry!' he began in a soft, rich baritone. 'Seems I've chosen a rotten time to come barging in here and forcing you to make an exception in my case. I can see you're up to your eyes! Well now, this is what I've come about, Mr Editor. Tomorrow I have to go to Odessa on a very important business matter. Had I been able to postpone my trip until Saturday then, believe me, I wouldn't have asked you to make an exception in my case. Normally I abide by the rules, because I like to do things the right way . . .'

'God, how he goes on and on!' I thought, stretching my hand towards my pen to show that I was terribly busy. At such times visitors really got on my nerves!

'I'll take only one minute of your time,' my hero continued in an apologetic tone. 'But first allow me to introduce myself . . . Ivan Petrovich Kamyshev, LL.B, former investigating magistrate. I don't have the honour of belonging to the writing fraternity. All the same, my purpose in coming here is purely literary. Before you there stands a person who wants to make a start, despite his forty-odd years. Better late than never!'

'Delighted . . . How can I help you?'

The gentleman who wanted to make a start sat down and gazed at the floor with imploring eyes.

'I've brought you a little story,' he continued, 'which I'd like you to print in your paper. I'm telling you quite frankly, Mr Editor, I haven't written this story either for literary fame or to express "sweet sounds" in words.[2] I'm too old now for admirable things like that. No, I'm setting out on the writer's path for purely commercial considerations . . . I want to earn some money . . . At the moment I'm completely unemployed. You know, I was investigating magistrate in S— district. I worked there for just over five years, but I didn't make much money – nor did I preserve my innocence.'

Kamyshev glanced at me with his kind eyes.

'The work there was a real bore,' he added, softly laughing. 'I simply slaved away until I called it a day and left. Now I'm out of a job and just about broke. If you published my story, regardless of any merits it may have, you'd be doing me more than a favour – you'd be helping me. I'm well aware that a newspaper isn't a charitable institution, nor an old people's home, but . . . if you'd be good enough to . . .'

'You're lying,' I thought.

Those little trinkets and that diamond ring on his little finger didn't tally at all with having to write for a living. What's more, a barely perceptible cloud – something that the experienced eye can detect on the faces of those who only rarely lie – passed over Kamyshev's face.

'What's the subject of your story?' I asked.

'Subject? What can I say? It's nothing new . . . it's about love, murder. Read it and you'll see. It's called *From the Memoirs of an Investigating Magistrate*.'

I probably frowned, as Kamyshev blinked in embarrassment, gave a start and quickly added:

'My story's written in the hackneyed style of previous investigating magistrates but . . . you'll find facts in it . . . the *truth*. Everything that's depicted in it, from start to finish, happened before my eyes . . . I was both eyewitness and even an active participant.'

'It's not a question of truth . . . You don't necessarily have to see something in order to describe it – that's not important. The point is, for far too long now our poor readers have had their teeth set on edge by Gaboriau[3] and Shklyarevsky.[4] They're sick and tired of all these mysterious murders, these detectives' artful ruses, the phenomenal quick-wittedness of investigating magistrates. Of course, there are different kinds of public, but I'm talking about the public that reads my paper. What's your story called?'

'*The Shooting Party.*'

'Hmm, doesn't sound much. And to be quite honest with you I'm so piled up with stuff here at the moment that it's impossible to take on anything new, even if its merits cannot be questioned.'

'But *please* take my story . . . *please*. You say it's nothing much, but you can't condemn something out of hand without even having seen it! Surely you must admit that even investigating magistrates are capable of writing seriously?'

Kamyshev said all this with a stutter, twiddling his pencil between his fingers and gazing at his feet. Finally he became extremely flustered and couldn't stop blinking. I felt quite sorry for him.

'All right, leave it here,' I said. 'But I can't promise that your story will be read soon. You'll have to wait.'

'For very long?'

'I can't say . . . come back in a month . . . or two . . . or three.'

'That's absolutely ages! But I dare not insist. You must do as you please.' Kamyshev stood up and reached for his cap. 'Thanks for the audience,' he said. 'I'm off home now and I'll feed myself on hope. Three months of hoping! But I can see that you've had enough of me. I wish you good day, sir!'

'Just one more word, if you don't mind,' I said, turning the pages of his thick notebook that were filled with very small handwriting. 'You write here in the first person . . . So, by investigating magistrate I take it you mean yourself?'

'Yes, but under a different name. My part in the story is rather scandalous . . . it would have been awkward to use my real name. Well then, in three months?'

'Perhaps . . . but not earlier.'

The former investigating magistrate bowed gallantly, gingerly grasped the door handle and vanished, leaving his story on my desk. I took the notebook and put it away in the table drawer.

That handsome Kamyshev's story reposed in my drawer for two months. One day, as I was leaving the office for my summer villa, I remembered it and took it with me.

After taking my seat in the railway compartment I opened the notebook and started reading from the middle: it excited my curiosity. That same evening, although I didn't really have the time, I read the story from the beginning to the words 'The End', written with a flourish. That night I read the story right through again and when dawn came I was pacing my veranda and rubbing my temples as if I wanted to banish some new and painful thought that had suddenly entered my head. And this thought really was painful, unbearably intense . . . It struck me that I, who was no investigating magistrate and even less a forensic psychologist, had stumbled upon one man's terrible secret, a secret that was no business of mine. I walked up and down the veranda, trying to persuade myself not to believe what I had discovered.

Kamyshev's story was not published for the reasons given at the end of my chat with the reader. I shall meet my reader again, but for the moment I'm taking leave of him for a long time and I offer Kamyshev's story for his perusal.

It's really a very ordinary story, containing many longueurs and in places the style is very uneven. The author has a weakness for striking effects and resounding phrases. Obviously he's writing for the very first time, with an inexperienced, untrained hand. For all that, his story makes for easy reading. There's a plot, it makes sense and – most important of all – it's original, with a very distinctive character – it's what one would call *sui generis*.[5] And it does have *some* literary merit. It's worth reading . . . here it is.

THE SHOOTING PARTY

(From the Memoirs of an Investigating Magistrate)

I

'A husband murdered his wife! Oh, you're so stupid! Now, will you please give me some sugar!'

This cry woke me up. I stretched myself and felt a heavy weight and lifelessness in every limb. You can get pins and needles in the legs and arms by lying on them, but now I felt that I'd made my whole body go to sleep, from head to foot. An after-dinner nap, in a stuffy, dry atmosphere, with flies and mosquitoes buzzing around, has a debilitating rather than invigorating effect. Jaded and bathed in sweat, I got up and went over to the window. It was after five in the afternoon. The sun was still high and was burning just as zealously as three hours earlier. The sunset and the cool of evening were still a long way off.

'A husband murdered his wife!'

'Enough of your nonsense, Ivan Demyanych!' I said, giving Ivan Demyanych's beak a gentle flick. 'Husbands murder their wives only in novels or in the tropics, where African passions run high, dear chap. We've enough of such horrors as burglaries or false identities as it is . . .'

'Burglaries . . .' Ivan Demyanych intoned through his hooked beak. 'Oh, you're so stupid!'

'But what can I do about it, dear chap? How are we humans to blame if we're born with limited brainpower? What's more, Ivan Demyanych, there's nothing to be ashamed of if one behaves like an idiot in temperatures like these. You're my clever little birdie, but it seems that your brains have curdled and grown stupid in this heat.'

My parrot's called Ivan Demyanych, not Pretty Polly or any other bird name. He acquired this name purely by chance. My servant Polikarp was once cleaning his cage when he suddenly made a discovery without which my noble bird would have been called Pretty Polly to this day. For no apparent reason, it suddenly struck that lazy servant of mine that my parrot's beak closely resembled the nose of Ivan Demyanych, our village shopkeeper, and ever since the name and patronymic of that long-nosed shopkeeper has stuck to my parrot. Thanks to Polikarp the entire village christened my remarkable bird *Ivan Demyanych*; thanks to Polikarp the bird became a real person, while the shopkeeper lost his real name: to the end of his days he'll be spoken of by country bumpkins as the 'magistrate's parrot'.

I bought Ivan Demyanych from the mother of my predecessor, investigating magistrate Pospelov, who passed away shortly before my appointment. I bought him together with some old-fashioned oak furniture, sundry trashy kitchen utensils and in general all the various household effects left by the deceased. To this day my walls are embellished with photographs of his relatives, and a portrait of the former owner still hangs over my bed. The deceased, a lean, wiry man with red moustache and thick underlip, sits goggling at me from his discoloured walnut frame, never taking his eyes off me while I'm lying there in his bed. I haven't taken down one photograph from the walls – briefly, I've left the flat exactly as I found it. I'm too lazy to think of my own comfort and I would have no objection to the living as well as the dead hanging on my walls – if the living should so desire.*

Ivan Demyanych found it as stifling as I did. He ruffled his feathers, spread his wings and screeched phrases out loud that he had learned from my predecessor Pospelov and from Polikarp. To occupy myself somehow during my post-prandial

* I apologize to the reader for using such expressions. The unfortunate Kamyshev's story abounds with them, and if I haven't deleted them it's only because I considered it necessary, in the interests of providing the reader with a complete portrait of the author, to print his story *in toto* (without omissions). A. C.

leisure time I sat down in front of the cage and started observing the movements of my parrot, who was making a determined effort to escape from the torments inflicted by the stifling heat and the insects that resided in his feathers, but without success. The poor thing seemed as miserable as sin.

'What time does 'e get up?' boomed a voice from the hall.

'It all depends!' Polikarp replied. 'Sometimes he'll wake up at five, sometimes he'll carry on sleeping till morning. There's nothing I can do about it, you know.'

'Are you 'is valet?'

'His house servant. Now, don't bother me and shut up . . . Can't you see I'm reading?'

I peeped into the hall. There was my Polikarp, lolling on the large red trunk and reading some book, as usual. Peering into it with his drowsy, unblinking eyes, he kept twitching his lips and frowning. He was clearly irritated by the presence of that stranger – a tall, bearded peasant who was standing by the trunk and trying in vain to engage him in conversation. On my appearance the peasant took one step away from the trunk and stood to attention like a soldier. Polikarp pulled a dissatisfied face and rose slightly without taking his eyes off his book.

'What do you want?' I asked the peasant.

'I'm from the Count, yer 'onner. The Count begs to send 'is compliments and asks you to come over right away.'

'Is the *Count* back?' I asked in amazement.

'That's right, yer 'onner. Came back last night, 'e did. 'Ere's a letter for you, sir.'

'Just look what the devil's brought in!' exclaimed my Polikarp. 'For two years we led nice quiet lives while he was away and now he'll go and turn the whole district into a pigsty again. There'll be no end to the shameful goings-on!'

'Shut up, I'm not asking you!'

'You don't *have* to ask me! I'm telling you straight. You'll leave his place filthy drunk and then you'll go swimming in the lake, just as you are, with your suit on. And I'm the one who'll have to clean it afterwards! That's at least a three-day job!'

'What's the Count doing just now?' I asked the peasant.

' 'E was just sitting down to 'is dinner when 'e sends me over.

Before that 'e was fishing in the bathing-pool, sir. What shall I tell 'im?'

I opened the letter and read the following:

My dear Lecoq![6]

If you're still alive and well and haven't forgotten your ever-intoxicated friend, don't waste another minute, attire yourself and ride over post-haste! I got back only last night, but already I die of boredom! The impatience I wait for you with knows no bounds. I wanted to come for you myself and carry you off to my lair, but the heat has fettered my limbs! All I can do is sit still and fan myself. Well, how are you? And how is that very clever Ivan Demyanych of yours? Do you still do battle with that old pedant Polikarp? Come quickly and tell me everything . . .

Your A. K.

I didn't need to look at the signature to recognize in that large, ugly scrawl the drunken hand of my friend, Count Karneyev, who rarely put pen to paper. The brevity of the letter, its pretensions to a certain degree of playfulness and liveliness, showed beyond doubt that my dull-witted friend had torn up a large quantity of notepaper before managing to complete it. Pronouns such as 'which' were absent from the letter and all gerunds were sedulously avoided – the Count rarely managed to employ both at one sitting.

'What answer shall I give, sir?' asked the peasant.

I didn't reply to this question immediately and any decent man in my place would have hesitated as well. The Count was very fond of me and most sincerely thrust his friendship upon me. But I felt nothing like friendship for him and I even disliked him. Therefore it would have been more honest to reject his friendship once and for all than go and visit him and play the hypocrite. Besides, going over to the Count's meant plunging once again into the kind of life that my Polikarp dignified by the name of 'pigsty' and which, for the entire two years before the Count left his estate for St Petersburg, had been shattering my robust health and drying my brains out. That dissipated, abnormal life, so full of dramatic incident and mad drunkenness, had failed to undermine my organism. But on the other hand it made me notorious all over the province . . . I was popular . . .

My reason told me the whole truth, the basic truth; a blush of shame for my recent past spread over my face and my heart sank at the thought that I wouldn't have the courage to say no to that trip to the Count's. But I didn't hesitate for long: the struggle lasted no longer than a minute.

'Convey my respects to the Count,' I told the messenger, 'and thank him for thinking of me . . . tell him I'm busy and that . . . tell him I'm . . .'

And just at that moment, when a definitive 'no' was about to roll off my tongue, I was suddenly overcome by a painful feeling. A young man, so full of life, strength and desire, cast by fate into that rural backwater, was gripped by feelings of melancholy and loneliness . . .

I remembered the Count's garden, with all the splendour of its cool conservatories, and the semidarkness of its narrow, neglected avenues. These avenues, protected from the sun by a canopy of the green, intertwined branches of ancient limes, know me very well. And they know those women who sought my love and the semidarkness . . . I remembered the luxurious drawing-room with the sweet repose of its velvet sofas, those heavy curtains and carpets soft as down, that indolence so adored by healthy young animals . . . I recalled my drunken recklessness that knew no bounds, my satanic pride and contempt for life. And my large body, weary with sleep, once more yearned for movement.

'Tell him I'm coming.'

The peasant bowed and left.

'I wouldn't have let that devil in had I known!' Polikarp growled as he swiftly and aimlessly turned the pages of his book.

'Put that book down and go and saddle Zorka,' I said sternly. 'And look lively!'

'Lively? Oh, of course . . . I'll dash off and see to it right away . . . There'd be some excuse if he was going there on business, but he'll ride over and bring the old devil to his knees!'

This was said in an undertone, but loud enough for me to hear. My servant who had whispered this impertinence stood erect, scornfully smirking and expecting some retaliatory outburst, but I pretended not to have heard. Silence was my most effective, my sharpest weapon in my battles with Polikarp. The contemptuous way I usually turned a deaf ear to his vitriolic remarks would disarm him and take the wind out of his sails. As a punishment it worked better than any clout on the ear or torrent of abuse. When Polikarp had gone out into the yard to saddle Zorka, I peeped into the book I had stopped him reading. It was *The Count of Monte Cristo*,[7] Dumas' spine-chilling novel. My cultured fool read everything, from pub signs to Auguste Comte,[8] who was lying in my trunk together with my other abandoned, unread books. Out of all that mass of printed and written matter, however, he recognized only terrifying, extremely exciting novels with distinguished 'personages', with poison and subterranean passages – everything else he styled 'rubbish'. I shall have occasion to discuss his reading later on, but now it was time to go!

A quarter of an hour later my Zorka's hoofs were already raising dust along the road from the village to the Count's estate. The sun was close to its resting place for the night, but the heat and humidity continued to make themselves felt. The burning air was motionless and dry, despite the fact that my path skirted the banks of the most enormous lake. To the right I could see a great watery expanse; to the left the young vernal foliage of an oak grove caressed my eyes, but at the same time my cheeks had to endure a Sahara-like heat.

'There's sure to be a storm!' I reflected, having visions of a fine, cooling downpour.

The lake was peacefully sleeping. It did not greet Zorka's flight with a single sound and only the cry of a young woodcock broke the sepulchral silence of that motionless giant. The sun looked at itself in it as though it were a huge mirror and flooded its entire breadth, from the road to the far bank, with its blinding light. To my dazzled eyes nature seemed to be receiving its light from the lake instead of from the sun.

The stifling heat also lulled into drowsiness the life in which the lake and its green banks were so rich. The birds were in hiding, the fish made no splash in the water, the grasshoppers and crickets were quietly waiting for the cool to set in. All around everything was deserted. Only now and then did my Zorka bear me into a thick cloud of mosquitoes that lived along the banks; and far out on the lake there barely stirred the three little black boats belonging to old Mikhey, our fisherman, who had fishing rights to the whole lake.

II

I did not ride in a straight line, but followed the curving banks of the circular lake. Travelling in a straight line was possible only by boat, but those who went overland were forced to describe a great circle, which meant a detour of about six miles. As I rode along and glanced at the lake, I had a continuous view of the clayey bank on the far side, where the white strip of a blossoming cherry orchard gleamed, while beyond the cherry trees were the Count's barns, dotted with many-coloured doves, and then the white belfry of the Count's church. By the clayey bank stood a bathing-hut, its sides nailed down with canvas; sheets were hanging up to dry on the railings. As I surveyed all this, a mere half mile appeared to separate me from my friend the Count, whereas in fact I had to ride about another ten miles to reach the estate.

On the way I considered my peculiar relationship with the Count. I found it interesting to take stock of this, to try and see where the two of us stood. But alas! This exercise was beyond my powers. However much I reflected, in the end I was forced to conclude that I was a poor judge of myself and of people in general. Those who knew both the Count and myself interpreted our mutual relationship in different ways. Those with limited brainpower, who couldn't see further than their noses, were fond of claiming that the distinguished Count had found an excellent drinking companion and stooge in that 'poor and undistinguished examining magistrate'. As they saw it, I, the author of these lines, went crawling and grovelling around the Count's table for a few crumbs and titbits! In their opinion, that distinguished Croesus, the bugbear, the envy of the whole of S— district, was extremely intelligent and liberal-minded. Otherwise, the fact that he so graciously condescended to be friends with an impoverished investigating magistrate, together with the genuine tolerance with which he accepted my over-familiarity with him, would have been incomprehensible. But those who were more intelligent explained our great intimacy as 'community of spiritual interests'. The Count and I were contemporaries. We had both graduated from the same university, we were both lawyers and we both knew very little. I myself knew a few things, but the Count had forgotten or drowned in alcohol all he had ever known. We were both proud men and for reasons known only to ourselves we lived like recluses, shunning society. We were both indifferent to what society thought of us (I mean the society in S— district), we were both immoral and we would both certainly come to a bad end. Such were the 'spiritual interests' that bound us. Those who knew us could have said no more than this about our relationship.

Of course, they would have had more to say had they known how spineless, pliant and complaisant my friend's nature was – and how strong and firm I was. They would have had a great deal to say had they known how fond that vain man was of me and how I detested him! He was first to offer me his friendship and I was first to address him as an intimate – but what a difference in tone! In an excess of noble feelings he had embraced me and humbly begged my friendship. But on one occasion, overcome by contempt and disgust, I told him:

'That's enough rubbish from *you*!'[9]

And he considered this familiarity an expression of friendship and took advantage of it, repaying me with his own honest, brotherly brand.

Yes, I would have acted more honestly and decently if I'd turned my Zorka around and ridden back to Polikarp and Ivan Demyanych. Later on I thought more than once about how many misfortunes I could have avoided bearing on my shoulders, how much good I could have done those who were close to me, if only I'd had the determination that evening to turn back, if only Zorka had bolted and borne me far away from that terrifying, vast lake! How many painful memories would not be oppressing my brain now, making me constantly drop my pen and clutch my head! But I shall not anticipate, especially as later I shall be compelled to dwell many more times on pain and sorrow: now for cheerful matters!

My Zorka bore me right up to the gates of the Count's courtyard. Just as we were going through she stumbled, so that I lost a stirrup and was almost thrown to the ground.

'A bad omen, sir!' shouted some peasant who was standing by one of the doors in the Count's long row of stables.

I believe that anyone who falls from his horse can break his neck, but I don't believe in omens. Handing the bridle to the peasant and beating the dust off my riding-boots with my whip, I ran into the house. No one was there to greet me. The windows and doors of the rooms were wide open, but despite that there was an oppressive, peculiar smell in the air – a blend of the odours of ancient, deserted apartments with the pleasant if pungent, narcotic scent of hothouse plants that had recently been brought into the rooms from the conservatories. In the drawing-room, on one of the sofas upholstered in light-blue silk, lay two crumpled cushions and on a round table in front of it I saw a glass containing a few drops of liquid that smelt of potent Riga balsam.[10] All this led me to believe that the house was inhabited, but I did not meet a living soul in any of the eleven rooms through which I passed. The same desolation that surrounded the lake reigned in that house.

From the so-called 'mosaic' drawing-room, large French windows led into the garden. They made a loud noise as I opened them and went down the marble terrace steps into the garden. After I'd taken a few strides along the avenue I met Nastasya, an old crone of about ninety who had been the Count's nanny. She was a tiny, wrinkled creature whom death had forgotten, with bald head and piercing eyes. Whenever you looked at her face you couldn't help remembering the nickname that the other servants had given her: Owlet. When she saw me she shuddered and almost dropped the jug of cream she was carrying in both hands.

'How are you, Owlet?' I asked.

She gave me a sidelong glance and silently walked past. I grasped her shoulder.

'Don't be scared, you old fool . . . where's the Count?'

The old woman pointed at her ears.

'Are you deaf? Have you been like that long?'

Despite her advanced age the old crone could hear and see very well, but she found it not unprofitable to calumniate her sensory organs. I wagged my finger and let her go.

After a few more steps I heard voices and before long I saw people. Just where the avenue widened out into an open space, surrounded by cast-iron benches and shaded by tall, white acacias, stood a table with a gleaming samovar on it. People were sitting around the table, talking. I quietly made my way across the grass to the little open space, hid behind a lilac bush, and sought out the Count with my eyes.

My friend, Count Karneyev, was sitting at the table on a folding cane chair, drinking tea. He was wearing that same multicoloured dressing-robe in which I'd seen him two years before, and a straw hat. His face had an anxious, preoccupied look and was deeply furrowed, so that those who didn't know him might have thought that some grave thought or problem was troubling him at that precise moment. In appearance the Count hadn't changed one bit during our two-year separation: there was that same small, thin body, as frail and sluggish as a corncrake's, those same narrow, consumptive's shoulders and that small head with reddish hair. His nose was as red as ever, and his cheeks were the same as they had been two years ago, sagging like limp rags. There was nothing bold, strong or manly in his face. Everything was weak, apathetic and flaccid. Only his long, drooping moustache made any impression. Someone had told my friend that a long moustache suited him: he believed him and every morning he would measure how much that hairy growth over his pale lips had lengthened. That moustache put you in mind of a bewhiskered but very young and puny kitten.

Next to the Count, at the same table, sat a stout gentleman I didn't know, with a large, closely cropped head and jet-black eyebrows. This gentleman's face was plump and shiny as a ripe melon. His moustache was longer than the Count's, his forehead low, his lips tightly pressed and his eyes were gazing lazily at the sky. His features had run to fat, but despite that they were as stiff as dried-up leather. He wasn't the Russian type. This stout gentleman was without jacket or waistcoat and simply wore a smock stained with dark patches of sweat. He was drinking seltzer water instead of tea.

At a respectful distance from the table stood a portly, stocky man with a plump red neck and protruding ears. This was Urbenin, the Count's estate manager. In honour of His Excellency's arrival he had donned a new black suit and was now suffering agonies. The sweat simply streamed from his red, sunburnt face. Next to the manager stood the peasant who had brought me the letter. It was only then that I noticed that he had one eye missing. Holding himself stiffly to attention and not daring to budge, he stood there like a statue as he waited to be questioned.

'I'd like to take your whip from you, Kuzma, and thrash the living daylights out of you,' the manager was telling him in a drawling, admonitory, soft, deep voice. 'How can you be so slapdash about the Master's orders? You should have asked the gentleman to come right away and found out exactly when we could expect him.'

'Yes, yes,' agreed the Count nervously. 'You should have found everything out! So, he told you he'd come. But that's not good enough! I *need* him here, this very minute! Right away – wi-th-out fail! He couldn't have understood you when you asked him.'

'Why do you need him so badly?' the stout gentleman asked the Count.

'I have to see him!'

'Is that all? If you ask me, Aleksey, that investigating magistrate of yours would be best advised to stay at home today. *I* don't feel up to visitors at the moment.'

I opened my eyes wide. What did that imperious, peremptory 'I' imply?

'But he's not just a visitor,' my friend pleaded. 'He won't prevent you from resting after your journey. You don't have to stand on ceremony with *him* – you'll soon see what a fine fellow he is. You'll take to him immediately and you'll be the best of friends, my dear chap!'

I emerged from my hiding place behind the lilac bush and went towards the table. When the Count saw me and recognized me his face lit up with a smile.

'Here he is, here he is!' he exclaimed, flushed with pleasure and leaping from the table. 'It's so *very* nice of you to come!' After running up to me he performed a little jig, embraced me and scratched my cheeks several times with his bristly moustache. The kisses were followed by prolonged handshaking and peering into my eyes.

'You haven't changed one bit, Sergey! Still just the same! As handsome and as strong as ever! Thanks for doing me the favour of coming!'

Freeing myself from the Count's embrace, I greeted the manager, whom I knew very well, and took my place at the table.

'Ah, my dear chap!' the Count continued, at once anxious and overjoyed. 'If you only knew how pleasant it is to behold your grave countenance! . . . You haven't met? Allow me to introduce you – my good friend Kaetan Kazimirovich Pshekhotsky . . . And this is . . .' he went on, introducing me to the fat gentleman, 'my good, long-standing friend Sergey Petrovich Zinovyev! He's our district investigating magistrate.' The stout, black-browed gentleman rose slightly and offered me his chubby, dreadfully sweaty hand.

'Delighted!' he mumbled, eyeing me up and down. 'Absolutely delighted!'

After he had unbosomed himself and calmed down, the Count poured me a glass of cold, dark-brown tea and pushed a box of biscuits towards me.

'Help yourself . . . I bought them at Eynem's[11] as I was passing through Moscow. But I'm angry with you, Seryozha – so angry that I even felt like terminating our friendship! It's not simply that you haven't written me a single line over the past two years – you haven't even deigned to answer any of my letters. That's not very friendly!'

'I'm no good at writing letters,' I said. 'And besides, I don't have time for letter-writing. Please tell me – what was there to write about?'

'There must have been plenty of things!'

'But there weren't, honestly. I acknowledge only three kinds of letter: love letters, congratulatory letters and business letters. I didn't write the first, as you're not a woman and I'm not in love with you. You don't need the second and we can do without the third, as neither of us has had any mutual business since the day we were born.'

'That may well be true,' replied the Count, who was ready and willing to agree to everything. 'All the same, you could at least have written a line. And on top of that, as Pyotr Yegorych so rightly says, for those entire two years you never once set foot here, just as if you were living a thousand miles away or as if . . . you were put off by my wealth. You could have lived here, done a spot of shooting. Just think what might have happened while I was away!'

The Count spoke a great deal and at great length. Once he started, his tongue would wag incessantly, interminably, however footling and trivial the subject.

He was as indefatigable as my Ivan Demyanych in his articulation of sounds and for me this ability made him barely tolerable. On this occasion he was stopped by his servant Ilya, a lanky, thin man in shabby, badly stained livery, who brought the Count a wine glass of vodka and half a tumbler of water on a silver tray. The Count downed the vodka, took a sip of water, frowned and shook his head.

'So, you still haven't lost your habit of swilling vodka at the first opportunity!' I remarked.

'No, I haven't, Seryozha!'

'Well, you could at least give up that drunken frowning and waggling your head! It's frightful!'

'I'm giving *everything* up, old man. My doctors have forbidden me to drink. I'm only having a little drink now as it's unhealthy to kick bad habits all in one go . . . it has to be done *gradually* . . .'

I looked at the Count's sickly, worn face, at the wine glass, at the footman in yellow shoes; I looked at the black-browed Pole who from the very start for some reason struck me as a scoundrel and crook; at the one-eyed peasant standing to attention – and I felt uneasy, stifled. Suddenly I had the urge to escape from that filthy atmosphere, but not before opening the Count's eyes to my boundless antipathy towards him. For one moment I was actually on the point of getting up and leaving there and then. But I didn't leave. I'm ashamed to admit that sheer physical laziness held me back.

'Bring me a glass of vodka too!' I ordered Ilya.

Oblong-shaped shadows began to fall on the avenue and on the open space where we were sitting. And now the distant croaking of frogs, the cawing of crows and the song of orioles greeted the setting sun. The spring evening was drawing in.

'Let Urbenin sit down,' I told the Count. 'He's standing there in front of you like a little boy.'

'Oh, how thoughtless of me, Pyotr Yegorych!' the Count exclaimed, turning to his manager. 'Please take a seat, you've been standing there long enough!'

Urbenin sat down and looked at me with grateful eyes. Invariably healthy and cheerful, this time he struck me as ill and depressed. His face had a wrinkled, sleepy look and his eyes gazed at us lazily and reluctantly.

'What's new, Pyotr Yegorych?' Karneyev asked him. 'What's new? Anything special to report, anything out of the ordinary?'

'Everything's the same, Your Excellency . . .'

'Are there any . . . nice new girls around, Pyotr Yegorych?'

The deeply virtuous Pyotr Yegorych blushed.

'I don't know, Your Excellency. I don't concern myself with such things.'

'There *are* a few, Your Excellency,' boomed one-eyed Kuzma; who had been silent up to now. 'And very nice ones they be too!'

'Pretty?'

'There's all kinds, Your Excellency, for every taste. Dark ones, fair ones . . . all sorts.'

'You don't say! Hold on a minute . . . I remember you now, you're that former Leporello[12] of mine, the clerk at the council offices . . . Your name's Kuzma, isn't it?'

'That's right, sir.'

'I remember, I remember. So, which ones would you recommend? All village girls, I dare say?'

'Oh yes, most of 'em, but there's some what's better-class, like.'

'And where did you find these "better-class" ones?' asked Ilya, winking at Kuzma.

'At Holy Week the postman's sister-in-law came to stay ... her name's Nastasya Ivanna ... A well-oiled girl she is. I'd 'ave taken a bite meself, but I didn't 'ave no money. All rosy-cheeked – and everything in the right place! And there's an even better one ... She's been waiting for you, Your Excellency. Ever so young, nice and plump, very jolly – a real smasher! Such a smasher as you've never seen the likes of, even in St Pittiburg, Your Excellency!'

'Who is she?'

'Olenka, the forester Skvortsov's little daughter.'

Urbenin's chair cracked under him. Supporting himself with his hands on the table and turning purple, the manager slowly stood up and turned towards one-eyed Kuzma. The expression of weariness and boredom on his face gave way to violent anger.

'Shut up, you oaf!' he snarled. 'You one-eyed reptile! You can say what you want, but don't you dare talk about respectable people like that!'

'I weren't talking about *you*, Pyotr Yegorych!' replied Kuzma, quite unruffled.

'I don't mean myself, you idiot! Oh, please forgive me, Your Excellency,' the manager said, turning to the Count. 'Forgive me for making a scene, but I would ask Your Excellency to stop that Leporello of yours – as you were pleased to call him – from extending his enthusiasm to people who are in every way deserving of respect!'

'It's all right,' babbled the naïve Count. 'He didn't say anything particularly bad.'

Insulted and excited beyond all measure, Urbenin walked away from the table and stood sideways to us. With his arms crossed on his chest and blinking, he hid his purple face from us behind some small branches and became very thoughtful: did this man foresee that in the very near future his moral feelings would have to suffer insults a thousand times more bitter?

'I can't understand why he's taking it so badly,' the Count whispered. 'What a queer fish! Nothing offensive was said at all.'

After two years of sobriety the glass of vodka had a slightly intoxicating effect on me. A feeling of lightness, of pleasure, flooded my brain and my whole body. What's more, I began to feel the cool of evening gradually replacing the stifling heat of the day. I suggested going for a stroll. The Count and his new Polish friend's jackets were brought from the house and off we went, with Urbenin following us.

III

The Count's garden, through which we were strolling, deserves a very special description on account of its striking luxuriance. In botanical, horticultural and many other respects it is richer and grander than any other garden I have seen. Besides the romantic avenues described above, with their green vaults, you'll find everything there that the most fastidious eye might demand from a garden. Here there is every possible kind of indigenous and foreign fruit tree, ranging from cherry and plum, to apricot trees with enormous fruit the size of goose eggs. Mulberries, barberries, French bergamot trees and even olives are to be found at every step. Here there are half-ruined mossy grottoes, fountains, small ponds reserved for goldfish and tame carp, little hillocks, summer-houses, expensive hothouses. And this uncommon luxury, assembled by the hands of grandfathers and fathers, this wealth of large, full roses, of romantic grottoes and endless paths, had been barbarously neglected and left to the mercy of weeds, thieves' axes and the crows that unceremoniously built their ugly nests on the rare trees. The lawful proprietor of this domain walked at my side and not one muscle of his haggard and self-satisfied face twitched at the sight of all that neglect and blatant human slovenliness, just as though he wasn't the owner of that garden. Only once, for want of something to do, did he tell the manager that it wouldn't be a bad idea to scatter a little sand over the paths. Yes, he could pay attention to the absence of sand that no one needed, but he didn't notice the bare trees that had died during the cold winter and the cows that were straying through the garden! To this observation Urbenin replied that it would take ten workers to look after the garden, and, since His Excellency didn't wish to live on his estate, any money spent on the garden would be an unnecessary and unproductive luxury. Of course, the Count agreed with this argument.

'And I must confess – I don't have the time!' Urbenin said dismissively. 'I have to work in the fields in summer, in winter I have to sell grain in town. There's no time for gardens in this place!'

The main, so-called 'general' avenue, whose whole charm lay in its broad lime trees and masses of tulips that stretched in two multicoloured strips along its entire length, ended in the distance in a yellow patch. This was the yellow stone summer-house where once there had been a bar and billiard table, skittles and Chinese board games. Aimlessly, we walked towards it. At the entrance we were met by a living creature that rather unsettled the nerves of my not very courageous companions.

'A serpent!' the Count suddenly screamed, gripping my shoulder and turning pale. 'Just look!'

The Pole took a step backwards, stopped as if rooted to the spot and spread his arms out, just as though he were barring the path of a ghost. On the topmost step of the dilapidated flight of stone steps lay a young snake – a common Russian viper. When it spotted us it raised its tiny head and started moving. The Count screamed again and hid behind my back.

'Don't be afraid, Your Excellency!' Urbenin said lazily, planting his foot on the first step.

'What if it bites me?'

'It won't bite . . . Incidentally, the harm from this type of snakebite is usually greatly exaggerated. I was once bitten by an old snake and – as you can see – I didn't die. Human bites are more dangerous than a snake's!' sighed Urbenin, unable to resist pointing a moral.

And in fact the manager barely had time to climb two or three more steps before the snake stretched to its full length and darted into a crevice between two flagstones with lightning speed. When we entered the summer-house we saw another living creature. On the old, faded, torn baize of the billiard table lay an old, shortish man, in blue jacket, striped trousers and jockey cap. He was sleeping sweetly and serenely. Around his toothless, cavernous mouth and sharp nose, flies were disporting themselves. As thin as a skeleton, motionless and open-mouthed, he resembled a corpse just brought from the morgue for dissection.

'Franz!' Urbenin said, nudging him. 'Franz!'

After five or six nudges, Franz closed his mouth, sat up, looked round at all of us and lay down again. A minute later his mouth was wide open again and the flies that had been frolicking near his nose were once again disturbed by the gentle tremors of his snoring.

'He's sleeping, the dissolute pig!' sighed Urbenin.

'Isn't that our gardener, Tricher?' asked the Count.

'The man himself . . . he gets into this state every day. During the day he sleeps like a log and at night he plays cards. I'm told that last night he played until six in the morning.'

'What does he play?'

'Games of chance . . . mainly *stukolka*.'[13]

'Yes, men of his sort are bad at their work. They get paid for doing absolutely nothing.'

'I didn't say that by way of complaint or to express my dissatisfaction, Your Excellency . . . I simply . . . well . . . I just felt sorry that such an able man should be slave to his passions. Besides, he's hard-working – a good man, who earns his money.'

We looked once more at Franz the cardsharp and left the summer-house. From there we headed for the garden gate that led out into the fields.

There are few novels where garden gates don't play a leading part. If you haven't noticed this, then ask my Polikarp – he has devoured piles of dreadful and not so dreadful novels in his time and will no doubt confirm that trivial but nonetheless basic fact.

My novel isn't free of garden gates either. But my gate is different from the others in that my pen will be leading through it many unfortunate wretches and hardly a single happy person – the reverse of what happens in other novels. And worst of all, I've already had occasion to describe this gate once, not as a novelist but as an investigating magistrate. In my novel it will let more criminals than lovers pass through.

A quarter of an hour later, leaning on our walking-sticks, we were trudging up the hill that we all knew as 'Stone Grave'. In neighbouring villages there exists the legend that under this pile of stones rests the body of a Tatar khan who, fearing that his enemies might desecrate his ashes after his death, left instructions in his will for a heap of stones to be piled up over him. But this legend has little truth in it. Those layers of stone, their size and relation to each other, rule out the agency of human hands in the origin of the hill. It stands by itself in a field and resembles an upturned night-cap.

When we had clambered to the top we could see the entire lake in all its enchanting expanse and indescribable beauty. The sun was no longer reflected in it – it had set, leaving a broad crimson strip that illuminated everything around with a pleasant pinkish-yellow light. At our feet lay the Count's estate, with manor house, church and garden, while in the distance, on the far side of the lake, was the small greyish village where fate had decreed I should reside. As before, the surface of the lake was motionless. Old Mikhey's little boats had separated from each other and were hurrying towards the bank.

To one side of my little village was the dark railway station, where small clouds of steam rose from locomotives, while behind us, on the other side of Stone Grave, a new vistas opened up. At the foot of Stone Grave stretched a road, bordered by lofty, ancient poplars. This road led to the Count's forest, that reached to the very horizon.

The Count and I stood on the top of the hill. Urbenin and the Pole, being rather unadventurous people, preferred to wait for us on the road down below.

'Who's that bigwig?' I asked the Count, nodding towards the Pole. 'Where did you fish him out from?'

'He's a very nice chap, Seryozha, *very* nice!' the Count said in alarm. 'You'll soon be best of friends!'

'Oh, I hardly think so. Why does he never say a word?'

'He's quiet by nature. But he's really very clever!'

'And what sort of person is he?'

'I met him in Moscow. He's very nice. I'll tell you all about it later, don't ask me now. Shall we go down?'

We descended Stone Grave and walked along the road towards the forest. It was growing noticeably darker. From the forest came the cries of cuckoos and the warbling of a tired and probably young nightingale.

'Ooh! Ooh!' came the shrill cry of a child as we approached the forest. 'Try and catch me!'

Out of the forest ran a little girl of about five, in a light-blue frock, her hair as white as flax. When she saw us she laughed out loud, skipped over to Urbenin and put her arms around his knee. Urbenin lifted her and kissed her on the cheek.

'It's my daughter Sasha,' he said. 'A lovely girl!'

In hot pursuit of Sasha, Urbenin's fifteen-year-old schoolboy son dashed out of the forest. The moment he saw us he hesitantly doffed his cap, put it on and then pulled it off again. A patch of red slowly followed him. At once our attention was riveted by this patch.

'What a magical vision!' exclaimed the Count, grasping my hand. 'Just look! How charming. Who is this girl? And I never knew that such naiads dwelt in my forest!'

I glanced at Urbenin to ask him who the girl was and – strange to relate – only then did I notice that the estate manager was terribly drunk. Red as a lobster, he gave a wild lurch and grabbed my elbow, enveloping me in alcoholic fumes as he whispered in my ear:

'Sergey Petrovich, I beg you, *please* stop the Count from making any more remarks about this girl. He might go too far – from sheer habit! That girl's a most worthy person, in the highest degree!'

This 'most worthy person, in the highest degree' was a girl of about nineteen, with beautiful fair hair, kind blue eyes and long curls. She was dressed in a bright red frock, halfway between a child's and a young girl's. Her little legs, as straight as needles in their red stockings, reposed in tiny, almost childish shoes. The whole time I admired her, those round shoulders kept shrinking coquettishly, as if they were cold and as if my gaze were biting them.

'What a well-developed figure for a girl with such a young face!' whispered the Count. Ever since his earliest days he had lost all capacity for respecting women and could only look upon them from the viewpoint of a depraved animal.

As for me, I well remember the fine feelings that began to glow within me. I was still a poet and in the presence of forests, a May evening and the first glimmerings of the evening star I could only view women with the eyes of a poet. I looked at the 'girl in red' with the same veneration with which I was accustomed to look at the forests, at the azure sky. At that time I still possessed a modicum of sentimentality, inherited from my German mother.

'Who is she?' asked the Count.

'She's the daughter of Skvortsov the forester, Your Excellency,' replied Urbenin.

'Is she the same Olenka whom the one-eyed peasant was talking about?'

'Yes, he did mention her name,' the manager replied, looking at me with large, beseeching eyes.

The girl in red let us go by without paying us the least attention, it seemed. Her eyes were looking somewhere to the side, but as someone who was an expert on women I felt that the pupils of her eyes were fixed on me.

'Which one is the Count?' I heard her whisper behind me.

'The one with the long moustache,' the schoolboy replied.

And we heard silvery laughter behind us. But it was the laughter of disenchantment. She had thought that *I* was the Count, owner of those vast forests and the wide lake – not that pigmy with the haggard face and long moustache.

I heard a deep sigh from Urbenin's chest. That man of iron could barely move.

'Tell your manager to go away,' I whispered to the Count. 'He's either ill . . . or drunk.'

'You don't look very well, Pyotr Yegorych,' the Count said, turning to Urbenin. 'I don't need you just now, so I won't detain you.'

'Don't worry, Your Excellency. Thank you for your concern, but I'm not ill.'

I looked back. The red patch didn't move and watched us as we left.

Poor little fair-haired girl! Did I imagine for one moment, on that serenest of May nights, that she would later become the heroine of my troubled novel?

And now, as I write these lines, the autumn rain angrily lashes my warm windows and somewhere above me the wind is howling. I gaze at the dark window and against a background of nocturnal gloom I try hard to recapture in my imagination that dear heroine of mine. I can see her with her innocently childlike, naïve, kind little face and loving eyes, and I want to throw down my pen, tear up, burn all that I have written so far. Why disturb the memory of that young, innocent creature?

But here, next to my inkwell, is her photograph. There that fair little head appears with all the vain grandeur of a beautiful woman who has plumbed the depths of depravity. Her eyes, so weary but proud in that depravity, are motionless: here she is that very snake, the harmfulness of whose bite Urbenin would not have considered exaggerated.

She blew a kiss to that storm – and the storm broke the flower off at its very root. Much was taken – but then, too high a price had been paid. The reader will forgive her sins.

IV

We walked through the forest.

Pine trees are boring in their silent monotony: they are all the same height, they all look exactly the same and they do not change with the seasons, knowing neither death nor vernal renewal. On the other hand they are attractive in their very gloominess – so still, so silent, as if they are thinking melancholy thoughts.

'Shouldn't we go back?' suggested the Count.

This question was unanswered. The Pole couldn't have cared less where he went, Urbenin didn't think he had any say in the matter and I was only too delighted with the cool of the forest and the resinous air to turn back. Besides, we had to while away the time somehow until nightfall, even if this meant simply strolling about. The very thought of the wild night that was approaching was accompanied by a delicious sinking of the heart. I'm ashamed to admit this, but I was dreaming of it and already mentally anticipating its pleasures. Judging by the impatience with which the Count constantly looked at his watch, it was obvious that he too was going through agonies of expectation. We felt that we understood one another.

Near the forester's cottage that nestled in a small clearing among the pines, we were greeted by the loud melodious barking of two flame-coloured dogs, glossy and as supple as eels, and of a breed that was unfamiliar to me. When they recognized Urbenin they joyfully wagged their tails and ran towards him, from which I gathered that the manager was a frequent visitor to the forester's cottage. Next to the cottage we were met by a bootless and capless lad with large freckles on his astonished face. For a minute he surveyed us in silence, with wide-open eyes and then, when he recognized the Count, he produced a loud 'Ah!' and dashed headlong into the cottage.

'I know why he ran off,' laughed the Count. 'I remember him . . . it's Mitka.'

The Count was not mistaken. Less than a minute later Mitka emerged from the cottage with a glass of vodka and half a tumbler of water on a tray.

'Your good health, Your Excellency,' he said, smiling all over his stupid, surprised face as he served the Count.

The Count downed the vodka and then took a drink of water – but for once he didn't frown. About a hundred paces from the cottage stood an iron bench, as old as the pines. We sat down on it and contemplated the May evening in all its tranquil beauty. Frightened crows flew cawing above our heads, the song of nightingales drifted towards us from all sides – nothing else broke the all-pervading silence.

The Count was incapable of remaining silent, even on calm evenings in May, when the voice of humans is least agreeable.

'I don't know whether you'll be satisfied,' he said, turning to me. 'I've ordered fish soup and game for supper. We'll have some cold sturgeon and sucking-pig with horseradish to go with the vodka.'

As if they were angered by these prosaic words, the poetic pines suddenly shook their crowns and a gentle rustle ran through the forest. A fresh breeze wafted over the clearing and played with the grass.

'Down boys!' Urbenin shouted to the flame-coloured dogs that were preventing him from lighting his cigarette with their endearments. 'I think it's going to rain tonight, I can feel it in the air. It's been so terribly hot today that you don't have to be a learned professor to forecast rain. It will be good for the corn.'

'And what's the good of corn to you,' I wondered, 'if the Count's going to squander the money on drink? No point in the rain troubling itself either.'

Again a breeze ran through the forest, but this time it was stronger. The pines and grass made a louder murmur.

'Let's go home.'

We stood up and lazily ambled back to the cottage.

'It's better to be a fair-haired Olenka,' I said, turning to Urbenin, 'and live here among the wild animals than an investigating magistrate and live among people. It's more peaceful . . . isn't that so, Pyotr Yegorych?'

'It doesn't matter what you are, as long as you have peace of mind, Sergey Petrovich.'

'And does this pretty Olenka have peace of mind?'

'The secrets of another's soul are known to God alone, but it strikes me that she has no reason to fret – no sorrow, and her sins are simply those of a child. She's a very good girl! Well, at last the heavens are talking of rain!'

We could hear a rumble, rather like a distant carriage or the clatter of skittles. From somewhere, far beyond the forest, came a great thunderclap. Mitka, who had been following us the whole time, shuddered and quickly crossed himself.

'A thunderstorm!' exclaimed the Count in alarm. 'I didn't expect that! Now we'll be caught in the rain on our way back. And it's got so dark! I said we should go back. But no, we carried on.'

'We can wait in the cottage until it's passed over,' I suggested.

'Why the cottage?' asked Urbenin, blinking peculiarly. 'It's going to rain all night, so do you really want to stay so long in the cottage? Now, please don't worry. Mitka will run on ahead and send the carriage to collect you.'

'It's all right – perhaps it won't rain all night,' I said. 'Storm clouds usually pass over very quickly. Besides, I don't know the new forester yet and I'd like to have a little chat with this Olenka, to find out what kind of dicky-bird she is.'

'No objections!' agreed the Count.

'But how can you go there if the place is all in a mess?' Urbenin anxiously babbled. 'Why sit in that stuffy place, Your Excellency, when you could be at home? I can't imagine what pleasure it can give you. And how can you get to know the forester if he's ill?'

It was patently obvious that the manager was violently opposed to our entering the forester's cottage. He even spread out his arms as if wanting to bar our way. I could see from his face that he had reasons for stopping us. I respect other people's reasons and secrets, but on this occasion my curiosity was greatly excited. I insisted – and into the cottage we went.

'Into the parlour, please!' barefooted Mitka said with a peculiar hiccup, almost choking with delight.

Imagine the tiniest parlour in the world, with unpainted wooden walls hung with oleographs from *The Cornfield*,[14] photographs in mother-of-pearl (as we call them here 'cockleshell') frames, and testimonials: one expressed a certain baron's gratitude for many years of service; the remainder were for horses. Here and there ivy made its way up the walls. In one of the corners, in front of a small icon, a tiny blue flame, faintly reflected in its silver mounting, was softly burning. Along the wall, chairs, evidently recently purchased, were ranged closely together. In fact, more had been bought than were needed, but they had still been placed there as there was nowhere else to put them. Crowded together were armchairs, a couch with snow-white, lace-frilled covers, and a round, polished table. A tame hare was dozing on the couch. It was cosy, clean and warm. A woman's presence was evident everywhere. Even the bookcase had an innocent, feminine look, as if it too wanted to declare that nothing but undemanding novels and light poetry were on its shelves. The charm of such warm, cosy little rooms is felt not so much in spring as in autumn, when you seek refuge from the cold and damp.

With much puffing and panting, and noisy striking of matches, Mitka lit two candles and placed them on the table as carefully as if they were milk. We sat down in the armchairs, exchanged glances and burst out laughing.

'Nikolay Yefimych is ill in bed,' Urbenin said, explaining the master's absence. 'And Olga Nikolayevna must have gone off to accompany my children.'

'Mitka! Are the doors locked!' came a weak tenor voice from the next room.

'Yes, they are, Nikolay Yefimych!' Mitka shouted hoarsely and rushed headlong into the next room.

'Good! See that every door is properly shut,' said that same feeble voice. 'And securely locked as well. If thieves should try to get in you must tell me . . . I'll shoot those devils with my rifle . . . the bastards!'

'Without fail, Nikolay Yefimych!'

We burst out laughing and looked quizzically at Urbenin. He turned red and started tidying the window curtains to hide his embarrassment. What was the meaning of this 'dream'? Once more we looked at each other.

But there was no time for wondering. Outside hurried footsteps could be heard again, followed by a noise in the porch and a door slamming. The girl in red flew into the room.

' "I lo-ove the storms of early Ma-ay",'[15] she sang in a shrill, strident soprano, punctuating her high-pitched singing with laughter. But the moment she saw us she suddenly stopped and fell silent. Deeply embarrassed, she went as meek as a lamb into the room from which we had just heard the voice of her father, Nikolay Yefimych.

'She wasn't expecting you!' laughed Urbenin.

Shortly afterwards she quietly returned, sat on the chair nearest the door and started inspecting us. She looked at us boldly, intensely, as if we were zoo animals and not new faces to her. For a minute we too looked at her, silently, without moving. I would willingly have sat there for a year, quite still, just to gaze at her, so beautiful did she look that evening. Her flushed cheeks as fresh as the air, that rapidly breathing, heaving bosom, those curls scattered over her forehead and shoulders and over that right hand with which she was adjusting her collar, her big, sparkling eyes – all this in one small body that you could take in at a single glance. Just one look at this tiny creature and you would see more than if you stared at the boundless horizon for centuries. She looked at me seriously, questioningly, with an upward glance. But when her eyes turned from me to the Count or the Pole, I began to read in them the complete reverse: a downward glance . . . and laughter.

I was the first to speak.

'Allow me to introduce myself,' I said, getting up and going over to her. 'Zinovyev . . . And this is my good friend Count Karneyev. Please do forgive us for barging into your pretty little cottage uninvited. Of course, we would never have done this if we hadn't been forced to take shelter from the storm.'

'But you won't make the cottage fall down!' she said, laughing and offering her hand.

She revealed her beautiful teeth. I sat down on a chair next to her and told her how we had been caught by a storm on our walk, quite unexpectedly. We started discussing the weather – the beginning of all beginnings. While we were chatting, Mitka had already managed to bring the Count two glasses of vodka and the water that invariably accompanied it. Taking advantage of the fact that I wasn't looking at him, the Count sweetly wrinkled his face after both glasses and shook his head.

'Perhaps you'd like some refreshments?' Olenka asked – and she left the room without waiting for a reply.

The first drops of rain beat against the panes. I went over to the window. By now it was completely dark and through the glass I could see nothing but raindrops trickling down and the reflection of my own nose. Lightning flashed and illuminated several of the nearest pines.

'Are the doors locked?' came that weak tenor voice again. 'Mitka! Come here you little devil and lock the doors! Oh God, this is sheer torment!'

A peasant woman with a bulging, tightly belted stomach and a stupid, worried face entered the parlour, bowed low to the Count and spread a white cloth over the table. Mitka gingerly followed her with the hors d'oeuvres. A minute later vodka, rum, cheese and a dish with some kind of roast fowl made their appearance on the table. The Count drank a glass of vodka but he did not start eating. The Pole sniffed the bird suspiciously and started carving.

'It's simply pelting now. Just look at that!' I told Olenka, who had come into the room again.

The girl in red came over to my window and just then, for one fleeting moment, we were lit up by a white radiance. There was a fearful crackling sound from above and something large and heavy seemed to have been ripped from its place in the sky, plummeting to earth with a great crash. The window panes and the wine glasses that were standing in front of the Count tinkled. It was an extremely violent thunderclap.

'Are you scared of storms?' I asked Olenka.

She pressed her cheek to her round shoulder and looked at me with the trustfulness of a child.

'Yes I am,' she whispered after a moment's thought. 'My mother was killed by a storm. It was even in the papers . . . Mother was crossing an open field and she was crying. She led a really wretched life in this world. God took pity on her and killed her with his heavenly electricity.'

'How do you know there's electricity in heaven?'

'I've learned about it. Did you know that people killed in storms or in war, and women who have died after a difficult labour, go to paradise! You won't find that in any books, but it's true. My mother's in paradise now. I think that one day I'll be killed in a storm and I too will go to paradise. Are you an educated man?'

'Yes.'

'Then you won't laugh at me. Now, this is how I'd like to die. To put on the most fashionable, expensive dress – like the one I saw that rich, local landowner Sheffer wearing the other day – and deck my arms with bracelets . . . Then to stand on the very top of Stone Grave and let myself be struck by lightning, in full view of everyone. A terrifying thunderclap, you know, and then – the end!'

'What a wild fantasy!' I laughed, peering into those eyes that were filled with holy terror at the thought of a terrible but dramatic death. 'So, you don't want to die in an ordinary dress?'

'No,' replied Olenka, with a shake of the head. 'To die, so that everyone can see me!'

'The frock you're wearing now is nicer than any fashionable and expensive dress. It suits you. It makes you look like a red flower from the green woods.'

'No, that's not true,' Olenka innocently sighed. 'It's a cheap dress, it can't possibly be nice.'

The Count came over to the window with the obvious intention of having a little chat with pretty Olenka. My friend can speak three European languages, but he can't speak to women. He looked somewhat out of his element as he came and stood near us, smiled inanely, mumbled an inarticulate 'Hmmm . . . y-y-yes . . .' and then retraced his steps to the carafe of vodka.

'When you came into the room,' I told Olenka, 'you were singing "I love the storms of early May". Haven't those lines been set to music?'

'No, I just sing all the poetry I know, after my own fashion.'

Just then I happened to look round. Urbenin was watching us. In his eyes I could read hatred and malice, which didn't in the least suit his kind, gentle face. 'He can't be jealous, can he?' I wondered.

The poor devil noted my quizzical look, rose from his chair and went out into the hall to fetch something. Even from his walk it was obvious that he was highly agitated. The thunderclaps, each louder and more resounding than the last, became more and more frequent. The lightning continually tinted the sky, the pines and the wet earth with its pleasant but dazzling light. It would be ages before the rain stopped. I walked away from the window to the book stand and started inspecting Olenka's library. 'Tell me what you read and I'll tell you what you are' – but for all that wealth of books, arranged in perfect symmetry on those shelves, it was difficult to assess in any way Olenka's intellectual level and 'educational attainments'. It was all a rather peculiar hotchpotch: three readers; one of Born's books;[16] Yevtushevsky's *Mathematics Problem Book*;[17] Lermontov (vol. 2); Shklyarevsky; the journal *The Task*;[18] a cookery book; *Miscellany*.[19] I could enumerate even more books, but just as I was taking *Miscellany* from the shelf and began turning the pages, the door to the other room opened and in came a person who immediately distracted my attention from Olenka's 'educational attainments'. This was a tall, muscular man in cotton-print dressing-gown, tattered slippers and with a rather original face: a mass of dark blue veins, it was embellished with a pair of sergeant's whiskers and sideburns, and on the whole it put me in mind of a bird's. The entire face seemed to have thrust itself forward in an apparent attempt to converge at the tip of the nose. Such faces, I think, are called 'pitcher-snouts'.[20] This character's small head reposed on a long, thin neck with a large Adam's apple and rocked like a starling-box in the wind. With his dull green eyes this strange man surveyed us, and then he stared at the Count.

'Are all the doors locked?' he asked in a pleading voice.

The Count glanced at me and shrugged his shoulders.

'Don't worry, Papa!' Olenka said. 'They're all locked. Go back to your room.'

'Is the barn locked?'

'He's a bit funny in the head . . . he gets like that sometimes,' Urbenin whispered, appearing from the hall. 'He's afraid of burglars and as you can see he's always fussing about the doors. Nikolay Yefimych!' he said, turning to this strange individual. 'Go back to your room and sleep. Don't worry, everything's locked.'

'Are the windows locked?'

Nikolay Yefimych quickly went to every window, checked the locks and then, without so much as a glance at us, shuffled back to his room in his slippers.

'Now and then he comes over all peculiar, poor devil,' Urbenin started explaining the moment he'd left the room. 'He's a fine, decent chap really, a family man . . . it's really very sad. Almost every summer he goes a bit dotty.'

I glanced at Olenka. Sheepishly, hiding her face from us, she began tidying the books I had disturbed. She was obviously ashamed of her crazy father.

'The carriage is here, Your Excellency!' Urbenin announced. 'You can drive back now if you wish.'

'But how on earth did that carriage get here?' I asked.

'I sent for it.'

A minute later I was sitting in the carriage with the Count, fuming as I listened to the peals of thunder.

'So, that Pyotr just bundled us out of the cottage, blast him!' I growled, getting really angry. 'He didn't let us have a proper look at Olenka! I wouldn't have eaten her! Silly old fool! He was simply bursting with jealousy the whole time. He's in love with that girl.'

'Oh yes! Fancy that – I noticed it too! And he was so jealous he didn't want to let us into the cottage – he only sent for the carriage out of sheer jealousy! Ha ha!'

' "The later love comes the more it burns" . . . Really, it's very hard not to fall for that girl in red, my friend, if you see her every day as we saw her today! She's devilishly pretty! Only, she's not his sort. He ought to understand that and not be so egotistically jealous. All right, love if you like, but don't stop others – all the more so if you realize the girl's not meant for you! Really, what a blockhead!'

'Do you remember how he flared up when Kuzma mentioned her name over tea?' sniggered the Count. 'I thought he was going to thrash the lot of us then – you don't go defending a woman's good name so fiercely if you've no feelings for her.'

'But some men will do that . . . however, that's not the point. The crux of the matter is this: if he could order *us* around like that today, how does he treat small fry who are at his beck and call? He probably won't let stewards, managers, huntsmen and other nobodies of this world go anywhere near her. Love and jealousy can make a man unjust, callous, misanthropic. I'll wager that because of Olenka he's tormented the life out of more than one servant under his command. Therefore you'd do well to take his complaints about your poor employees, about the need to dismiss this one or the other, with a pinch of salt. In general, his authority must be curbed for the time being. Love will pass – and then there'll be nothing to fear. He's really quite a decent fellow.'

'And how do you like her papa?' laughed the Count.

'He's insane . . . should be in a lunatic asylum, not managing forests. You wouldn't be far wrong if you went and hung the sign "Lunatic Asylum" on the gates to your estate. It's sheer Bedlam here! This forester, Owlet, that card-mad Franz, that old man in love, an overexcited girl, a drunken Count – what more do you want?'

'And I pay that forester wages! How can he work if he's insane?'

'It's obvious that Urbenin's keeping him on solely because of the daughter. Urbenin says that Nikolay Yefimych goes off his rocker every summer. But that's not so . . . that forester's constantly off his rocker, not only during the summer. Fortunately your Pyotr Yegorych rarely lies and he'd soon give himself away if he did.'

'Last year Urbenin wrote to inform me that our old forester Akhmetyev was going to Mount Athos[21] to become a monk and he recommended the "experienced, honest and worthy Skvortsov". Of course, I agreed, as I invariably do. After all, letters aren't faces: they don't show it if they lie!'

The carriage drove into the courtyard and stopped at the main entrance. We climbed out. By now it had stopped raining. Giving off flashes of lightning and angrily rumbling, a storm cloud was racing towards the north-east, revealing an ever-increasing expanse of starry blue sky. It seemed as if some heavily armed power, having wrought wholesale devastation and exacted terrible tribute, was now rushing on to new conquests. Small clouds that had been left behind hurried after it in hot pursuit, as if afraid they would not catch up with it. Peace was being restored to Nature.

And this peace was apparent in the calm aromatic air, filled with languor and nightingale melodies, in the silence of the sleeping garden, in the caressing light of the rising moon. The lake awoke after its daytime slumbers and made itself audible to man with its gentle murmur.

At such times it is pleasant to drive through open country in a comfortable carriage, or to row on a lake. But we went into the house: there a different kind of poetry was awaiting us.

V

The man who, under the influence of mental pain or plagued with unbearable suffering, puts a bullet in his brains is called a suicide. But for those who give full rein to their pathetic, spiritually debasing passions during the sacred days of their youth there is no name in the language of man. Bullets are followed by the peace of the grave, ruined youth is followed by years of grief and agonizing memories. Anyone who has profaned his youth will understand my present state of mind. I'm not old yet, I'm not grey, but I'm no longer alive. Psychiatrists tell of a soldier who, wounded at Waterloo, went mad, subsequently assuring everyone (and he believed it himself) that he had been killed at Waterloo and that the person they now took to be him was merely his ghost, an echo of the past. And now I'm experiencing something similar to that half-death.

'I'm very glad you didn't have anything to eat at the forester's and haven't spoilt your appetite,' the Count told me as we entered the house. 'We're going to have an excellent supper, just like old times. You can serve us now,' he told Ilya, who was helping him off with his jacket and putting on his dressing-robe.

Off we went to the dining-room. Here, on a side-table, life was already 'bubbling away'. Bottles of every colour and conceivable size stood in rows, as they do on the shelves of theatre bars, reflecting the light from the lamps and awaiting our attention. Salted, marinaded meats, all kinds of savouries stood on another table, together with a carafe of vodka and another of English bitters.[22] Close to the wine bottles were two dishes: one with sucking-pig, the other with cold sturgeon.

'Well, gentlemen,' began the Count, filling three glasses and shuddering as if he felt cold. 'Good health! Take your glass, Kaetan Kazimirovich!'

I emptied mine, but the Pole shook his head negatively. He drew the sturgeon closer to him, sniffed it and started eating.

Here I must crave the reader's forgiveness, for now I have to describe something which is not in the least 'poetic'.

'Well now, you've had your first,' said the Count, refilling the glasses. 'Be bold, my dear Lecoq!'

I took my glass, glanced at it and put it down. 'To hell with it, it's ages since I last had a drink,' I said. 'Why not remember the good old days?' And without further hesitation I filled five glasses and, one after the other, poured their contents down my throat. That was the only way I knew how to drink. Little schoolboys learn from big ones how to smoke cigarettes. The Count looked at me as he poured himself five glasses, arched his body, wrinkled his face, shook his head and tossed them all back. My own five glasses struck him as an act of bravado, but I didn't drink at all to flaunt my talent for drinking: far from it. I *craved* intoxication, pure and utter intoxication such as I had not known for a very long time, living as I did in a tiny little village. After drinking my fill I sat at the table and started on the sucking-pig.

Intoxication was not long in coming. Soon I felt a slight dizziness. Then I experienced a pleasant, cool sensation in my chest – this was the start of a blissful, expansive state. Suddenly, without any particularly noticeable transition, I became extremely merry. My feelings of boredom and emptiness gave way to a sensation of perfect joy and euphoria. I started smiling. Suddenly I yearned for conversation, laughter, people. As I chewed the sucking-pig I began to experience life in all its plenitude, almost complete contentment with life, almost perfect happiness.

'Why aren't you drinking?' I asked the Pole.

'He doesn't drink,' said the Count. 'Don't try and force him.'

'All the same, you must at least drink something!' I exclaimed. The Pole popped a large slice of sturgeon into his mouth and shook his head dismissively. His silence only egged me on.

'Listen, Kaetan . . . what's your second name? . . . why do you never say a word?' I asked. 'So far I haven't had the pleasure of hearing your voice.'

His eyebrows rose like a swallow in flight and he looked at me.

'Do you vish me to speak?' he asked with a strong Polish accent.

'I vish very much.'

'And vy is zat?'

'Vy indeed! On board ship, during dinner, strangers and people who've never met manage to get into conversation. But we, who have known each other for several hours now, simply gape at one another – and so far we haven't spoken a single word to each other. It's unheard of!'

The Pole said nothing.

'But vy are you so silent?' I asked after a brief interval. 'Give me some sort of reply.'

'I don't vish to reply. I can detect laughter in your voice and I don't like being ridiculed.'

'But he's not laughing at you at all!' the Count said in alarm. 'Where did you get that idea from, Kaetan? He's just being friendly.'

'Counts and princes have never taken zat tone with me!' Kaetan said, frowning. 'I don't like zat tone.'

'So, you won't honour us with a little conversation?' I persisted, polishing off another glass and laughing.

'Do you know my real reason for coming back here?' interrupted the Count, wishing to change the subject. 'Haven't I told you yet? In St Petersburg I went to see a doctor friend who's always treated me, complaining about not feeling well. He listened, tapped, poked me all over and asked: "You're not a coward, are you?" Well, although I'm no coward, I went white and replied that I wasn't.'

'Cut it short, old man, you're boring me!'

'He diagnosed that I would die very soon if I didn't leave St Petersburg and go abroad. My whole liver was diseased from chronic drinking. So I decided to come here. Yes, it would have been stupid to have stayed on there. This estate is magnificent, so rich . . . the climate alone is priceless! Here one can at least get on with some work! Hard work is the best, the most effective medicine. Isn't that so, Kaetan? I'll do a spot of farming and give up drink. The doctor forbade me a single glass . . . not even one glass!'

'Then don't drink!'

'I *don't* drink any more – today's the very last time, just to celebrate my reunion' – here the Count leant over and gave me a resounding kiss on the cheek – 'with my dear, good friend. But not a drop tomorrow! Today Bacchus takes leave of me forever! So, how about a little farewell glass of brandy, Sergey?'

We drank some brandy.

'I'll get well again, my dear Seryozha, and I'll busy myself with farming. Rationalized farming! Urbenin is a good, kind man, he understands everything – but is he really the managerial type? No, he's simply a slave to routine! We should subscribe to journals, read, follow all the news, exhibit at agricultural shows. But he's too ignorant for that! Surely he can't be in love with Olenka? Ha ha! I'll take charge of things myself and make him my assistant. I'll take part in the elections, cheer local society up a bit . . . eh? Come off it, you're laughing! Yes, laughing! Really, it's impossible to discuss anything with you.'

I felt cheerful and amused. The Count, the candles, the bottles, the plaster hares and ducks that adorned the dining-room walls all amused me. The only thing that didn't amuse me was Kaetan's sober physiognomy. That man's presence irritated me.

'Can't you tell your lousy Pole to go to hell?' I whispered to the Count.

'*What* did you say? For God's sake!' mumbled the Count, seizing both my arms as if I were about to thrash that Pole of his. 'Leave him alone!'

'But I just can't bear the sight of him!' I said. 'Listen,' I went on, turning to Pshekhotsky. 'You refuse to talk to me, but please forgive me – I haven't abandoned all hope yet of gaining a closer acquaintance with your conversational ability . . .'

'Stop it!' exclaimed the Count, tugging my sleeve. 'I *beg* you!'

'I won't leave you alone until you reply to my questions,' I continued. 'Vy are you frowning? Do you detect laughter in my voice even now?'

'If I'd drunk as much as you, I'd be able to have a conversation vith you. But I'm not your sort,' the Pole growled.

'"Not my sort" – that's exactly what needs to be proven . . . that's exactly what I meant to say. A goose is no companion for a pig . . . a drunkard cramps a sober man's style and the sober man cramps the drunkard. In the next room there are the most excellent soft sofas! You can go and sleep off your sturgeon with horseradish. You won't be able to hear me from there. Don't you vish to head in zat direction?'

The Count clasped his hands in despair, blinked and walked up and down the dining-room. He was a coward and scared of 'angry exchanges'. But when I was drunk, misunderstandings and unpleasantness only amused me.

'I don't understand. I don't under-stand!' moaned the Count, at a loss what to say or do.

He knew that I would take some stopping.

'I don't really know you yet,' I continued. 'Perhaps you *are* a very fine person and therefore I wouldn't want to start quarrelling with you so early in the day. I *don't* have any quarrel with you, I'm simply inviting you to try and get into your head that there's no place for the sober amongst the drunk. The presence of a sober person has an irritating effect on the drunken organism! Please understand that!'

'You can say vot you like,' Pshekhotsky sighed. 'Nothing you say vill get my back up, young man!'

'Nothing? What if I called you an obstinate pig – wouldn't you take offence at that?'

The Pole turned crimson – and that was all. White as a sheet, the Count came over to me with an imploring look and opened his arms wide.

'Please moderate your language, I beg you!'

I was now relishing my drunken role and wanted to carry on, but fortunately for the Count and the Pole some footsteps rang out and into the dining-room came Urbenin.

'I wish you good appetite!' he began. 'I've come to inquire if you have any orders for me, Your Excellency.'

'None at the moment, but I do have a request,' replied the Count. 'I'm really delighted you've come, Pyotr Yegorych. Sit down and have some supper with us and let's discuss farming.'

Urbenin sat down. The Count quaffed some brandy and started explaining his plans for the future 'rational' management of the estate. He spoke lengthily, tiresomely, constantly repeating himself and changing the subject. Urbenin listened to him attentively, as serious people listen to the chatter of women and children. He ate some fish soup and sadly gazed into his plate.

'I've brought some first-class plans back with me,' the Count said. 'Remarkable plans! Would you like me to show you them?'

Karneyev jumped up and ran to his study to fetch them. Taking advantage of his absence, Urbenin quickly poured himself half a tumbler of vodka and swallowed it, without taking any food with it.

'Vodka's a disgusting drink!' he said, looking hatefully at the carafe.

'Why don't you drink while the Count's here, Pyotr Yegorych?' I asked him. 'You're not scared, are you?'

'Sergey Petrovich, it's better to play the hypocrite and drink on the sly, than when you're with the Count. You know he's very odd. If I were to steal twenty thousand from him and he got to know, he wouldn't be concerned and he'd say nothing. But if I forgot to account for a ten-copeck piece that I'd spent, or if I drank some vodka in front of him, he'd start moaning that his manager was a crook. You know very well what he's like.'

Urbenin poured himself another half tumbler and swallowed it.

'You never used to drink, Pyotr Yegorych,' I said.

'No – but I do now. A hell of a lot!' he whispered. 'A hell of a lot, day and night, never stopping for a breather! Even the Count never drank as much as I do now. Things are very hard for me, Sergey Petrovich. God alone knows how heavy my heart is. That's exactly why I drink – to drown my sorrows . . . I've always been fond of you and respected you, Sergey Petrovich, and to tell you quite frankly . . . I'd willingly go and hang myself!'

'Why is that?'

'Because of my own stupidity. It's not only children who are stupid . . . there are fools at fifty. Don't ask the reason.'

The Count came in again and put a stop to his effusions.

'A most excellent liqueur!' he exclaimed, putting a pot-bellied bottle with the Benedictine seal on the table instead of his 'first-class plans'. 'I picked it up at Depré's[23] when I was passing through Moscow. Would you care for a drop, Seryozha?'

'But I thought you'd gone to fetch the plans,' I said.

'Me? What plans? Oh yes! But the devil himself couldn't sort my suitcases out, old chap. I kept rummaging and rummaging but I gave it up as a bad job. It's a very nice liqueur. Would you care for a drop?'

Urbenin stayed a little longer, then he said goodbye and left. When he had gone we started on the red wine: this completely finished me off. I was intoxicated exactly the way I wanted to be when I was riding to the Count's. I became extremely high spirited, lively, unusually cheerful. I wanted to accomplish some truly extraordinary, amusing, dashing deed . . . At such moments I felt I could have swum right across the lake, solved the most complicated case, conquered any woman. The world, with all its diversity of life, sent me into raptures. I loved it, but at the same time I wanted to find fault with someone, to sting with venomous witticism, to mock . . . I simply had to ridicule that black-browed Pole and the Count, to wear them down with biting sarcasm, to make mincemeat of them.

'Why are you so quiet?' I began. 'Speak and I'll listen! Ha ha! I simply *adore* it when people with serious, respectable physiognomies spout puerile nonsense! It's such a mockery, such a mockery of the human brain! Your faces don't correspond to your brains! To tell the truth, you should have the physiognomies of idiots, but you have the faces of Greek sages!'

I didn't finish. My tongue became tied in knots at the thought that I was talking to nobodies who weren't even worth a mention! I needed a crowded ballroom, brilliant women, thousands of lights . . . I got up, took my glass and started wandering through all the rooms. On a drunken spree you don't set limits to your space, you don't restrict yourself to a dining-room, but roam over the whole house, even the entire estate.

I selected an ottoman in the 'mosaic' room, lay down and surrendered myself to fantasies and building castles in the air. Drunken dreams, each more grandiose and boundless than the last, took possession of my young brain. Now I could see a new world, full of stupefying pleasures and beauty beyond description. All that was lacking was for me to talk in rhyme and start having hallucinations.

The Count came up to me and sat on the edge of the ottoman. He wanted to tell me something. I had begun to read in his eyes this desire to communicate something rather unusual very soon after the above-mentioned five glasses: I knew what he wanted to discuss.

'I've had so much to drink today!' he told me. 'For me it's more harmful than any poison. But today's the last time. Word of honour, the last time! I do have will-power.'

'Of course, of course.'

'For the last . . . for the last time, Seryozha, old chap, shouldn't we send a telegram to town?'

'By all means . . . send one . . .'

'Let's have a real orgy – for the last time. Come on, get up and write it.'

The Count had no idea how to write telegrams – they always turned out too long and incomplete. So I got up and wrote:

TO LONDON RESTAURANT GIPSY CHOIR OWNER KARPOV DROP EVERYTHING COME IMMEDIATELY TWO O'CLOCK TRAIN THE COUNT

'It's a quarter to eleven now,' the Count said. 'My man can ride to the station in three quarters of an hour – one hour *maximum*. Karpov will get the telegram before one. So he'll have time to catch the express. Should he miss it he can *take the goods train. Yes?*'

VI

One-eyed Kuzma was dispatched with the telegram, Ilya was instructed to send carriages to the station one hour later. To kill time I slowly started lighting the lamps and candles in every room. Then I opened the grand piano and tried a few notes.

And then I remember lying on the same ottoman, thinking of nothing and silently waving away the Count, who was pestering me with his incessant chatter. I was in a kind of semi-conscious state, half-asleep, aware only of the bright light from the lamps and my serene and cheerful state of mind. A vision of the girl in red, her little head inclined towards her shoulder, her eyes filled with horror at the prospect of that dramatic death, appeared before me and gently shook its tiny finger at me. A vision of another girl, in black dress and with a pale, proud face, drifted past and looked at me half-imploringly, half-reproachfully.

Then I heard noise, laughter, people running about. Deep black eyes came between me and the light. I could see their sparkle, their laughter. A joyful smile flickered on luscious lips . . . it was my gipsy girl Tina smiling at me.

'Is it you?' she asked. 'Are you asleep? Get up, my darling . . . I haven't seen you for ages.'

Without a word I pressed her hand and drew her to me.

'Let's go into the other room . . . we've all arrived.'

'Let's stay here . . . I like it here, Tina . . .'

'But there's too much light . . . you're crazy . . . someone might come in.'

'If anyone does I'll wring their neck. I like it here, Tina. It's two years since I last saw you.'

Someone was playing the piano in the ballroom.

> 'Ah, Moscow, Moscow,
> Moscow with your white stone walls . . .'[24]

several voices bawled at once.

'Can you hear? They're all in there singing . . . no one will come in.'

My encounter with Tina roused me from my half-conscious state. Ten minutes later she led me into the ballroom, where the choir was standing in a semicircle. The Count was straddling a chair and beating time with his hands. Pshekhotsky stood behind his chair, watching those songbirds with astonished eyes. I grabbed Karpov's balalaika from his hands, performed a wild flourish and started singing:

'Down Mo-other Vo-olga
Do-own the Riv-er Vo-olga . . .'[25]

And the choir responded:

'Oh burn, oh speak . . . speak!'[26]

I waved my arm and in an instant, as quick as lightning, there followed another rapid transition:

'Nights of madness, nights of gladness . . .'[27]

Nothing stimulates and titillates my nerves so much as abrupt transitions like these. I trembled with delight. With one arm around Tina and waving the balalaika in the other, I sang *Nights of Madness* to the end. The balalaika crashed to the floor and broke into small splinters . . .

'More wine!'

After that my memories verge on the chaotic. Everything becomes muddled, confused, everything grows vague and blurred . . . I remember the grey sky of early morning . . . We are in rowing-boats. The lake is slightly ruffled and seems to be grumbling at the sight of our debauchery. I stand reeling in the middle of the boat. Tina tries to convince me that I'll fall into the water and she begs me to sit down. But I complain out loud that there are no waves on the lake as high as Stone Grave and my shouts frighten the martins that dart like white spots over the blue surface.

Then follows a long, hot day with its interminable lunch, ten-year-old liqueurs, bowls of punch, drunken brawls. I remember but a few moments of that day, I remember rocking on the garden swing with Tina. I'm standing at one end of the seat, she at the other. I work with my whole body, in a wild frenzy, with my last ounce of strength and I cannot really say whether I want Tina to fall off the swing and be killed, or to fly right up to the clouds. Tina stands there as pale as death, but she is proud and vain, and has clenched her teeth in order not to betray her fear with the least sound. Higher and higher we fly and I cannot remember how it all ended. Then came a stroll with Tina down that distant avenue with the green vault screening it from the sun. Poetic half-light, black locks, luscious lips, whispers . . . And then at my side there walks a small contralto singer, a fair-haired girl with a sharp little nose, the eyes of a child and a very slender waist. I stroll with her until Tina, who has been following us, comes along and makes a scene. The gipsy girl is pale and furious. She damns me and is so offended that she prepares to return to town. Pale-faced and with trembling hands, the Count runs around us and as usual cannot find the words to persuade Tina to stay. Finally Tina slaps my face. It's strange: the most innocuous, barely offensive words spoken by a man send me into a frenzy, but I'm quite indifferent to the slaps women give me . . . And then again those long hours after dinner, again that snake on the steps, again sleeping Franz with flies around his mouth, again that garden gate. The girl in red stands on the top of Stone Grave but disappears like a lizard as soon as she sees us.

By evening Tina and I are once again friends. There follows the same wild night, music, rollicking songs with titillating, nerve-tingling transitions . . . and not one moment's sleep!

'This is self-destruction!' whispers Urbenin, who has dropped in for a moment to listen to our singing.

Of course, he was right. I later recalled the Count and myself standing in the garden, face to face, arguing. Nearby strolls that black-browed Kaetan, who had taken no part in our jollification but who nevertheless had not slept and who kept following us like a shadow. The sky is pale now and the rays of the rising sun are already beginning to shed their golden light over the highest tree top. All around I can hear the chatter of busy sparrows, the singing of starlings, rustling, the flapping of wings that had grown heavy during the night. I can hear the lowing herd and shepherds' cries. Close by is a small, marble-topped table. A Shandor candle[28] stands on it, burning with a pale light . . . there are cigarette ends, sweet wrappers, broken glasses, orange peel . . .

'You must take this!' I say, handing the Count a bundle of banknotes. 'I shall force you to take them!'

'But it was I who invited the gipsies, not you!' cries the Count, trying to grab one of my buttons. 'I'm master here, I treated you . . . so why on earth should you pay? Please understand that I even take this as an insult!'

'But I engaged them too, so I'll pay half. You refuse to accept it? Well, I don't understand the reason for these favours! Surely you don't think that because you're stinking rich you have the right to offer me such favours? Damn it – *I* engaged Karpov, so *I'll* pay him! I don't need your "half". And *I* wrote the telegram!'

'In a restaurant, Seryozha, you can pay as much as you like, but my house isn't a restaurant. And then, I really don't understand why you're making all this fuss, I don't understand why you're so eager to pay. You don't have much money, but I'm rolling in it. Justice itself is on my side!'

'So you won't take it? No? Well, don't!'

I hold the banknotes up to the faint candlelight, set fire to them and throw them on the ground. A groan suddenly bursts from Kaetan's chest. He becomes wide-eyed, turns pale and falls heavily to the floor, trying to put out the flames with the palms of his hands . . . in this he succeeds.

'I don't understand!' he says, stuffing the singed banknotes into his pocket. 'Burning money! Just as if it were last year's chaff or love letters! Better give it all away to some beggar than consign it to the flames.'

I enter the house . . . there, in every room, sprawled over sofas and carpets, sleep the gipsies – exhausted, completely worn out. My Tina is sleeping on the ottoman in the 'mosaic' drawing-room.

She lies stretched out and she's breathing heavily. Her teeth are clenched, her face pale. She's probably dreaming of swings. Owlet wanders through all the rooms, looking malignantly with her sharp eyes at those who had so rudely disturbed the deathly silence of that forgotten estate. Not for nothing does she go around tiring her old bones.

That's all that remains in my memory after two wild nights – the rest either hasn't been preserved by my inebriated brain cells or cannot be described here with any decency. But enough of that!

Never before had Zorka borne me so zealously as on that morning after the burning of the banknotes. She too wanted to go home. The lake gently rolled its foamy waves: reflecting the rising sun, it was preparing for its daytime slumber. The woods and willows along the banks were motionless, as if at morning prayer. It is difficult to describe my state of mind at the time. Without going into too much detail I shall merely say that I was delighted beyond words – and at the same time I was almost consumed with shame when, as I turned out of the Count's estate, I saw by the lakeside old Mikhey's saintly face, emaciated by honest toil and illness. Mikhey resembles a biblical fisherman. His hair is as white as snow, he has a large beard and he gazes contemplatively at the sky. When he stands motionless on the bank, following the racing clouds with his eyes, you might fancy he sees angels in the sky . . . I'm very fond of such faces!

When I saw him I reined in Zorka and gave him my hand, as if wishing to cleanse myself through contact with his honest, calloused hand. He looked up at me with his small, sagacious eyes and smiled.

'Good morning, sir!' he said, awkwardly offering me his hand. 'Why've you come galloping over here again? Is that old layabout back?'

'He is.'

'I thought so, I can see it from your face. 'Ere I be standing and looking. What a world! Vanity of vanities, says I! Just look! That German deserves to die – all 'e bothers 'isself with is worthless things. Can you see 'im?'

The old man pointed his stick at the Count's bathing-place. A rowing-boat was swiftly moving away from it and a man in a jockey cap and blue jacket was sitting in it. It was Franz the gardener.

'Every morning 'e takes something out to the island and hides it. That fool can't get it into 'is head that sand and money are worth the same as far as 'e's concerned – can't take 'em with 'im when 'e dies. Please give me a cigarette, sir!'

I offered him my cigarette case. He took three out and stuffed them into his breast pocket.

'They're for me nephew . . .'e can smoke 'em.'

My impatient Zorka gave a start and flew off. I bowed to the old man, thankful that he'd let my eyes rest upon his face. For a long time he stood there watching me go.

VII

At home I was greeted by Polikarp. With a contemptuous, crushing look, he inspected my noble body, as if trying to find out whether on this occasion I'd been bathing fully dressed in my suit or not.

'Congratulations!' he growled. 'I can see you had a good time!'

'Shut up, you fool!' I replied.

I was incensed by his stupid face. After quickly undressing I covered myself with a blanket and closed my eyes.

My head was in a spin and the world became enveloped in mist. In that mist familiar shapes flashed by . . . the Count, the snake, Franz, those flame-coloured dogs, the girl in red, crazy Nikolay Yefimych . . .

'A husband murdered his wife! Oh, how stupid you are!' The girl in red wagged her finger at me, Tina blotted out the light with her black eyes and I . . . I fell asleep.

'How sweetly, how peacefully he sleeps! When you look at that innocent child's smile and listen closely to that regular breathing you might think that this is no investigating magistrate lying there on the bed but the living embodiment of a pure conscience! You might even think that Count Karneyev hadn't returned, that there had been neither drunkenness nor gipsy girls, nor scandals on the lake. Get up, you most spiteful of men! You are not worthy of enjoying such bliss as peaceful slumber. Arise!'

I opened my eyes and stretched myself voluptuously. From the window to my bed streamed a broad ray of sunlight in which minute white specks of dust were chasing each other in great agitation, so that the ray itself seemed tinted dull white. The sunbeam kept disappearing from sight, then reappearing, depending on whether our charming district doctor, Pavel Ivanovich Voznesensky – who was walking around my bedroom – entered or left the field of light. In his long, unbuttoned frock-coat that hung loosely, as if from a clothes peg, his hands thrust deep into the pockets of his unusually long trousers, the doctor paced from corner to corner, from chair to chair, from portrait to portrait, screwing up his short-sighted eyes at everything they happened to fall upon. True to his habit of poking his nose and snooping into everything wherever he could, he would bend down and then stand bolt upright again, peering at the wash basin, at the folds of the lowered curtains, at chinks in the door, at the lamp, just as if he were looking for something or wanting to satisfy himself that all was in order. As he stared through his spectacles at some chink, or some stain on the wallpaper, he would frown, assume a worried expression, sniff with his long nose and studiously scratch away with his fingernail. All this he performed mechanically, involuntarily, from sheer habit. Nevertheless, he gave the impression of a surveyor carrying out some inspection as his eyes swiftly passed from one object to the other.

'Get up! You're being spoken to!' he said, waking me up with his melodious tenor voice, peering into the soap dish and removing a hair from the soap with his fingernail.

'A . . . a . . . a . . . good morning, Dr Screwy!' I yawned when I spotted him bending over the washstand. 'It's been ages since I last saw you!'

The whole district teased the doctor by calling him 'Screwy' on account of his habit of constantly screwing up his eyes. And I too teased him with that nickname. When he saw that I was awake, Voznesensky came over to me, sat on the edge of the bed and immediately raised a matchbox to his screwed-up eyes.

'Only idlers or those with a clear conscience sleep like you do,' he said. 'And as you're neither one nor the other, it might be more becoming if you got up a bit earlier, dear chap.'

'What's the time?'

'Just gone eleven.'

'To hell with you, silly old Screwy! No one asked you to wake me so early! Do you know, it was after five when I got to bed and if it hadn't been for you I'd have slept until this evening.'

'That's right!' came Polikarp's deep voice from the next room. 'As if he hasn't slept enough! It's the second day he's been sleeping, but it's still not enough! Do you know what day it is?' Polikarp asked, entering the bedroom and looking at me the way clever people look at fools.

'It's Wednesday,' I said.

'Oh yes, of course it is! They've arranged for a week to have two Wednesdays, specially for you!'

'Today's Thursday!' said the doctor. 'So, my dear chap, you managed to sleep through the whole of Wednesday! Very nice! Very nice! And how much did you have to drink, may I ask?'

'I hadn't slept for two days and I drank – I just can't remember how much I drank.'

After I had dismissed Polikarp I started dressing and describing to the doctor those recently experienced 'nights of madness, wild words' that are so fine, so touching in songs but so ugly in reality. In my description I tried not to overstep the limits of the 'light genre', to keep to the facts and not to lapse into moralizing, although all this was alien to the nature of one with a passion for summarizing and making deductions. As I spoke I pretended to be talking about trifles that didn't worry me in the least. Respecting Pavel Ivanovich's chaste ears and conscious of his revulsion for the Count, I concealed a great deal, touched on many things only superficially – but for all that, despite my playful tone and grotesque turn of phrase, the doctor looked me gravely in the eye throughout my narrative, constantly shaking his head and impatiently jerking his shoulders. Not once did he smile. Evidently my 'light genre' made a far from light impression on him.

'Why aren't you laughing, Screwy?' I asked after I'd finished my description.

'If it weren't *you* who was telling me all this, and if it hadn't *been for a certain incident*, I'd never have believed a word of it. But it's absolutely shocking, old man!'

'What incident are you talking about?'

'The peasant whom you so indelicately treated to a taste of the oar called on me yesterday evening . . . Ivan Osipov . . .'

'Ivan Osipov?' I said, shrugging my shoulders. 'It's the first I've heard of him.'

'He's tall, red-haired, with freckles. Try to remember! You hit him on the head with an oar.'

'I'm really at a complete loss . . . I don't know any Osipov. I never hit anyone with an oar. You must have been dreaming, old boy!'

'If only it were a dream! He came to me with an official letter from the Karneyev district authorities and asked for a medical certificate. In the letter it states – and he's not telling any lies – that it was *you* who inflicted the wound. Still don't remember? You bruised him above the forehead, just at the hairline – went right down to the bone, dear chap!'

'I can't remember,' I whispered. 'Who is he? What does he do?'

'He's just an ordinary peasant from the Karneyev estate. He was one of the oarsmen when you were making merry on the lake.'

'Hm . . . it's possible . . . I can't remember. I was probably drunk . . . and then, somehow, by accident . . .'

'No sir, it wasn't by accident. He says that you lost your temper with him for some reason, kept swearing at him – and then you became really furious, leapt over and struck him in front of witnesses. What's more, you shouted: "I'll kill you, you rotten bastard!" '

I went red and paced from corner to corner.

'For the life of me I can't remember,' I said, making a great effort of memory. 'I can't remember! You say I lost my temper – when I'm drunk I'm usually unforgivably loathsome!'

'So, what more need I say!?'

'That peasant obviously wants to create a scandal, but that's not what's important . . . what's important is the fact itself, the blow I inflicted. Surely you don't think I'm capable of fighting? And why should I strike a miserable peasant?'

'Well, my dear sir . . . Of course, I couldn't refuse him a medical certificate, but I didn't forget to advise him to come and see you about it. You'll sort it all out with him one way or the other. It's only a slight bruise, but from an official point of view any head wound penetrating the skull is a serious matter. You frequently come across cases where apparently the most trivial head wound that had been considered relatively minor led to necrosis of the skull bones and therefore a journey *ad patres*.'[29]

Carried away, Screwy stood up, paced the room close to the walls, waved his arms and started expounding his knowledge of surgical pathology for my benefit. Necrosis of the skull bones, inflammation of the brain, death and other horrors, simply poured from his lips, together with interminable explanations of the macroscopic and microscopic processes that are normally to be found in that hazy *terra incognita*[30] which was of no interest to me.

'That's enough, you old windbag!' I said, putting an end to his medical chatter. 'Don't you realize how boring all this stuff is for me!'

'Boring or not – that isn't the point. You must listen and show a little remorse. Perhaps you'll be more careful another time and not do such stupid, unnecessary, things. You could lose your job because of that oaf Osipov – if you don't patch things up with him. For one of the high priests of Themis[31] to be taken to court for common assault would be simply scandalous!'

Pavel Ivanovich is the only person whose pronouncements I can listen to with a light heart, without frowning, whom I can allow to peer into my eyes questioningly and to lower his probing hand into the convolutions of my soul. We're friends in the very best sense of the word and we respect one another, although there do exist between us grievances of an unpleasant, rather ticklish nature. Like a black cat, a woman had come between us. This eternal *casus belli*[32] had given rise to many conflicts, but it didn't make us fall out and we continued to live in peace.

Screwy is a very fine fellow . . . I love his simple and far from supple face with its big nose, screwed-up eyes and thin, small, reddish beard. I love his tall, slim, narrow-shouldered figure from which his frock-coat and overcoat dangle as if from a clothes peg.

His badly made trousers hang in ugly folds at the knees and his boots are shamelessly down at heel. His white tie is never in the right place. But please don't think he's slovenly. One look at his kind, serious face is enough to tell you that he has no time to bother about his appearance – and he wouldn't know how to, anyway. He's young, honest, unpretentious and he loves medicine. He's always on the go – that suffices to explain in his favour all the shortcomings of his unpretentious attire. Like an artist, he doesn't know the value of money: without turning a hair he sacrifices his own comfort and life's blessings to some trivial vices of his own, and as a result he gives the impression of a man without means, of someone who can barely make ends meet. He neither smokes nor drinks; he doesn't spend money on women. All the same, the two thousand he earns from hospital work and private practice passes through his hands as quickly as my own money does when I'm on a drinking spree. Two passions drain his resources: one is lending money, the other is ordering items from newspaper advertisements. He'll lend money to anyone who asks, without a murmur, without any mention of repayment. No tool could ever root out his reckless faith in people's conscientiousness and this faith is even more blatantly obvious in his perpetual ordering of items extolled in newspaper advertisements. He orders *everything*, whether he needs it or not. He writes away for books, telescopes, humorous magazines, hundred-piece dinner services, chronometers. And it's not surprising that patients who call on Pavel Ivanovich take his room for an arsenal or a museum. He's always been cheated and is still being cheated, but his faith remains as firm and rocklike as ever. He's really a splendid fellow and we shall meet him more than once in the pages of this novel.

'Heavens, I've really outstayed my welcome!' he suddenly realized, looking at the cheap watch with one lid that he'd ordered from Moscow – it had a 'five-year guarantee' but nonetheless had twice been back to the repairer's. 'Well, time I was off, old man! Goodbye – and mark my words, these sprees of the Count's will get you into hot water! And I don't only mean your health! Ah, yes! Are you going to Tenevo tomorrow?'

'What's happening there tomorrow?'

'A church fête! *Everyone* will be there. You simply must come! I promised that you'd come, without fail. Now, don't make me out to be a liar.'

To whom he had given his word there was no need to ask. We understood each other. After saying goodbye the doctor put on his shabby coat and drove off.

I was left alone. To stifle the unpleasant thoughts that were starting to swarm around my head, I went over to my writing-desk and started opening my letters, trying not to think or take stock. The first envelope that caught my eye contained the following letter:

> My darling Seryozha,
> I'm sorry to trouble you, but I'm so stunned I don't know whom to turn to. It's really shocking! Of course, I can't get them back now and I have no regrets, but just judge for yourself: if you let thieves have their way, then a respectable woman can't feel safe anywhere. After you left I woke up on the couch and found lots of my things were missing: they'd stolen a bracelet, a gold stud, ten pearls from my necklace and about a hundred roubles were taken from my purse. I wanted to complain to the Count, but as he was asleep I left. It's shocking! The house of a *Count*, yet they steal there as if it were a pub. You must tell the Count.
>
> Love and kisses
> Your affectionate Tina

That His Excellency's house was alive with thieves was nothing new to me and I added Tina's letter to the information on that score I'd already preserved in my memory. Sooner or later I would be obliged to put this information into action. I knew who the thieves were . . .

VIII

Black-eyed Tina's letter, her florid, flamboyant handwriting reminded me of the mosaic drawing-room and gave me the urge, so it seemed, to have a 'morning-after drink'. But I took a grip on myself and by sheer willpower forced myself to work. At first I found it boring beyond words to decipher the bold handwriting of district police officers, but then my attention gradually became fixed on a burglary and I began to enjoy my work. All day long I sat at my desk, while Polikarp constantly walked past, incredulously watching me at work. He had no confidence in my powers of abstinence and expected me to get up from my desk any minute and order him to saddle Zorka. But towards evening, when he saw how doggedly I was working, he was reassured and that sullen look of his gave way to an expression of satisfaction. He started walking around on tiptoe and speaking in whispers. When some youths went past the windows playing their accordions, he went out into the street and shouted:

'What you devils making such a racket for? Can't you go down another street? Or don't you know, you infidels, that the Master's working?'

When he brought the samovar into the dining-room that evening, he quietly opened the door and amiably asked me to come and have some tea.

'Please have some tea!' he said, gently sighing and respectfully smiling.

And while I was drinking it he quietly came up behind me and kissed me on the shoulder.

'Now, that's better, Sergey Petrovich,' he muttered. 'To hell with that tow-haired devil, may he damned well . . . Is it right for someone of your lofty intellect, an educated man like you, to concern himself with such weak characters? Your work is noble. Everyone should respect your wishes, fear you, but if you go around with that devil, breaking people's heads and swimming fully clothed in the lake, people will say: "He's got no brains at all! What a trivial man!" And this reputation will follow you everywhere! One expects irresponsible behaviour from a shopkeeper, but not from a gentleman! Gentlemen need to be knowledgeable, they have a job of work to do . . .'

'All right! Enough is enough!'

'Don't get mixed up with that Count, Sergey Petrovich. If you need a friend, then why not Dr Pavel Ivanych. I know he goes around like a tramp, but he's really highly intelligent!'

Polikarp's sincerity touched me deeply. I wanted to say a few kind words to him.

'What novel are you reading now?' I asked.

'*The Count of Monte Christo*. Now, there's a Count for you! A real Count, not like that scruffy devil of yours!'

After tea I got down to work again and carried on until my eyelids began to droop and my weary eyes began to close. When I went to bed I told Polikarp to wake me at five o'clock.

IX

After five o'clock next morning, gaily whistling and knocking the heads off the flowers in the meadows with my walking-stick, I made my way on foot to Tenevo, where the church fête was being held and to which my friend Screwy had invited me. It was a delightful morning. Happiness itself seemed to be hovering over the earth – it was reflected in every diamond-like drop of dew and was beckoning the soul of every passer-by. Bathed in morning sunlight, the woods were quiet and motionless, as if listening to my footsteps and to the chirping of the feathered fraternity who greeted me by voicing their mistrust and alarm. The air was saturated with the exhalations of vernal greenery and caressed my healthy lungs with its softness. I breathed it in, and as I surveyed the open prospect with my enraptured eyes, I sensed the presence of spring, of youth – and it seemed that those young birches, the grass by the wayside and the incessantly humming cockchafers were sharing my feelings.

'But why is it back there, in the world,' I reflected, 'that men herd themselves together in wretched, cramped hovels, confine themselves to narrow, constricting ideas, while there's such freedom and scope for life and thought here? Why don't they come out here?'

And my imagination that had waxed so poetic had no desire to encumber itself with thoughts of winter and earning a living – those two afflictions that drive poets into cold, prosaic St Petersburg and filthy Moscow, where they pay fees for poetry, but provide no inspiration.

Peasants' carts and landowners' carriages, hurrying to Mass and the fête, kept passing me. Constantly I had to doff my cap and acknowledge friendly bows from peasants and some squires I knew. Everyone offered me a lift, but walking was better than riding and I refused all their offers. Amongst others, the Count's gardener Franz, in his blue jacket and jockey cap, passed me in a racing droshky. He lazily glanced at me with his sleepy, sour-looking eyes. Tied to the droshky was a twelve-gallon, iron-hooped barrel evidently containing vodka. Franz's repulsive mug and his vodka barrel somewhat spoiled my poetic mood, but poetry soon triumphed again when I heard the sound of carriage wheels behind me. As I looked back, I saw a lumbering wagonette drawn by a pair of little bays. On a leather, box-shaped seat in the wagonette I saw my new acquaintance, the 'girl in red', who two days before had spoken to me of the 'electricity' that had killed her mother. Olenka's pretty, freshly washed and rather sleepy little face shone and flushed slightly when she saw me striding out along the boundary path that separated the forest from the road. She nodded cheerfully to me and smiled welcomingly, the way only old friends smile at each other.

'Good morning!' I shouted to her.

She waved her hand and disappeared from sight, together with the lumbering wagonette, without giving me the chance to have a good look at her pretty, fresh little face. This time she wasn't dressed in red, but in some dark-green costume with large buttons, and a broad-brimmed straw hat. Despite this, I liked her no less than before. It would have given me great pleasure to talk to her and listen to her voice. I wanted to peer into her blue eyes in the brilliance of the sunlight, just as I had looked into them that evening when the lightning was flashing.

I wanted to take her down from that ugly wagonette and suggest she walk the rest of the way with me – I would certainly have done so but for the conventions of society. For some reason I felt that she would have eagerly agreed to my suggestion. Not for nothing did she look back twice at me when the wagonette turned off behind some tall alders.

It was about four miles from my abode to Tenevo – an almost negligible distance on a fine morning for a young man. Shortly after six o'clock I was already making my way between carts and booths to the church there. The air was already filled with the sound of trade, despite the early hour and the fact that Mass hadn't finished. The creaking of carts, neighing of horses, lowing of cows, blowing of toy trumpets – all this mingled with the shouts of the gipsy horse dealers and the songs of peasants who had already managed to 'get sozzled', as they say. So many cheerful, festive faces, so many different types! So much charm and movement in the mass of people, with their brightly coloured clothes, bathed in the morning sunshine! By the thousand, these people swarmed and moved around, making a great din, trying to complete their business in a few hours and disperse by evening, leaving behind them on the open space – as if they were mementoes – scattered wisps of hay, oats spilled here and there, nutshells . . . People were flocking in dense crowds to and from the church.

The cross on the church gave off golden rays as bright as the sun itself. It glittered and seemed to be burning with golden fire. Below it the cupola was aflame with the same fire and the newly painted green dome gleamed in the sun, while beyond the glittering cross the transparent blue sky stretched into the far distance.

I passed through the crowded churchyard and made my way into the church. Mass had only just started and when I entered they were still reading from the Gospels. In the church silence reigned, broken only by the reader's voice and the footsteps of the priest with his censer. The congregation stood humbly, motionless, gazing reverentially at the wide-open holy altar gates and listening to the long drawn-out reading. Rural etiquette – rather, rural propriety – clamps down very heavily on any violation of the awesome quiet of a church. I always used to feel ashamed when something there made me smile or speak. Unfortunately, only on rare occasions did I fail to meet some of my friends in church and of these, I regret to say, I had great numbers. Usually, the moment I entered the church, some member of the local 'intelligentsia' would immediately come up to me and, after a long preamble about the weather, would start talking about his own footling, trivial affairs. I would usually reply yes or no, but I'm so punctilious that I could never bring myself to ignore that person altogether. And my punctiliousness cost me dear. I would chat away and look awkwardly at my neighbours at prayer, afraid that they would take offence at my idle prattle.

And on this occasion too I failed to escape from my friends.

Just as I was entering the church I saw my heroine – that very same 'girl in red' whom I had met on my way to Tenevo. That poor girl, red as a lobster and perspiring, was standing in the middle of the congregation, looking around at all those faces with imploring eyes, in search of a deliverer. She was stuck fast in that dense crowd; unable to move either forwards or backwards, she resembled a bird held tightly squeezed in a fist. When she saw me she smiled bitterly and nodded at me with her pretty little chin.

'For goodness' sake, take me to the front!' she said, seizing my sleeve. 'It's terribly stuffy and cramped here . . . I beg you!'

'It's just as crowded at the front!' I replied.

'But there everyone's well dressed and respectable, while here there's only common peasants. Besides, we have a place reserved for us at the front. And *you* should be there too.'

So, she wasn't red in the face because it was stuffy and crowded in the church – oh no! Her pretty little head was tormented by thoughts of precedence! I took note of that vain girl's entreaties and by carefully pushing people aside managed to lead her as far as the pulpit, where the whole flower of our provincial *beau monde*[33] had already assembled. After settling Olenka in a position that was in keeping with her aristocratic pretensions, I stationed myself behind the *beau monde* and began observing all that was going on.

As usual, the ladies and gentlemen were whispering and giggling. Kalinin, the Justice of the Peace, gesticulating with his fingers and rolling his head, was telling Squire Deryaev about his ailments in an undertone. Deryaev was cursing doctors in an almost inaudible voice and advised the JP to go and get treatment from a certain Yevstrat Ivanych. When the ladies saw Olenka they seized upon her as a good subject for gossip and started whispering among themselves. Only one girl was apparently praying. She was kneeling and kept moving her lips as she stared in front of her with her blue eyes. She didn't notice the lock of hair that had come loose under her hat and was hanging untidily over her pale temple. She didn't notice when Olenka and I came and stood beside her.

She was Nadezhda Nikolayevna, the JP's daughter. When I spoke earlier of the woman who had run like a black cat between myself and the doctor, I was referring to her. The doctor loved her as only such fine natures as my dear old Screwy's were capable of loving. Now he stood beside her, stiff as a poker, hands on trouser seams and craning his neck. Now and then he cast his loving, questioning eyes on her intent face. It was as if he were watching over her prayers and in his eyes there shone a melancholy, passionate yearning to be the object of her prayers. But, sadly for him, he knew for whom she was praying . . . it was not for him.

I motioned to Pavel Ivanovich when he looked round and we both left the church.

'Let's have a little wander around the fair,' I suggested.

We lit our cigarettes and went over to the booths.

'How's Nadezhda Nikolayevna?' I asked the doctor as we entered a tent where they sold toys.

'All right . . . I *think* she's well,' the doctor replied, screwing up his eyes at a toy soldier with lilac face and crimson uniform. 'She was inquiring about you.'

'And what precisely was she inquiring about?'

'Well, things in general . . . she's angry with you for not having visited them for so long. She wants to see you and discover the reasons for this sudden cooling off towards their house. You used to go there every day and then – well, I ask you! It's as if you'd simply cut them off . . . and you don't even bow when you meet them . . .'

'That's nonsense, Screwy. In fact, I stopped visiting the Kalinins as I didn't have the time. The truth is the truth. My relationship with that family is as excellent as ever. I always bow if I happen to meet one of them.'

'But when you met her father last Thursday, for some reason you didn't think it necessary to acknowledge his greeting.'

'I don't care for that blockhead of a JP,' I replied, 'and I just can't look at his ugly mug calmly. All the same, I still have the strength to bow to him and shake his outstretched hand. I probably didn't notice him last Thursday, or I didn't recognize him. You're not yourself today, Screwy, and you keep picking on me.'

'I'm fond of you, dear chap,' Pavel Ivanovich sighed, 'but I don't believe you. "Didn't notice, didn't recognize . . ." – I need neither your explanations nor your excuses. What's the point of them if there's so little truth in them? You're a splendid, fine fellow, but in your sick brain there's some section which, I'm sorry to say, is capable of any mean trick.'

'My most humble thanks.'

'Now don't get angry, dear chap. I hope to God that I've made a mistake, but you strike me as something of a psychopath. Sometimes, against your better judgement and the general tenor of your fine nature, you suddenly have such cravings, you act so wildly that everyone who knows you as a respectable man is completely baffled. It's simply staggering how those lofty moral principles of yours, with which I have the honour to be acquainted, can coexist with these sudden urges that culminate in such blatant abominations! What kind of animal is this?' Pavel Ivanovich suddenly asked the stall-keeper in a completely different tone of voice as he raised to his eyes a wooden creature with human nose, a mane and grey stripes down its back.

'It's a lion,' yawned the stall-keeper. 'But it could be some other animal. Damned if I know!'

From the toy stalls we went to the textile stalls, where business was already in full swing.

'Those toys only mislead children,' observed the doctor. 'They give the most distorted ideas about flora and fauna. That lion, for example. It's striped, it's purple and it squeaks. Whoever heard of squeaking lions?!'

'Listen, Screwy,' I said. 'It's obvious that you've something to tell me, but you can't bring yourself to do it. Out with it! I enjoy listening to you, even when you say unpleasant things!'

'Whether it's pleasant or not, old boy, you *must* listen. There's a lot I have to tell you.'

'Fire away . . . I'm turning into one enormous ear.'

'I've already told you that I suspect you're a psychopath. Now, would you care to hear the evidence? I shall express myself frankly and perhaps rather harshly at times. My words will jar on you, but please don't get angry, old chap. You know how I feel towards you – I'm fonder of you than anyone else in the district and I respect you. I'm telling you this not by way of reproach or criticism, or even to hurt you. Let's both be objective, old man. Let's examine your psyche with an impartial eye, as if it were the liver or stomach.'

'Fine, let's be objective,' I agreed.

'Excellent. So, let's begin with your relationship with the Kalinins. If you care to consult your memory, it will tell you that *you* started visiting the Kalinins immediately on your arrival in our blessed district. *They* did not seek your acquaintance. From the start, the JP didn't take to you because of your arrogant look, your sarcastic tone and your friendship with that raffish Count – and you would never have been invited there if you yourself hadn't first paid them a visit. Do you remember? You got to know Nadezhda Nikolayevna and started going to the JP's house almost every day. Whenever I visited the house you were invariably there . . . They gave you the warmest of welcomes. Those people were as nice as pie to you . . . both the father and mother, and the little sisters. They grew attached to you, as if you were one of the family. They were in raptures over you, they pampered you, they went into fits of laughter over your feeblest joke. For them you were the very paragon of wit, high-mindedness, gentlemanliness. You seemed to be aware of this and you repaid attachment with attachment – you used to go there every single day, even on the eve of church festivals when they were busy cleaning and up to their eyes in preparations. Finally, the ill-fated love you aroused in Nadenka is no secret to you – isn't that so? Knowing full well that she was head over heels in love with you, you went there day after day. And what then, old man? A year ago, for no earthly reason, you suddenly stopped visiting them. They waited a week, a month – they're still waiting, but you never turn up. They write to you, but you don't reply. Finally, you don't even send them your regards. For someone like you, who attaches so much importance to etiquette, your behaviour must appear the height of rudeness! What prompted you to steer clear of the Kalinins, so abruptly, so dramatically? Had they offended you? Did you get bored with them? In that case you could have broken away gradually, not in that insultingly brusque, quite uncalled-for manner.'

'So, I've stopped visiting them,' I laughed, 'and therefore I've joined the ranks of psychopaths! How naïve you are, Screwy! Isn't it all the same whether one ends a friendship suddenly or gradually? It's even more honest if you make a clean break – it's not so hypocritical. But all this is so trivial!'

'Let's admit it's all very trivial, or that some hidden reasons that are no concern of an outside observer compelled you to cold-shoulder them so abruptly. But how can one explain this latest action of yours?'

'What, for instance?'

'For instance, one day you turned up at a local government meeting – I don't know what business you had there – and when the chairman asked why you were no longer to be seen at the Kalinins you replied – just try and remember what you said! – "I'm scared of being married off!" That's what slipped off your tongue! And you said this during a meeting, loud and clear, so that all hundred members in the room could hear you. Your remark met with laughter and obscene jokes about fishing for husbands. Some rotter catches up your words, goes to the Kalinins and repeats them to Nadezhda while they are all having dinner. Why all these insults, Sergey Petrovich?'

Pavel Ivanovich barred my way, planting himself in front of me and continuing to stare into my face with imploring, almost tearful eyes.

'Why such insults? For what? Because this fine girl loves you? Let's admit that her father – like every father – has designs on you. Like a good father he has everyone in his sights – you, me, Markuzin . . . All parents are alike. There's no doubt that she was head over heels with you and perhaps hoping to become your wife. So why give her such a resounding slap in the face? Weren't *you* responsible for these designs on your person? You went there every day – ordinary visitors don't call so frequently. During the day you went fishing with her, in the evening you strolled in the garden, jealously keeping your little tête-à-têtes a secret. You discovered that she loved you – and you didn't alter your behaviour one little bit! After that, could anyone have doubted your intentions? I was convinced that you would marry her! And you . . . you complained, you laughed. What for? What has she done to you?'

'Don't shout, Screwy, people are looking,' I said, walking around Pavel Ivanovich. 'Let's finish this conversation, old man, it's all old women's talk. But I'll just say a few things – and then I don't want to hear any more from you! I used to visit the Kalinins because I was bored and because I was interested in Nadenka. She's a fascinating girl. Perhaps I might even have married her, but when I found out that you preceded me as aspirant for her heart, that you were not indifferent towards her, I decided to retire from the scene. It would have been cruel on my part to have cramped the style of such a splendid chap as you!'

'*Merci* for the favour! I didn't ask for this very gracious indulgence and as far as I can tell from your expression you're not telling the truth now, you're talking idly, not thinking about what you're saying. And then the fact that I'm a splendid chap didn't prevent you – on one of your last visits – from suggesting something to Nadenka in the summer-house which wouldn't have done this "splendid chap" any good, had he married her!'

'Hold on! How did you find out about my "suggestion", Screwy? So, things can't be so bad with you if people can trust you with such secrets! But you've turned white with rage and it almost looks as if you're about to hit me any minute. And just now *you* agreed to be objective! How funny you are, Screwy! Come, enough of this nonsense . . . Let's go to the post office.'

We set off for the post office, which looked gaily onto the market place with its three little windows. Through the grey fence we could see the many-coloured flowerbed of our postmaster Maksim Fyodorovich, famous throughout the district for his expertise in laying out flowerbeds, borders, lawns, etc.

We found Maksim Fyodorovich very pleasantly occupied. Red-faced and beaming with pleasure, he was sitting at his green table leafing through a thick bundle of one-hundred rouble notes as if they were a book. Clearly, even the sight of someone else's money was capable of lifting his spirits.

'Hullo, Maksim Fyodorovich!' I greeted him. 'Where did you get that pile of money from?'

'Well now, it's to be sent to St Petersburg,' the postmaster replied, smiling sweetly and pointing his chin at the corner where a dark figure was sitting on the only chair in the post office. When it saw me the figure rose and came over to me. I recognized it as my newly created enemy whom I had so deeply offended when getting drunk at the Count's.

'My most humble respects,' he said.

'Good morning, Kaetan Kazimirovich,' I replied, pretending not to notice his outstretched hand. 'How's the Count?'

'Well, thank God . . . but he's rather in the dumps. He's expecting you over any minute.'

On Pshekhotsky's face I could detect a desire to have a little chat with me. What could the reason be for this, seeing that I'd called him 'pig' that evening? And why such a change in his attitude?

'That's a lot of money you've got there,' I said, looking at the packets of hundred-rouble notes he was preparing for dispatch.

And it was just as if someone had prodded my grey matter! On one of those banknotes I saw charred edges, with one corner completely burnt off. It was that very same one-hundred rouble note that I had wanted to burn on the Shandor candle when the Count refused to accept it from me in payment for the gipsies and which Pshekhotsky had picked up when I had thrown it on the floor.

'I'd do better giving it to some beggar than consigning it to the flames' he had said then.

To which 'beggars' was he sending it now?

'Seven thousand five hundred roubles,' Maksim Fyodorovich said, taking ages to count them. 'Exactly right!'

It's awkward prying into someone else's secrets, but I desperately wanted to know whose money it was and to whom in St Petersburg that black-browed Pole was sending it. In any event, the money wasn't his – and the Count had no one in St Petersburg to send it to.

He's cleaned that drunken Count out, I thought. If that stupid, deaf Owlet can rob the Count, then what problem will this goose have thrusting his paw into his pocket?

'Oh, by the way, I'm sending some money off too,' Pavel Ivanovich suddenly remembered. 'Do you know what, gentlemen? You'll never believe it! For fifteen roubles you can get five items, carriage paid. A telescope, chronometer, calendar and some other things. Maksim Fyodorych, please lend me a sheet of paper and an envelope.'

Screwy sent off his fifteen roubles. I collected my newspapers and letters and we left the post office.

We set off for the church. Screwy strode along behind me, pale and miserable as an autumn day. Contrary to expectations, he was deeply distressed by the conversation in which he had attempted to portray himself as 'objective'.

In the church they were ringing the bells. A dense and apparently endless crowd was descending the porch steps and above it rose ancient banners and the dark cross that headed the procession. The sun played gaily on the priests' vestments and the icon of the Holy Virgin gave off dazzling rays.

'There's our lot,' said the doctor, pointing to our local *beau monde* that had detached itself from the crowd and was standing to one side.

'Your lot, not mine,' I said.

'It's all the same . . . let's go and join them.'

I went up to my friends and exchanged bows. Kalinin the JP, a tall, broad-shouldered man with a grey beard and crab-like, bulging eyes, stood in front of everyone, whispering something in his daughter's ear. Pretending not to notice me, he did not make one movement in acknowledgement of the 'general' salutation I aimed in his direction.

'Goodbye, my sweet little angel!' he said tearfully, kissing his daughter's pale forehead. 'Drive home on your own – I'll be back by evening. My visits won't take very long.'

After kissing his daughter once more and sweetly smiling at the *beau monde*, he frowned grimly and turned sharply on one heel towards a peasant with a village constable's badge who was standing behind him.

'Will I ever get my carriage and horses?' he said hoarsely.

The constable shuddered and waved his arms.

'Watch out!' Kalinin shouted.

The crowd that was following the procession made way and the JP's carriage drove up to Kalinin in great style, the bells of the horses jingling away. Kalinin climbed in, bowed majestically, alarming the crowd with his 'Watch out!!', and disappeared from view without so much as a glance at me.

'What a majestic swine!' I whispered in the doctor's ear. 'Let's get out of here!'

'But surely you want a word with Nadezhda Nikolayevna?' Pavel Ivanych asked.

'No, I must be off . . . I haven't the time . . .'

The doctor gave me an angry look, sighed and turned away. I performed a 'general' bow and went over to the booths. As I fought my way through the dense crowd I turned round to glance at the JP's daughter. She followed me with her eyes and seemed to be trying to see if I could bear her pure, penetrating gaze, so full of bitter resentment and reproach.

'But why?' her eyes were saying.

Something stirred within me and I felt pained and ashamed of my stupid behaviour. Suddenly I had the urge to go back and, with all the strength of my gentle (and so far not completely corrupted) soul, to caress and fondle that girl who loved me so passionately and whom I had so dreadfully insulted, and to tell her that it was not I who was to blame, but my damned pride, which prevented me from living, from breathing and from taking the decisive step. That stupid, foppish pride of mine, so brimful of vanity! Could such a shallow person as myself hold out an olive branch, when I knew and could see very well that the eyes of the local gossips and sinister old crones[34] were watching my every movement? Rather let them shower *her* with scornful looks and smiles than lose faith in that 'inflexibility' and pride of mine, which silly women found so pleasing.

When I discussed earlier with Pavel Ivanych the reasons that made me suddenly stop visiting the Kalinins, I was being dishonest and quite inaccurate. I concealed the real reason – I concealed it because I was ashamed of its triviality. This reason, as flimsy as gossamer, was as follows. On my last visit, after I had handed Zorka to the coachman, the following phrase reached my ears as I was entering the Kalinins' house:

'Nadya, where are you? Your *fiancé's* arrived!'

These words were spoken by her father, the JP, who had probably not expected me to hear him. But hear him I did and my vanity was aroused.

'Me a *fiancé*?' I asked myself. 'Who allowed you to call me a *fiancé*? And on what basis?'

And something seemed to snap deep inside me . . . My pride welled up and I forgot all that I had remembered when riding to the Kalinins . . . I forgot that I had captivated the girl and that I in turn had been so taken with her that I was unable to spend a single evening without her company. I forgot her lovely eyes that never left my memory day and night, her kind smile, her melodious voice. I forgot those quiet summer evenings which would never be repeated, either for me or for her . . . Everything crumbled under the pressure of devilish arrogance, aroused by that stupid phrase of her simpleton father. Infuriated, I had swept out of the house, mounted Zorka and galloped off, vowing to be revenged on Kalinin, who had dared enlist me as fiancé for his daughter without my permission.

'Besides, Voznesensky's in love with her,' I thought, trying to justify my sudden departure as I rode home. 'He started buzzing around her before me and he was already considered her fiancé when I first met her. I won't cramp his style!'

From that time onwards I never set foot in Kalinin's house again, although there were moments when I suffered from longings for Nadya and my heart was yearning, simply yearning, for a renewal of the past. But the whole district knew about the break that had occurred, knew that I had 'cut and run' from marriage. But my vanity could not make any concessions!

Who can tell? If Kalinin hadn't used that phrase and if I hadn't been so foolishly vain and touchy, perhaps there would have been no need for me to look back, or for her to look at me with such eyes. But better such eyes, better that feeling of injury and reproach than what I saw in them several months after the meeting in the church at Tenevo. The sadness that was shining now in the depths of those black eyes was only the beginning of that terrible disaster which wiped the girl off the face of the earth, like a sudden, onrushing train. It was like comparing little flowers to the berries that were already ripening in order to pour awful venom into her frail body and pining heart.

After leaving Tenevo, I took the same road I had walked along that morning. From the sun I could tell that it was already noon. As they had done earlier that morning, peasant carts and landowners' carriages seduced my ears with their creaking and the metallic jingle of their bells. Once again gardener Franz drove past with his sour eyes and touched his cap. His revolting face jarred on me, but this time the disagreeable impression from meeting him was erased at one stroke by the appearance of Olenka, the forester's daughter, who had caught up with me in her cumbersome wagonette.

'Give me a lift!' I shouted to her.

She nodded gaily at me and stopped the vehicle. I sat beside her and the wagonette rumbled noisily along the road that ran like a bright strip across a two-mile cutting in the Tenevo forest. For two minutes we silently surveyed each other.

'How pretty she really is!' I thought, glancing at her slender neck and plump little chin. 'If I were asked to choose between Nadenka and her I'd settle for this one. She's more natural, fresher, her nature is more expansive and happy-go-lucky. If she fell into the right hands one could do a lot with her! As for the other one, she's so gloomy, so dreamy, so cerebral!'

Two pieces of linen and several parcels were lying at Olenka's feet.

'So many purchases!' I said. 'Why do you need so much linen?'

'I don't really need all of it right now,' Olenka replied. 'I just bought it, amongst other things. You just can't imagine the running around I've had to do! Today I spent a whole hour walking all over the fair and tomorrow I have to go shopping in town. And then there's the sewing on top of it. Listen – do you know any women who could come and do some sewing for me?'

'No, I don't. But why did you have to go and buy so much? Why all this sewing? For heaven's sake, your family's not so big, is it? You can count them on one hand!'

'How strange you men are! You understand nothing, you'd be angry enough if your wife came to you dressed like a slut right after getting married. I know Pyotr Yegorych isn't hard up, but still, it would be a bit embarrassing if I didn't look like a decent housewife right from the start.'

'What's Pyotr Yegorych got to do with it?'

'Hm . . . you're laughing – as if you didn't know!' Olenka said, blushing slightly.

'You, young lady, are talking in riddles.'

'Surely you must have heard? I'm going to marry Pyotr Yegorych!'

'Marry?' I asked in a startled voice, opening my eyes wide. 'Which Pyotr Yegorych?'

'For heaven's sake! Why . . . *Urbenin*!'

I glanced at her blushing, smiling face.

'You . . . getting married . . . to Urbenin? I see you like to have your little joke!'

'It's not a joke at all . . . I really don't see what's so surprising or peculiar about it,' Olenka said, pouting.

A minute passed in silence. I looked at that beautiful girl, at her young, almost childish face and I was amazed – how could she make such awful jokes? At once I pictured that elderly, fat, red-faced Urbenin standing next to her with his protruding ears and rough hands, whose touch could only scratch a young female body that had just begun to live. Surely the thought of such a sight must scare this pretty, sylvan fairy, who could look at the sky with romantic eyes when lightning flashed across it and thunder angrily rumbled. I was really frightened!

'True, he's on the elderly side,' Olenka sighed, 'but then he loves me. His love is the reliable sort.'

'It's not a question of reliability, but of happiness.'

'I'll be happy with him. He's not short of money, thank God. He's not some sort of beggar, but a gentleman. Of course, I'm not in love with him, but are only those who marry for love happy? I know all about these love matches!'

'My child!' I exclaimed, looking at her bright eyes in horror. 'When did you manage to stuff your poor little head with this terrible worldly wisdom? Granted you're only telling me jokes, but where did you learn to joke so crudely, like an old man! Where? When?'

Olenka looked at me in amazement and shrugged her shoulders. 'I don't understand what you're talking about,' she said. 'You don't like it when a young girl marries an old man. True?'

Olenka suddenly blushed, her chin twitched nervously and without waiting for a reply she hastened to add:

'You don't like it? Then please go into the forest yourself, into that boredom, where there's nothing but merlins and a mad father, sitting and twiddling your thumbs until a young fiancé turns up! You liked it there that evening, but you should take a look in winter – then you're glad that death is round the corner.'

'Oh, all this is so silly, Olenka, so immature, so stupid! If you're not joking then . . . I really don't know what to say, really I don't! You'd better say nothing and not pollute the air with your little tongue! In your position I would have hanged myself on seven aspens, but you calmly go and buy linen . . . and you're smiling! A-ah!'

'At least he'll get treatment for my father with the money *he*'s got,' she whispered.

'How much do you need for your father's treatment?' I shouted. 'Take the money from me! A hundred? Two hundred? A thousand? You're lying, Olenka! It's not treatment for your father that you need!'

The news conveyed by Olenka excited me so much that I didn't notice that our wagonette had passed my village, driven into the Count's courtyard and stopped at the manager's front door. When I saw the children running out and the smiling face of Urbenin, who had jumped up to help Olenka out, I leapt from the wagonette and ran into the Count's house without even saying goodbye. Here some fresh news awaited me.

'Well timed! Well timed!' the Count greeted me, scratching my face with his long, prickly moustache. 'You couldn't have picked a better time! We've only this minute sat down to lunch. Of course, you've met . . . perhaps you've had more than one little confrontation in the legal department . . . ha ha!'

With both hands the Count pointed out two gentlemen sitting in soft armchairs and eating cold tongue. One of them I had the pleasure of recognizing as Kalinin, the JP. But the other, a little grey-haired old gentleman with a large, moon-shaped bald patch, was my good friend Babayev, a rich landowner who held the position of permanent member in our district council. After I had exchanged bows I looked at Kalinin in astonishment. I knew how much he hated the Count and the rumours he had spread in the district about the man at whose house he was now tucking into tongue and peas with such relish and drinking ten-year-old liqueurs. How could any self-respecting man explain this visit of his? The JP caught my glance – and most likely he clearly guessed its meaning.

'I've devoted today to visits,' he told me. 'I've been running around the whole district. And, as you can see, I've also dropped in on His Excellency.'

Ilya brought the fourth course. I sat down, drank a glass of vodka and started lunch.

'It's bad, Your Excellency . . . very bad!' Kalinin said, continuing the conversation which had been interrupted by my arrival. 'For us small fry it's no sin, but you're rich, a brilliant celebrity – it's a sin to neglect things as you do.'

'That's true, it's a sin,' agreed Babayev.

'What's all this about?' I asked.

'Nikolay Ignatych has given me a good idea,' the Count said, nodding towards the JP. 'Here he comes visiting me, sits down to lunch and I complain to him that I'm bored . . .'

'Yes, he complains he's bored,' Kalinin interrupted the Count.

'He's bored, miserable, this and that. In short, he's *disenchanted*. A kind of Onegin.[35] "But you yourself are to blame, Your Excellency," I say. "And why is that?" Very simple. "You," I tell him, "should do a spot of work to avoid being bored, you should busy yourself with farming. Farming is excellent, wonderful." He replies that he intends taking it up, but he's still bored. He lacks – in a manner of speaking – a stimulating, uplifting element. He lacks . . . what shall I say? . . . er . . . powerful sensations!'

'Well, what sort of idea did you give him?'

'As a matter of fact, I didn't give him any idea, but simply ventured to rebuke His Excellency. "How is it, Your Excellency," I say, "that such a young, educated, brilliant man can shut himself off like this? Surely it's a sin? You never go anywhere, you're like some old man or hermit. How much effort would it take to arrange social gatherings, at-homes, so to speak?" I ask.'

'Why should he give "at-homes",' I asked.

'You ask *why*? Firstly, His Excellency would get acquainted with local society if he held at-homes, he'd learn all about it, so to speak. Secondly, society in turn would have the honour of becoming more closely acquainted with one of our richest landowners. There would be a mutual exchange of ideas, so to speak, conversation, conviviality. Come to think of it, how many educated young ladies, how many gallants we have among us! What musical evenings, dances, picnics could be arranged – just think of it! The rooms here are enormous, there's summerhouses in the garden, and so on. Such amateur dramatics and concerts could be given that were never dreamt of in this province. Yes, I swear it. Judge for yourselves! And now all this is almost going for naught, buried in the ground. But then . . . you must only try and understand! If I had His Excellency's means I'd show you all how to live! And he says he's bored! My God, just listening to him makes me laugh . . . ashamed even!'

And Kalinin blinked – he wanted to show that he really did feel ashamed.

'That's all perfectly true,' the Count said, getting up and thrusting his hands into his pockets. 'I could give superb evenings . . . concerts, private theatricals – all that could in fact be arranged most charmingly. What's more, these evenings would not only amuse society, they would have an educational influence as well! Isn't that so?'

'Oh yes,' I agreed. 'The moment our young ladies see your mustachioed physiognomy they'd be immediately saturated with the spirit of civilization.'

'You're always joking, Seryozha,' said the Count, taking offence. 'But you *never* give me friendly advice! Everything's a joke with you! It's time, my friend, you dropped these student habits of yours!'

The Count started pacing from corner to corner and describing to me in lengthy, boring terms the benefit that his parties might bestow on humanity. Music, literature, drama, riding, hunting. Hunting alone could bring together all the local elite!

'We'll talk about it later!' the Count told Kalinin, taking leave of him after lunch.

'So, if I may make so bold, the district has grounds for hope, Your Excellency?' the JP asked.

'Of course, of course . . . I'll work on the idea, I'll make an effort . . . I'm delighted, absolutely delighted. You can tell everyone that.'

One should have seen the utter bliss written all over the JP's face when he took his seat in his carriage and said: 'Let's go!' He was so pleased that he even forgot our disagreements and when we parted called me 'dear chap' and firmly shook my hand.

After the visitors had left, the Count and I sat at the table and continued our lunch. We lunched until seven o'clock in the evening, when the crockery was removed from the table and dinner was served. Young drunkards are expert at whiling away the long intervals between meals! We drank continuously, taking small nibbles in between, which enabled us to preserve our appetites, which would have been lost had we stopped eating altogether.

'Did you send some money to anyone today?' I asked the Count, remembering the packets of one-hundred rouble notes I'd seen that morning in the Tenevo post office.

'To no one.'

'Can you please tell me – is your new friend – what's his name . . . that . . . Kazimir Kaetanych or Kaetan Kazimirovich . . . is he wealthy?'

'No, Seryozha. He's an out-and-out pauper. But what a fine soul he has, what a heart! It's not right that you should speak contemptuously of him and . . . bully him. You must learn to be discerning with people, dear chap! Shall we have another glass?'

Pshekhotsky returned towards dinner-time. When he saw me sitting at the table drinking he frowned and after hovering for a while around our table considered it prudent to retire to his room. He declined dinner, pleading a headache, but he offered no objection when the Count advised him to have dinner in his room, in bed.

Urbenin made his entry during the second course. I barely recognized him. His broad, red face was beaming with pleasure. A contented smile seemed to be playing even on his protruding ears and on the thick fingers with which he constantly kept adjusting his dashing new tie.

'One of our cows is poorly, Your Excellency. I sent for our own vet but he seems to have gone away somewhere. Should we send for the vet in town, Your Excellency? If *I* send for him he won't take any notice and he won't come, but it would be a different matter if you wrote to him. It's probably something trivial, on the other hand it might be serious.'

'Very well, I'll write to him,' muttered the Count.

'My congratulations, Pyotr Yegorych,' I said, standing up and offering the estate manager my hand.

'On what?'

'You're getting married, aren't you?'

'Yes, fancy that – he's getting married,' said the Count, winking at the blushing Urbenin. 'What do you think of him! Ha ha! He kept it all hush-hush and then suddenly – right out of the blue! And do you know who he's marrying? Both of us guessed it that evening, didn't we? We, Pyotr Yegorych, had decided even then that something highly improper was brewing in your rascally heart! And when Sergey Petrovich looked at you and Olenka he even said that nice fellow's smitten! Ha ha! Sit down and have some dinner with us, Pyotr Yegorych!'

Urbenin gingerly and respectfully took his seat and motioned to Ilya with his eyes to bring him some soup.

I poured him a glass of vodka.

'I don't drink,' he said.

'Rubbish! You drink more than we do!'

'I used to drink, sir, but not any more,' the manager smiled. 'I don't need to drink now, I've no reason to. Thank God everything's turned out so well, everything's settled to my heart's desire – even better than I could ever have hoped.'

'Well, you could at least drink this to celebrate,' I said, pouring him some sherry.

'Well, perhaps I will. I used to drink a great deal, in fact. Now I can admit it in front of His Excellency. I used to drink from dawn to dusk. The moment I got up my first thought was drink. Well, naturally, I'd go straight to the cabinet. But now, thank God, I've no reason to drown my sorrows in vodka!'

Urbenin downed the sherry. I poured him another. He drank that too and imperceptibly grew tipsy.

'I just can't believe it,' he said, suddenly laughing happily, like a child. 'As I look at this ring I recall her words when she gave her consent – and I still can't believe it! It's even quite funny – how could someone of my age and with my looks ever have dreamed that this worthy girl wouldn't turn her nose up at becoming my . . . the mother of my little orphans? Really, she's a beauty, as you saw for yourselves, an angel in the flesh! It's a sheer miracle! . . . Is that some more sherry you've poured me? Well, why not, for the very last time. I used to drink to drown my sorrows, now I'm drinking to celebrate. And how I suffered, gentlemen, what I went through! I first saw her a year ago and – would you believe it? – since then I didn't have one good night's sleep, not one day passed without my drowning that silly weakness of mine in vodka, without my blaming myself for my stupidity. I would look at her through the window and admire her – and I'd tear my hair out. I could have hanged myself at the time . . . But thank God I took a chance. I proposed and – you know – you could have knocked me down with a feather! Ha ha! I listened and I just couldn't believe my ears. She said: "I consent", but I thought she said: "Go to hell, you old fogey!" But afterwards, when she kissed me, I was certain . . .'

As he recalled the first time he kissed poetic Olenka the fifty-year-old Urbenin closed his eyes and blushed like a schoolboy. I found all this disgusting.

'Gentlemen,' he said, looking at us with happy, friendly eyes. 'Why don't you get married? Why are you wasting your lives, throwing them out of the window? Why are you avoiding the greatest blessing for any mortal on this earth? Surely the pleasure you derive from debauchery can't provide a fraction of what a quiet family life might offer! You're a young man, Your Excellency. And you too, Sergey Petrovich. I'm happy now and – as God is my witness – I'm so very fond of you both! Please forgive this stupid advice of mine, but I only want both of you to be happy. Why don't you get married? Family life is a blessing . . . it's every man's duty!'

The blissful, melting look of that elderly man who was about to marry a young girl and who was now advising us to exchange our dissipated existence for a quiet family life became too much to bear.

'Yes,' I said, 'family life is a duty. I agree with you. So, you're fulfilling this duty for the second time?'

'Yes, for the second time. In general, I like family life. To be a bachelor or widower is only half a life for me. Whatever you may say, gentlemen, matrimony is a wonderful thing!'

'Well, of course . . . even when the husband is almost three times his wife's age?'

Urbenin flushed. The hand bearing the spoonful of soup to his lips trembled and the soup spilled back into the plate.

'I understand what you wish to say, Sergey Petrovich,' he mumbled. 'Thank you for being so frank. And in fact I do ask myself: isn't this all rather low? Yes, I'm going through hell! But why should I question myself, make problems for myself when I feel constantly happy, when I can forget my old age and ugliness . . . everything! *Homo sum*,[36] Sergey Petrovich! And when the question of age difference enters my old noddle for one fleeting moment, I'm not lost for a reply and I calm myself as best I can. I feel that I've made Olenka happy, that I've given her a father and my children a mother. However, it's all rather like in a novel . . . my head's going round! You shouldn't have made me drink all that sherry!'

Urbenin got up, wiped his face with his napkin and sat down again. A minute later he downed another sherry at one gulp, gave me a long, pleading look as if asking for protection – and then his shoulders suddenly began to shake and he began sobbing like a child.

'It's nothing, sir, nothing,' he muttered, trying to overcome his tears. 'Now don't you worry. After what you said my heart was filled with some vague forebodings. But it's nothing, sir.'

Urbenin's forebodings were realized so soon that I hardly have time to change my pen and start a new page. With the next chapter my tranquil muse will exchange the serene expression on her face for one of anger and grief. The Preface is finished and the drama begins. The criminal will of man now comes into its own.

X

I remember a fine Sunday morning. Through the windows of the Count's church the diaphanous blue sky was visible and a dull shaft of light, where clouds of incense gaily played, lay across the church, from its painted cupola right down to the floor. Through the windows and doors came the songs of swallows and starlings. One sparrow, clearly a very bold fellow, flew in through the doorway; after circling and chirping over our heads and dipping several times into the beam of light, it flew out of the window. There was singing in the church too . . . The choir sang harmoniously, with feeling, and with that same enthusiasm of which our Ukrainian singers are capable when they feel that they are the heroes of the moment and that all eyes are constantly on them. Most of the tunes were cheerful and lively, like those tiny patches of sunlight that played on the walls and the clothes of the congregation. Despite the cheerful wedding melodies, my ear seemed to detect a note of melancholy in that unpolished, yet soft tenor voice, as if the singer felt sorry that pretty, romantic Olenka was standing beside that ponderous, bear-like has-been, Urbenin. And it was not only the tenor who felt sorry at the spectacle of that ill-matched couple. Even an idiot could have read pity on those numerous faces that filled my field of vision, however hard they tried to appear cheerful and unconcerned.

Attired in my new dress suit, I stood behind Olenka and held the garland over her head. I was pale and not feeling too well . . . yesterday's carousal and outing on the lake had given me a splitting headache and I constantly had to check that my hand wasn't trembling as it held the garland. Deep down I felt miserable and apprehensive, as if I were in a forest on a rainy, autumn night. I felt annoyed, repelled, regretful, I felt a nagging anxiety, as if I were suffering pangs of conscience. There in the depths, at the very bottom of my heart, dwelt a little demon that stubbornly, persistently whispered to me that if Olenka's marriage to that clumsy Urbenin was a sin, then I was guilty of it. Where could such thoughts have come from? Couldn't I have saved that silly young girl from the unbelievable risk she had taken, from her undoubted mistake?

'Who knows?' whispered the little demon. 'You should know this better than me!'

I'd seen many unequal marriages in my time, I'd stood more than once before Pukirev's picture,[37] read many novels based on disparity between husband and wife. Finally, I knew all about physiology, which peremptorily punishes unequal marriages – but not once in my life had I experienced such an appalling state of mind, that I could not shake off, however hard I tried, now as I stood behind Olenka, fulfilling a best man's duties. If my heart was troubled by regret alone, then why hadn't I felt this regret earlier, when I attended other weddings?

'It's not regret,' whispered the little demon. 'It's jealousy!'

But one can be jealous only of those one loves – and did I love that girl in red? If I were to love all the girls I met living under the moon, then my heart would not be large enough and I would really have been overreaching myself!

At the back of the church, just by the door, behind the

churchwarden's cupboard, stood my friend Count Karneyev, selling candles. His hair was smoothed down and heavily greased, and it gave off a narcotic, stifling smell of perfume. Today he looked such a dear that I couldn't resist remarking when I greeted him:

'Aleksey! You look the perfect quadrille dancer today!'

He escorted everyone who came in or out with a sugary smile and I could hear the clumsy compliments with which he rewarded every lady who bought a candle from him. He, that spoilt darling of fortune, who never kept brass coins and who had no idea how to use them, was constantly dropping five- and three-copeck coins on the floor. Nearby, leaning on the cupboard, stood the majestic Kalinin, with the Order of Stanislas around his neck. His face was radiant and shining – he was glad that his idea about 'at-homes' had fallen on such fertile soil and was already beginning to bear fruit. In his heart of hearts he was showering Urbenin with a thousand thanks: although the wedding was an absurdity, it was easy to seize upon it as an opportunity to arrange the first 'at-home'.

Vain Olenka must have been in her seventh heaven. From the nuptial lectern, right up to the main doors, stretched two rows of female representatives from our local 'flower-garden'. The lady guests were dressed as they would have been if the Count himself were getting married – one couldn't have wished for more elegant outfits. The majority of these ladies were aristocrats – not one priest's wife, not one shopkeeper's wife. There were ladies to whom Olenka had never before thought that she even had the right to curtsy. Olenka's groom was an estate manager, merely a privileged servant, but that could not have wounded her vanity. He was of the gentry and owned a mortgaged estate in the neighbouring district. His father had been district marshal of the nobility and he himself had already been a JP for nine years in his native district. What more could an ambitious daughter of a personal nobleman have wanted? Even the fact that her best man was celebrated throughout the whole province as a *bon vivant*[38] and a Don Juan could tickle her pride: all the ladies were ogling him. He was as impressive as forty thousand best men put together[39] and – more significant than anything else – had not refused to be best man to a simple girl like her, when it was a known fact that he had even refused aristocratic ladies when they invited him to be *their* best man!

But vain Olenka did not rejoice. She was as pale as the linen she had recently brought back from Tenevo fair. The hand which held the candle trembled slightly, now and then her chin quivered. Her eyes were filled with a kind of stupor, as if she had suddenly been surprised or frightened by something. There was not a trace of that gaiety that had shone in her eyes when, even as recently as yesterday, she had run around the garden and enthusiastically discussed the kind of wallpaper she would like to have in her drawing-room, on what days she would receive visitors, and so on. Now her face was far too serious – much more than the solemnity of the occasion demanded.

Urbenin was wearing a new dress suit. Although he was decently attired, his hair was brushed the way Orthodox Russians used to brush their hair back in 1812. As usual, he was red-faced and serious. His eyes seemed to be praying and the signs of the cross he made after each 'Lord have mercy' were not performed mechanically.

Behind me stood Urbenin's children from his first marriage – the schoolboy Grisha and a fair-haired little girl called Sasha. They were gazing at their father's red neck and protruding ears, and their faces resembled question marks. They just couldn't understand what their father wanted with that woman and why he was taking her into their house. Sasha was merely surprised, but fourteen-year-old Grisha was frowning and scowling. He would definitely have said 'no' if his father had asked his permission to marry.

The wedding ceremony was performed with particular solemnity. Three priests and two deacons were officiating. The service was long – so long that my arms grew weary from holding the garland, and the ladies, who normally like to witness weddings, let their eyes wander from the bridal pair. The rural dean read the prayers slowly, in measured tones, without omitting a single one. The choir sang an extremely long hymn from their music books. Taking the opportunity to show off his deep bass voice, the clerk read from the Acts of the Apostles with a 'doubly emphatic drawl'. But finally the senior priest took the garland from my hand, the couple kissed. The guests grew excited, the regular rows broke up, the sound of congratulations, kisses and sighing filled the air. Radiant and smiling, Urbenin took his young bride on his arm and we all went out into the fresh air.

If anyone who was with me in the church should find this account incomplete and not totally accurate, let him ascribe any omission to my headache and the above-mentioned depression that prevented me from observing and taking note of the proceedings. Of course, had I known at the time that I would be writing a novel, I wouldn't have gazed at the floor as I did that morning and I would have ignored my headache completely!

Fate sometimes allows itself to play bitter, nasty tricks. The bridal pair had barely left the church when they were greeted by an unwelcome and unexpected surprise. As the wedding procession – so gay in the sunshine with hundreds of different tints and colours – was making its way from the church to the Count's house, Olenka suddenly took a step backwards, stopped and tugged her husband's elbow so violently that he staggered.

'They've let him out!' she cried out loud, looking at me in horror.

Poor girl! Her insane father, the forester Skvortsov, was running down the avenue to meet her. Waving his arms and stumbling, rolling his eyes like one demented, he made quite a disagreeable spectacle. Even this would probably have been acceptable had he not been wearing his cotton-print dressing-gown and bedroom slippers, whose decrepitude clashed terribly with his daughter's luxurious wedding-gown. His face was sleepy, his hair fluttered about in the wind, his nightshirt was undone . . .

'Olenka!' he babbled as he approached the couple. 'Why have you left me?'

Olenka blushed and gave the smiling ladies a sidelong glance. The poor girl was burning with shame.

'Mitka didn't lock the doors!' the forester continued, turning to us. 'Do you think burglars would have any trouble getting in? Last year they stole the samovar from the kitchen and now *she* wants us to be robbed again!'

'I don't know who let him out!' Urbenin whispered to me. 'I gave orders for him to be locked in. Sergey Petrovich, my dear chap, please do us a favour and get us out of this mess somehow!'

'I know who stole your samovar,' I told the forester. 'Come on, I'll show you.'

Putting my arm around Skvortsov's waist, I led him towards the church. After taking him into the churchyard I talked to him, and when (according to my calculations) the wedding procession should have arrived back at the house, I left him, without showing him where his stolen samovar was.

However unexpected and extraordinary that encounter with the madman was, it was nevertheless soon forgotten. A new surprise that fate had in store for the couple was even weirder . . .

XI

An hour later we were all sitting down and having dinner at long tables.

Anyone who was used to the cobwebs, mildew and the uninhibited whooping of gipsies in the Count's apartments must have found it strange looking at that everyday, pedestrian crowd, now shattering the silence of those ancient, deserted rooms with its banal chatter. That gaily coloured, noisy crowd resembled a flock of starlings that had suddenly flown down to rest for a fleeting moment in a neglected cemetery or (and may that noble bird forgive the comparison!) a flight of migratory storks that had come to roost in their twilight days on the ruins of an abandoned castle.

I sat there, full of loathing for that crowd which was inspecting the decaying wealth of Count Karneyev with such idle curiosity. Those mosaic walls, the moulded ceilings, the luxurious, splendid Persian carpets and rococo furniture aroused delight and amazement. The Count's mustachioed face continually grinned with a self-satisfied smile. He accepted the rapturous flattery of his guests as something well deserved, although in fact he had not contributed one bit to the riches and luxury of his neglected mansion. On the contrary, he deserved the bitterest reproaches – contempt even – for his barbaric, grossly indifferent attitude to all the wealth assembled by his father and forefathers, which had taken decades rather than days to accumulate! Only the spiritually blind or poor could fail to see on every grey marble slab, in every painting, in every dark corner of the Count's garden, the sweat, tears and calloused hands of the people whose children now sheltered in those miserable little huts in the Count's wretched village. And among that vast assembly now seated at the wedding table – wealthy, independent people whom nothing was preventing from uttering the harshest truth – there wasn't a soul who would have informed the Count that his self-satisfied smile was stupid and inappropriate. Everyone found it necessary to smile obsequiously and sing his praises. If this was 'elementary' politeness (we love to lump the blame for many things on politeness and propriety) then I would have preferred ill-mannered louts who eat with their hands, take bread from someone else's plate at table and blow their noses between two fingers, to those fops.

Urbenin was smiling, but he had his own reasons for that. He smiled obsequiously and respectfully – and happily, like a child. His broad smile was a substitute for the happiness of a dog – a loyal, affectionate dog that had been petted and made happy, and which was wagging its tail now, cheerfully and devotedly, as a token of gratitude.

Like Risler Senior in Alphonse Daudet's novel,[40] beaming and rubbing his hands with pleasure, he gaped at his loving wife and was so overcome with emotion that he could not resist asking himself question after question.

'Who would have thought that this young beauty would fall in love with an old fogey like me? Surely she could have found someone a little younger and more refined? A woman's heart passes all understanding!'

And he even had the nerve to turn to me and blurt out:

'Just think – the times we live in! He he! When an old man can carry off such a beautiful fairy from under the noses of young men! Why didn't you keep your eyes open!? He he! The young men of today aren't what they were!'

Unable to stem the flood of gratitude that was bursting from his broad chest, he kept leaping up and holding out his glass to the Count's. In a voice that was trembling with emotion he said: 'You know how I feel towards you, Your Excellency. You've done so much for me today that my fondness for you seems a mere nothing, a trifle. What have I done to deserve such consideration from Your Excellency, such concern for my happiness? Only counts and bankers celebrate their weddings in such style! Such luxury, so many distinguished guests! Ah, what can I say? Believe me, Your Excellency, I'll never forget you, just as I'll never forget the best, the happiest day of my life!'

And so on. Evidently Olenka didn't care for her husband's flamboyant show of respect. She was noticeably pained by his speechifying, which produced smiles on the diners' faces, and she even seemed ashamed of it. Despite the glass of champagne she had drunk she was as gloomy and miserable as ever: there was that same pallor as in the church, that same dread in her eyes. She said nothing, replied lazily to all questions, forced herself to smile at the Count's jokes and barely touched those expensive dishes. As much as Urbenin (who was gradually getting drunk) considered himself the happiest of mortals, so her pretty little face was unhappy. Just looking at it made me feel sorry, and to avoid the sight of that little face I tried to fix my eyes on my plate.

How could this sadness of hers be explained? Was regret beginning to gnaw away at that poor girl? Or perhaps she was so vain that she expected even more pomp and ceremony?

When I glanced up at her during the second course I was so upset that my heart really began to ache for her. As she answered one of the Count's stupid questions, that poor girl tried hard to swallow. Sobs welled up in her throat. Instead of taking her napkin from her mouth she timidly, like a small, frightened animal, kept looking at us to see whether we had noticed how close she was to tears.

'Why are you looking so sour-faced today?' asked the Count. 'Hey, Pyotr Yegorych, it's your fault! Now please be good enough to cheer your wife up. Gentlemen, I demand a kiss. Ha ha! Not for myself, of course, but . . . I want *them* to kiss each other. Oh, it's so sad!'

'So sad!' repeated Kalinin.

Smiling all over his red face, Urbenin stood up and blinked. Prompted by the guests' whooping and exclamations, Olenka rose slightly and offered her motionless, lifeless lips to Urbenin. He kissed her. Olenka pressed her lips tightly together, as if afraid they might be kissed a second time and glanced at me. Most probably she didn't like the way I looked at her: taking note of this she suddenly blushed, reached for her handkerchief and started blowing her nose in an attempt to hide her terrible confusion one way or the other. It occurred to me that she felt ashamed in front of me, ashamed of that kiss, of her marriage.

'Why should I worry about you?' I thought. But at the same time I didn't let her out of my sight as I tried to find the reason for her confusion.

My gaze was too much for the poor girl. True, the blushes of shame soon vanished from her face, but then tears poured from her eyes – real tears, that I had never seen before. With her handkerchief pressed to her face she stood up and ran out of the dining-room.

'Olga Nikolayevna has a headache,' I hurriedly explained her exit. 'She was already complaining about it this morning.'

'Come off it, old man!' joked the Count. 'Headaches have nothing to do with it. It was the *kiss* that was to blame and embarrassed her. Ladies and gentlemen! I demand that the bridegroom be sternly reprimanded! He hasn't trained his wife in the art of kissing. Ha ha!'

Delighted by the Count's witticism, the guests burst out laughing. But it wasn't right of them to laugh . . .

Five minutes, ten minutes, passed and still the young bride did not return. Everything became quiet. Even the Count stopped joking. Olenka's absence was all the more noticeable because she had departed so suddenly, without saying one word. Not to mention the question of etiquette, which, more than anything else, had been badly breached, Olenka had left the table immediately after the kiss, as if she were angry at having been forced to kiss her husband. One could not assume that she had left out of embarrassment. It's possible to be embarrassed for a minute, for two minutes, but not for an eternity, which the first ten minutes of her absence appeared to be. So many evil, nasty thoughts must have flashed through the men's tipsy heads, so much slanderous talk was already on the lips of those charming ladies! The bride had risen from the table and left – what a dramatic and effective scene for a novel of provincial high society!

Urbenin started anxiously looking around.

'It's nerves,' he muttered. 'Or perhaps part of her dress has come undone. Who can understand them, these women! She'll be back in a jiffy, any minute now . . .'

But after another ten minutes had passed and she still hadn't appeared, he looked at me with such unhappy, imploring eyes that I felt sorry for him.

'What if I went to look for her?' his eyes said. 'Will *you* help me out of this dreadful mess, old chap? You're the most intelligent, the boldest and most resourceful man here – please help me!'

I noted the entreaty in his unhappy eyes and decided to help him. How I helped him the reader will discover later. All I shall say now is that the bear in Krylov's fable[41] that did a hermit a good turn, loses (in my opinion) all its animal majesty, pales and turns into innocent infusoria,[42] when I remind myself of the 'obliging fool' role I played. The only resemblance between myself and the bear consisted in both of us going to help someone, with sincere motives, without anticipating any nasty consequences as a result. But the difference between us was enormous: the stone that I hurled at Urbenin's head was much heavier.

'Where's Olga Nikolayevna?' I asked the footman who was serving me some salad.

'She's gone into the garden, sir,' he replied.

'This is simply unheard of, *mesdames*,' I told the ladies in a jocular tone of voice. 'The bride's left and my wine's turned sour! I must go and find her and bring her back, even if all her teeth are aching! A best man is like an official – and this one's going to demonstrate his authority!'

I stood up and to the loud applause of my friend, the Count, went from the dining-room into the garden. The direct, burning rays of the afternoon sun beat on my head that was inflamed with wine. Suffocating heat and humid air breathed right into my face. I walked haphazardly along one of the side paths, whistling some kind of tune and giving 'full steam ahead' to my investigatory capabilities as a simple detective. I checked all the bushes, summer-houses, grottoes and, just as I was beginning to feel pangs of regret at having turned right instead of left, I suddenly heard a strange noise. Someone was either laughing or crying. These sounds came from a grotto that I had left until last. I quickly entered and was immediately enveloped in dampness, the smell of mildew, mushrooms and lime – and then I saw the object of my search.

She was standing there, leaning against a wooden column that was covered in black moss, looking at me with eyes full of horror and despair, and tearing her hair. Tears poured from her eyes as from a squeezed sponge.

'What have I done?' she muttered. 'What have I done?'

'Yes, Olenka, what *have* you done?' I said, standing behind her with arms folded.

'Why did I marry him? Where were my eyes? Where were my brains?'

'Yes, Olya . . . the step you took is hard to explain. To put it down to inexperience is too lenient, to explain it by depravity – that I don't want to do!'

'Only today did I come to understand – only today! Why didn't I understand this yesterday? Now everything is irrevocable, all is lost! Everything, everything! And I could have married a man I love and who loves me!'

'And who might that be, Olya?' I asked.

'*You!*' she said, looking at me openly, directly. 'But I was in too much of a hurry! I was stupid! You're clever, high-minded, young . . . you're rich! You seemed so *unattainable*!'

'That's enough, Olya,' I said, taking her hand. 'Now, wipe your little eyes and let's go back. They're waiting for us. Come on, enough of those tears, enough!' I kissed her hand. 'Now, that's enough, little girl! You did something silly and now you must pay for it. It's your own fault . . . Come on, that's enough . . . calm down.'

'But you do love me, don't you? You're so big, so handsome! You do love me, don't you?'

'It's time to go, my dear,' I said, noticing to my great horror that I was kissing her forehead, putting my arm around her waist, that she was scorching me with her hot breath, and hanging on my neck.

'That's enough!' I muttered. 'Enough of this!'

XII

Five minutes later, when I had carried her out of the grotto in my arms and, wearied by new sensations, had set her down, I spotted Pshekhotsky almost at the entrance. He was standing there maliciously eyeing me and silently applauding. I looked him up and down, took Olenka by the arm and returned to the house.

'You'll be out of here *today*!' I told Pshekhotsky as I looked around. 'You won't get away with this spying!'

My kisses had probably been very passionate, as Olenka's face was burning as if it were on fire. There was no trace of the tears she had just shed.

'Now I couldn't give a damn, as the saying goes,' she murmured as she walked back with me towards the house, convulsively squeezing my elbow. 'This morning I didn't know what to do, I was so horrified . . . and now, my good giant, I'm beside myself with happiness. My husband's sitting back there, waiting for me. Ha ha! What do I care? Even if he were a crocodile or a terrible serpent . . . I'm afraid of *nothing*! I love you and that's all that matters.'

I looked at her face that was glowing with happiness, at her eyes that were full of joyful, satisfied love – and my heart sank with fears for the future of that pretty, blissful creature. Her love for me was only another push into the abyss. What would become of that smiling woman who had no thought for the future? My heart sank, turned over from a feeling that could be called neither pity nor compassion – it was stronger than both of these. I stopped and took Olenka by the shoulder. Never before had I seen a more beautiful and graceful creature, nor one that was at the same time more pathetic. There was no time for deliberating, weighing things up, taking stock. Overcome with emotion I told her:

'Let's go to my place right away, Olga! This very minute!'

'What? What did you say?' she asked, puzzled by my rather solemn tone.

'Let's go to my place right away.'

Olga smiled and pointed back towards the house.

'Well, what's the matter?' I asked. 'Isn't it all the same whether I take you away today or tomorrow? The sooner the better . . . let's go!'

'But it's all rather peculiar . . .'

'Are you afraid of a scandal, little girl? Yes, there'll be an almighty, magnificent scandal – but a thousand scandals are better than your staying here! I won't leave you here! I *can't* leave you here! Do you understand, Olga? Forget your faint-heartedness, your female logic and do what I say! Obey me, if you don't desire your own ruin!'

Olga's eyes told me that she didn't understand. Meanwhile, time did not stand still and ran its course, so that now it was impossible to stay in the avenue a moment longer, while they were waiting for us back *there*. A decision had to be made. I pressed the 'girl in red' to me (she was virtually my wife now) and at the time it struck me that I really did love her, that I loved her with a husband's love, that she was *mine* and that her fate rested on my conscience. I could see that I was bound up with that creature for ever, irrevocably.

'Listen to me, my darling, my treasure!' I said. 'This is a bold step. It will set us at loggerheads with our close friends, it will bring down on our heads a thousand reproaches and tearful complaints. It might even ruin my career, cause me thousands of insurmountable vexations! But it's all decided, my darling. You will be my wife. I couldn't ask for a better one and all those other women can go to hell! I shall make you happy, I'll look after you, like the apple of my eye, as long as I live. I'll educate you, make a woman of you. This I promise you – here is my honest hand on it!'

I spoke with genuine enthusiasm, with feeling, like a *jeune premier*[43] acting the most dramatic part of his role. I spoke beautifully – and as if to emphasize my words a female eagle flying over our heads touched me with its wings. My Olya took my outstretched hand, held it in her tiny hands and tenderly kissed it. But it wasn't a sign of consent: the stupid little face of that unworldly woman, who had never heard speeches before, expressed only bewilderment. Still she didn't understand me.

'You say that I should come to your place,' she said, thinking hard. 'I don't quite understand you. Surely you realize what *he* would have to say about it?'

'And how does what he would have to say concern you?'

'*Concern* me? No, Seryozha, you'd better not say any more. You must stop this, please! You love me and I need nothing more. With a love like yours I could live in hell . . .'

'But what will you do, you silly little girl?'

'I shall go on living here and you can ride over every day! I shall come out of the house to meet you.'

'I can't imagine that kind of life without shivers running up and down my spine! At night there'll be *him*; during the day – *me*! No, it's impossible, Olya. I love you so much now that . . . I'm even madly jealous . . . I didn't suspect for one moment that I was capable of such feelings.'

Such indiscretion! There I was, holding her around the waist and she was tenderly stroking my hand when at any moment someone might come down the avenue and see us.

'Let's go,' I said, taking my hands away. 'Put your coat on and let's go.'

'But you're in such a hurry,' she murmured tearfully. 'You're hurrying as if you're rushing to a fire . . . And God only knows what you've thought up! Running away right after my wedding! What will people say!'

And Olenka shrugged her shoulders. Her face was filled with such consternation, amazement and incomprehension that I gave everything up as hopeless and postponed my decision regarding this question of vital importance for her until the next time. Besides, there was no time to continue our conversation – as we went up the stone steps of the terrace we could hear people talking. Olenka tidied her hair at the dining-room door, checked her dress and went in. Her face showed no sign of embarrassment. Contrary to what I was expecting, she made a really brave entry.

'Gentlemen! I've brought you back the fugitive!' I announced, entering and taking my place at the table. 'I had great difficulty finding her . . . I'm absolutely exhausted. I went into the garden and looked around – and there she was, strolling down the avenue, if you please! "What are you doing here?" I asked. "Well, it's so stuffy in there!" she replied.'

She glanced at me, at the guests, at her husband and burst out laughing. Suddenly she felt amused, high-spirited. In her face I could read her longing to share the happiness that had come her way with all the company of diners. Unable to express it in words, she poured it out in her laughter.

'How ridiculous I am!' she said. 'Here I am laughing and I myself don't know the reason. Count, will you please laugh!'

'It's so sad!' Kalinin shouted.

Urbenin coughed and looked quizzically at Olenka.

'Well?' she asked with a fleeting frown.

'They keep shouting "It's so sad",' Urbenin said as he got up, smirking and wiping his lips with his napkin.

Olenka stood up and let him kiss her motionless lips. It was an impersonal kiss, but it only kindled all the more the fire that was smouldering in my breast and threatening to burst into flames any moment. I turned away, pressed my lips together and waited for the dinner to finish. Fortunately the end came quickly, otherwise I could have stood it no longer.

'Come here!' I said rudely, going over to the Count after the dinner.

The Count looked at me in amazement and followed me into the empty room where I led him.

'What do you want, old chap?' he said, unbuttoning his waistcoat and belching.

'You must choose one of us,' I replied, barely able to stand from the anger that gripped me. 'It's either me or Pshekhotsky! If you don't promise me that this scoundrel will be out of your estate within the hour I shall never set foot here again! I give you thirty seconds to reply!'

The Count let his cigar fall from his mouth and spread his arms out.

'What's the matter, Seryozha?' he asked, opening his eyes wide. 'You look terrible!'

'Please don't beat about the bush! I can't stand that spy, that scoundrel, that rotter, that friend of yours – Pshekhotsky – and for the sake of our good relations I insist he clears out immediately!'

'But what's he done to you?' the Count asked, greatly alarmed. 'Why are you attacking him like this?'

'I'm asking you: either me or him.'

'But my dear chap, you're putting me in an awfully ticklish position . . . wait, there's a little feather on your coat . . . You're asking me the impossible!'

'Goodbye,' I said. 'You're no longer a friend of mine.'

Turning sharply on my heels I went into the hall, put on my overcoat and hurried out of the house. As I was crossing the garden and making my way towards the servants' kitchen, where I wanted to give orders for my horse to be saddled, something made me stop. Nadezhda Kalinin was coming towards me with a small cup of coffee in her hand. She too had been at Urbenin's wedding, but some vague fear made me avoid conversation with her and the whole day I hadn't once gone up to her or said a single word.

'Sergey Petrovich,' she said in an unnaturally low voice as I passed her and slightly raised my hat. 'Stop!'

'What do you want?' I asked, going up to her.

'I don't want anything . . . you're not my lackey,' she said, staring at me and turning terribly pale. 'You're in a hurry to get somewhere. However, if you're not too rushed, may I detain you for a moment?'

'Of course . . . you don't have to ask!'

'In that case let's sit down. You, Sergey Petrovich,' she continued after we had sat down, 'constantly ignored me all day long, you avoided me like the plague. So, just today I decided to have things out with you. I'm proud and selfish . . . I don't want to thrust a meeting like this on you, but for once in my life I can sacrifice my pride.'

'What are you talking about?'

'Today I decided to ask you . . . it's such a difficult, humiliating question for me . . . I don't know how to put it. You don't even look at me when you reply! Don't you feel sorry for me, Sergey Petrovich?'

Nadya looked at me and feebly shook her head. Her face turned even paler, her upper lip trembled and twisted.

'Sergey Petrovich! It seems that a certain misunderstanding, some kind of idle whim has put a distance between us. I think that if we were to have things out everything would be as it used to be. If I didn't think this I wouldn't have the determination to ask the question you're about to hear. I'm unhappy, Sergey Petrovich. You must be able to see that. My life is no life at all . . . Everything has dried up. But the main thing is . . . there's a kind of uncertainty, when one doesn't know whether to hope or not. Your behaviour towards me is so hard to understand that it's impossible to draw any firm conclusions from it. Tell me – and then I'll know what to do. Then my life will at least have some direction. Then I can decide accordingly.'

'There's something you want to ask me, Nadezhda Nikolayevna,' I said, mentally preparing an answer to the question I felt was coming.

'Yes, I want to ask . . . it's a humiliating question . . . if anyone should overhear he'd think I'm imposing myself on you, like Pushkin's Tatyana.[44] But it's a question I'm forcing myself to ask.'

The question was in fact forced. When Nadya turned her face to me to ask it I took fright: she was trembling, convulsively pressing her fingers together as she squeezed out the fateful words depressingly slowly. She was terribly pale.

'Dare I hope?' she finally whispered. 'Don't be afraid, you can be quite frank with me. Whatever the answer, it's better than this uncertainty. Well, dare I hope?'

She waited for an answer, but at that moment my mood was such that I felt incapable of any reasonable answer. Drunk, excited by the incident in the grotto, infuriated at Pshekhotsky's spying and Olga's indecision, having endured that stupid conversation with the Count, I could barely listen to Nadya.

'Dare I hope?' she repeated. '*Please* give me an answer!'

'Well, I'm not up to giving any replies just now, Nadezhda Nikolayevna!' I said dismissively as I stood up. 'I'm incapable of giving *any* sort of answer at the moment . . . I'm sorry, but I neither heard nor understood you. I'm stupid and in a raging temper. But you're upsetting yourself for nothing, really.'

I waved my arm again and left Nadya. It was only later, when I came to my senses, that I realized how stupid and cruel I had been for not giving that girl an answer to her simple, straightforward question. Why hadn't I answered her?

Now, when I can view the past dispassionately, I cannot explain away my cruelty by my state of mind at the time. I feel that by not answering her I was flirting, play-acting. The hearts of other human beings are hard to comprehend, but it's even harder to fathom one's own. If in fact I was putting on an act, may God forgive me! However, mocking another's suffering is unforgivable.

XIII

For three days I paced my room like a wolf in a cage, trying with all the strength of my exceptional will-power to stop myself leaving the house. I didn't lay a finger on the piles of documents lying on the table and impatiently awaiting my attention. I received no one, argued with Polikarp, became irritable. I didn't venture onto the Count's estate and my obstinacy cost me enormous mental effort. A thousand times I must have picked up my hat – and thrown it down just as often. At times I decided to defy the whole world and go and see Olga, come what may, at others I would cold-bloodedly decide to stay at home.

My reason argued against riding over to the Count's estate. Once I had vowed to the Count never to set foot in his house again how could I sacrifice my self-esteem, my pride? What would that mustachioed fop have thought if, after our inane conversation, I'd gone up to him as if nothing had happened? Wouldn't that have been an admission of guilt?

Furthermore, as an honest man, I should have broken off all relations with Olga. Any future liaison could only bring about her ruin. She had blundered in marrying Urbenin and by having an affair with me she had blundered yet again. Wouldn't living with that elderly husband and simultaneously having a secret lover make her resemble a depraved doll? Not to mention how loathsome such a life would be in principle – one also had to think of the consequences.

What a coward I was! I feared the consequences, I feared the present and I feared the past. Any ordinary man would have laughed at my line of reasoning – he wouldn't have paced from corner to corner, clutched his head and drawn up all kinds of plans, but would have let life, which grinds even millstones into flour, take control. Life would have digested everything, without asking either for his help or permission. But I'm cautious to the point of cowardice. I paced from corner to corner, sick with pity for Olga and at the same time I was horrified at the thought that she might agree to the suggestion I had made in a moment of passion and come and stay with me – as I had promised her – for ever! What would have happened if she had done what I wanted and married me? How long would that 'for ever' have lasted and what would life with me have given poor Olga? I wouldn't have given her a family, therefore I wouldn't have given her happiness. No, it wasn't right to ride over to Olga!

But meanwhile my heart yearned passionately for her. I pined like a young boy, in love for the first time and not allowed out for a rendezvous. Tempted by the incident in the garden, I thirsted for a new meeting – and the seductive image of Olga, who, as I knew very well, was also waiting and pining for me, never left my head for one moment.

The Count sent me letter after letter, each more woeful and

self-degrading than the last. He implored me to forgive that 'kind, simple, but rather limited man' and he was amazed that I had decided to break off a long-standing friendship for some mere trifle. In one of his last letters he promised to come in person and if I so desired would bring along Pshekhotsky to apologize – although 'he didn't feel that he was in the least to blame'. I read the letters and replied by asking each messenger to leave me in peace. I was very good at putting on an act!

When my nervous agitation was at its peak, when I stood by the window and decided to go anywhere except the Count's estate, when I was tormenting myself with arguments, self-reproach and visions of the love-making that awaited me at Olga's, my door softly opened, I heard light footsteps behind me and my neck was immediately encircled by two pretty little arms.

'Is that you, Olga?' I asked, turning round.

I recognized her from her hot breath, from the way she clung to my neck and even from her smell. Pressing her small head against my cheek she struck me as extraordinarily happy. She couldn't speak for happiness – not one word. I pressed her to my breast – and then what became of all the anguish, of all those questions that had been tormenting me for three days on end? I laughed and skipped for joy, just like a schoolboy.

Olga was wearing a blue silk dress that beautifully suited her pale complexion and her magnificent flaxen hair. This dress was in the latest fashion and looked terribly expensive. Most probably it had cost Urbenin about a quarter of his salary.

'You *do* look pretty today!' I said, lifting Olga and kissing her neck. 'Well now, how are you? Are you well?'

'It's not very nice here, is it?' she replied, glancing around my study. 'You're a wealthy man, you get a large salary, yet how simply you live!'

'Not everyone can live in the lap of luxury like the Count,' I said. 'But enough said about my "wealth". What good genius has brought you to my lair?'

'Stop it, Seryozha, you're crumpling my dress . . . put me down! I've only dropped in for a moment, darling. I told everyone at home I was going to see Akatikha, the Count's laundrywoman – she doesn't live very far from here, about three houses away. Put me down, darling, it's embarrassing! Why haven't you been to see me for so long?'

I made some sort of reply, sat her down opposite me and began to contemplate her beauty. For a minute we looked at each other in silence.

'You're very pretty, Olga,' I sighed. 'It's even a pity and rather insulting that you're so pretty!'

'Why is it a pity?'

'Because the devil only knows who's got you in his clutches.'

'But what more do you want? Aren't I *yours*? I'm here, aren't I? . . . Now listen, Seryozha. Will you tell me the truth if I ask you?'

'Of course I'll tell you the truth.'

'Would you have married me if I hadn't married Pyotr Yegorych?'

'Probably not' was what I wanted to say, but why pick at a wound which was painful enough and which was tormenting poor Olga's heart?

'Of course I would,' I said in the tone of one speaking the truth. Olya sighed and looked down.

'What a mistake I made, what a terrible mistake! And what's worst of all, it can't be rectified! I can't divorce him, can I?'

'No, you can't.'

'I don't understand why I was in such a hurry! We girls are so stupid and empty-headed. There's no one around to give us a good thrashing! But there's no going back now and there's no point in arguing. Neither arguments nor tears will help. Yesterday I cried all night long, Seryozha. There he was . . . lying next to me . . . but I was thinking of you and I couldn't sleep. I even wanted to run away that night – even into the forest and back to Father. Better to live with an insane father than with this . . . what's his name?'

'Having second thoughts about it won't help, Olya. You should have thought about it then, when you drove with me from Tenevo and were so delighted to be marrying a rich man. But it's too late now to be practising eloquence . . .'

'Too late . . . then there's nothing I can do about it!' Olya said, decisively waving her arm. 'As long as it gets no worse I can go on living. Goodbye . . . I must go now.'

I drew Olya to me and showered her face with kisses, as if trying to reward myself for those three lost days. She snuggled up to me like a lamb, warming my face with her hot breath. There was silence.

'A husband murdered his wife,' screeched my parrot.

Olya shuddered, freed herself from my embrace and looked at me questioningly.

'It's only the parrot, darling,' I said. 'Now relax . . .'

'A husband murdered his wife!' Ivan Demyanych repeated.

Olya stood up, silently put on her hat and gave me her hand. Fear was written all over her face.

'And what if Urbenin finds out?' she asked, looking at me with wide-open eyes. 'He'll kill me!'

'Rubbish!' I laughed. 'I'd be a fine person if I let him kill you! But he's hardly capable of such an unusual act as murder. You're leaving? Well, goodbye my child . . . I shall wait . . . Tomorrow I'll be in the forest, near the cottage where you used to live. We'll meet there.'

After I had seen Olya out and returned to my study I found Polikarp there. He was standing in the middle of the room sternly eyeing me and contemptuously shaking his head.

'Mind that doesn't happen here again, Sergey Petrovich,' he said in the tone of a strict parent. 'I won't stand for it!'

'What do you mean?'

'Just what I say. Do you think I didn't see? I saw *everything*. She'd better not dare come here! I don't want any carryings-on here! There's other places for that.'

I was in the most splendid mood and therefore Polikarp's spying, his didactic tone, didn't make me angry. I laughed and dispatched him to the kitchen.

Barely giving me time to collect myself after Olya's visit, a new visitor arrived. A carriage rattled up to the door of my flat and Polikarp – spitting to each side and muttering oaths – announced the arrival of 'that damned fellow . . . may he go to hell!' – that is, the Count, whom he hated from the bottom of his heart. The Count entered, eyed me tearfully and shook his head.

'You keep turning your back on me, you don't want to talk.'

'I don't keep turning my back,' I replied.

'I was so fond of you, Seryozha, and you . . . just for some trifle . . . Why do you have to insult me? Why?'

The Count sat down, sighed and shook his head.

'Come on, stop playing the fool!' I said. 'It's all right.'

My influence over that weak, frail little man was strong – as strong as my contempt for him. My contemptuous tone didn't offend him – on the contrary. On hearing my 'It's all right', he leapt up and began embracing me.

'I've brought him with me . . . he's waiting in the carriage . . . do you want him to apologize in person?'

'Do you know *what* he's done wrong?'

'No.'

'That's fine. He can forget the apology, but you must warn him that if anything of the sort happens once again I shan't merely get mad – I shall take steps!'

'So, it's peace then, Seryozha? Excellent! You should have done this ages ago – the devil only knows what you were quarrelling about! Just like two schoolgirls! Oh, by the way, dear chap, I wonder if you've . . . half a glass of vodka? I'm absolutely parched.'

I ordered some vodka. The Count drank two glasses, sprawled out on the sofa and chattered away.

'I just bumped into Olga, dear chap. Splendid girl! I must tell you – I'm beginning to detest that Urbenin. Which means I'm beginning to fancy Olya. Devilishly pretty! I'm thinking of having a little flirtation with her.'

'You should keep away from married women!' I sighed.

'Come off it, he's an old man! There's no harm in pinching Pyotr Yegorych's wife. She's too good for him. He's just like a dog – can't guzzle himself, so he stops everyone else. Today I shall start my assault and go about it systematically. Such a sweetie! What style, old man! Simply makes you smack your lips!'

The Count drank a third glass and continued:

'Do you know who else I fancy here? Nadenka, that idiot Kalinin's daughter. A fiery brunette, pale complexion, with gorgeous eyes – you know the type! I must also cast my line there . . . I'm giving a party at Whitsun – a musical–vocal–literary party – just so that I can invite her. So, my friend, life's not too bad here – quite jolly in fact! There's the social life, women . . . and . . . mind if I have a little nap . . . just a few minutes?'

'You may. But what about Pshekhotsky in the carriage?'

'He can wait, damn him! I myself don't care for him, dear chap.' The Count raised himself on his elbow and said in a mysterious voice: 'I'm keeping him only out of necessity . . . I need him . . . Well, to hell with him!'

The Count's elbow gave way and his head flopped onto the cushion. A minute later I could hear snoring.

After the Count left that evening a third visitor arrived – Dr Pavel Ivanovich. He had come to tell me that Nadezhda Nikolayevna wasn't very well and that she had finally refused him. The poor devil was miserable and resembled a wet hen.

XIV

The poetic month of May went by . . . lilacs and tulips finished flowering – and with them fate had ordained that the joys of love should also shed their blossoms (despite its sinfulness and pain, love still occasionally afforded sweet minutes that can never be erased from the memory). But there are moments for which one would sacrifice months and years.

One evening in June, after the sun had set but when its broad trail – a crimson and golden strip – still glowed in the distant west, heralding a calm, bright day, I rode Zorka up to the outbuilding where Urbenin lived. That evening a musical soirée was to be held at the Count's. The guests had already started arriving, but the Count wasn't at home: he had gone for a ride and had promised to be back very soon. Shortly afterwards, holding my horse by the bridle, I stood at the porch and chatted with Sasha, Urbenin's little daughter. Urbenin himself was sitting on the steps with his head propped on his fists, peering at the distant prospect through the gates. He was gloomy and answered my questions reluctantly. I left him in peace and turned to Sasha.

'Where's your new mama?' I asked her.

'She's gone riding with the Count. She goes riding with him every day.'

'Every day,' muttered Urbenin with a sigh.

Much could be heard in that sigh. In it I could hear exactly what was troubling my heart too, what I was endeavouring to explain to myself but was unable to – and I became lost in speculation.

So, Olga went riding with the Count every day. But that didn't mean a thing. Olga could never have fallen in love with the Count, and Urbenin's jealousy was totally unfounded. It wasn't the Count of whom we should have been jealous, but *something else*, which had taken me so long to understand. This 'something else' stood like a solid wall between myself and Olga. She still loved me, but after the visit described in the previous chapter, she hadn't come to see me more than twice and when she met me somewhere outside my flat she would flush mysteriously and stubbornly evade my questions. She reciprocated my caresses passionately, but her responses were so abrupt, so nervous, that all I could remember of our brief trysts was an agonizing perplexity. Her conscience wasn't clear – that was obvious – but it was impossible to read the precise reason for this on Olga's guilty face.

'I hope your new mama is well?' I asked Sasha.

'Yes, she is. But last night she had toosache. She was kwying.'

'Crying?' Urbenin asked, turning his face to Sasha. 'Did you see her? You must have dreamt it, darling.'

Olga did not have toothache. If she had been crying, it was from something other than physical pain. I wanted to continue my conversation with Sasha, but this I didn't manage, since at that moment I heard the sound of horses' hoofs and soon we saw the riders – a gentleman awkwardly bouncing about in the saddle and a graceful horsewoman. To conceal my joy from Olga I lifted Sasha in my arms and kissed her forehead as I ran my fingers through her fair hair.

'What a pretty girl you are, Sasha!' I said. 'Such beautiful curls!'

Olga gave me a fleeting glance, replied to my bow in complete silence and went into the outbuilding, leaning on the Count's arm. Urbenin got up and followed her.

Five minutes later the Count emerged from the outbuilding. He was cheerful as never before, his face even seemed to have a fresher look.

'Congratulate me!' he said, taking my hand and giggling.

'On what?'

'On my conquest . . . Just one more of these rides and I swear by the ashes of my noble ancestors I'll pluck the petals from this flower.'

'So you haven't plucked them yet?'

'Yet? . . . Well, almost! During ten minutes of "your hand in mine"[45] not once did she take it away. I smothered it with kisses! But let's wait until tomorrow, we must be on our way now. They're expecting me. Oh yes! I need to talk to you about something, dear chap. Tell me, is it true what people are saying . . . that you have evil designs on Nadezhda Nikolayevna?'

'What of it?'

'If it's true, I won't stand in your way. It's not my policy to trip people up. But if you have no designs on her, then of course . . .'

'I have no designs.'

'*Merci*, my dear chap!'

The Count had visions of killing two hares at once and he was fully convinced that he would succeed. And on that evening I observed his pursuit of these hares. It was all as stupid and comical as a fine caricature. As I watched I could only laugh or be repelled by the Count's vulgarity; but no one could have thought that this puerile pursuit would end with the moral fall of a few, the ruin of some – and the crimes of others!

The Count did not kill two hares, but more! Yes, he killed them, but the skins and flesh went to someone else.

I saw him furtively squeeze the hand of Olga, who invariably greeted him with a friendly smile, but who watched him leave with a disdainful grin. Once, eager to show that there were no secrets between us, he even kissed her hand in my presence.

'What an idiot!' she whispered in my ear as she wiped her hand.

'Listen, Olga,' I said when the Count had left. 'I feel there's something you want to tell me. Yes?'

I looked searchingly into her face. She blushed crimson and blinked timorously, like a cat caught stealing.

'Olga,' I said sternly. 'You've got to tell me! I insist!'

'Yes, there *is* something I want to tell you,' she whispered, pressing my hands. 'I love you, I can't live without you, but don't come here to see me, my darling! Don't love me any more, don't call me Olya. I can't go on like this, it's impossible. And don't even let anyone see that you love me.'

'Why not?'

'Because that's what I want. You don't need to know the reason and I'm not going to tell you. Now leave me, they're coming.'

I didn't leave her and she herself had to bring our conversation to an end. Taking the arm of her husband, who just happened to be passing, she nodded at me with a hypocritical smile and left.

The Count's other 'hare' – Nadezhda Nikolayevna – enjoyed his undivided attention that evening. The whole time he buzzed around her, telling her anecdotes, joking and flirting, while she, pale and exhausted, twisted her mouth into an artificial smile. Kalinin the JP constantly watched them, stroked his beard and coughed meaningfully. The Count's flirtation with his daughter was very much to his liking: a Count as son-in-law! What dream could be sweeter for a provincial *bon vivant*? From the moment the Count started courting his daughter, he had grown two feet in his own estimation. And with what imperious glances he sized me up, how spitefully he coughed when he talked to me! 'You stood on ceremony and you deserted us,' he said, 'but we don't give a damn! Now we have a *Count*!'

The following evening I was once again at the Count's estate.

On this occasion I didn't chat with Sasha, but with her schoolboy brother, who led me into the garden and poured out his soul to me. These outpourings were provoked by my questions about life with his 'new mama'.

'She's a very good friend of yours,' he said, nervously unbuttoning his uniform. 'I know you'll go and tell her, but I'm not afraid. Go ahead, tell her whatever you like. She's wicked, vile!'

And he told me that Olga had taken his room from him, had dismissed the old nanny who had been with the Urbenins for ten years and that she was constantly in a bad temper, always shouting.

'Yesterday you praised my sister Sasha's hair. Yes, it's really beautiful! Just like flax! But this morning Olga went and cut it all off!'

It's sheer jealousy! I explained to myself Olga's excursion into the unfamiliar realm of hairdressing.

'It seems she was jealous because you praised Sasha's hair and not hers,' the boy said, confirming my thoughts. 'And she's tormented the life out of Papa. He keeps spending an awful lot on her, he's neglecting his work and he's started drinking again. Again! She's a stupid woman . . . all day long she cries because she has to live in poor surroundings, in such a small house. Is it Papa's fault that he doesn't have much money?'

The boy related many sad things. He could see what his blinded father could not or did not want to see. That poor boy's father had been wronged – and his sister and his old nanny too. He had been robbed of his little sanctuary, where he was accustomed to busy himself keeping his books in order and feeding the goldfinches he'd caught. Everyone had been wronged and that stupid and omnipotent stepmother was making a mockery of everything! But the poor boy could never have dreamt of the terrible insult that was inflicted on his family by that young stepmother and which I witnessed that very same evening after my conversation with him. Everything paled into insignificance before that outrage and Sasha's cropped hair seemed a mere trifle by comparison.

XV

Late that evening I was sitting at the Count's. As usual, we were drinking. The Count was completely drunk, myself only slightly.

'This morning Olga let me touch her waist "accidentally",' he muttered. 'That means we can take things a bit further tomorrow.'

'Well, what about Nadya? How's things with her?'

'I'm making progress! With her it's only just the start! So far it's only a period of eye contact. I love reading her mournful black eyes, old chap. Something that words cannot convey is written in them, something only the soul can understand . . . Another drink?'

'So, she must like you if she has the patience to talk to you for hours on end. Her Papa likes you too.'

'Her Papa? You mean that blockhead! Ha ha! That moron suspects I have honourable intentions!'

The Count had a coughing fit and took a drink.

'He thinks I'm going to marry her! Apart from the fact that I can't get married, it would be more honourable on my part – looking at things from an *honourable* viewpoint – to seduce the girl rather than marry her . . . Stuck for life with a drunken middle-aged sot who's always coughing?! Brrr! *Any* wife would wither away or clear out the next day. What's that noise?'

The Count and I leapt up. Several doors slammed almost simultaneously and Olga ran into the room. She was as white as a sheet and trembling like a violently plucked violin string. Her hair was dishevelled, the pupils of her eyes dilated. She was gasping for breath and kept crumpling the front of her nightdress with her fingers.

'Olga, what's wrong, dear?' I asked, grasping her arm and turning pale.

The Count ought to have been startled by my accidental use of 'dear', but he didn't hear. Transformed into one huge question mark, his mouth wide open and his eyes goggling, he stared at Olga as if she were a ghost.

'What's happened?' I asked.

'He keeps beating me,' Olga said and slumped sobbing into an armchair. 'He keeps beating me!'

'Who's *he*?'

'My husband, of course! I just cannot live with him. I've left him!'

'That's outrageous!' the Count exclaimed, banging his fist on the table. 'What right does he have? This is sheer tyranny . . . it's . . . it's the devil only knows what! Beating his wife! *Beating* her! Why does he do that to you?'

'For no reason at all,' Olga replied, wiping away the tears. 'I simply took my handkerchief from my pocket and out fell the letter you sent me yesterday. He leapt up, read it and started hitting me. He grabbed my hand and crushed it – just look, there's still red blotches on it – and he demanded an explanation. Instead of giving him an explanation I rushed over here . . . If only you would take my side! He has no right to treat his wife so roughly. I'm not a cook, I'm a gentlewoman!'

The Count paced from corner to corner and with his drunken, muddled tongue started jabbering some nonsense which, when translated into sober language, must have meant: 'On the position of women in Russia.'

'This is sheer barbarity! This is New Zealand! Does that peasant also think that his wife will have her throat cut at his funeral? As you know, when savages go to the next world they take their wives with them!'

I just couldn't come to my senses. How was I to interpret Olga's sudden visit in her nightdress? What should I think, what should I decide to do? If she had been beaten, if her dignity had been insulted, then why hadn't she run to her father or the housekeeper? Finally, why not to *me*, who despite everything, was still close to her? And had she really been insulted? My heart spoke to me of that simple-minded Urbenin's innocence: sensing the truth, it was afflicted with the same pain that the stunned husband must have been feeling now. Without asking questions and without knowing where to begin, I started calming Olga down and offered her some wine.

'What a mistake I made! What an awful mistake!' she sighed through her tears, raising the wine glass to her lips. 'And the look on his face when he was courting me – it was as if butter wouldn't melt in his mouth. I thought that this was no man, but an angel!'

'Did you expect him to be pleased about that letter which fell from your pocket?' I asked. 'Did you want him to have a good laugh about it?'

'Let's not talk about it,' the Count interrupted. 'Whatever happened, he behaved like a cad! That's no way to treat a woman! I shall challenge him to a duel. I'll show him! Believe me, Olga Nikolayevna, he won't get away with it!'

The Count puffed himself out like a young turkey, although no one had authorized him to come between husband and wife. I said nothing and didn't contradict him, because I knew that his taking revenge on behalf of someone else's wife would be limited to a drunken torrent of words within those four walls and that the duel would be completely forgotten by the morning. But why did Olga remain silent? I was reluctant to think that she wouldn't object to any services that the Count might offer her, I didn't want to believe that this silly, beautiful cat had so little pride that she would willingly agree for the drunken Count to be judge of man and wife . . .

'I'll rub his nose in the mud!' screeched this newly fledged knight in shining armour. 'And to finish with – a slap in the face! Yes, tomorrow!'

And she didn't succeed in silencing that scoundrel who in a drunken fit had insulted a man guilty only of making a mistake and being deceived himself. Urbenin had violently squeezed her hand – this was the reason for that scandalous flight to the Count's house. But now, right in front of her, that drunken reprobate was trampling a good name and emptying filthy slops over a man who must now be eating his heart out with anguish and uncertainty, who must have now come to realize that he had been deceived. But she didn't turn a hair!

While the Count was venting his anger and Olga was wiping away the tears, a manservant served some roast partridge. The Count offered his lady guest half a partridge. She refused with a shake of the head but then, like an automaton, took her knife and fork and started eating. The partridge was followed by a large glass of wine, and soon there were no more signs of tears – except for a few pink spots near the eyes and some isolated, deep sighs.

Soon we could hear laughter . . . Olga was laughing like a comforted child that had forgotten the injury done to it. The Count laughed too as he looked at her.

'Do you know – I've had an idea!' he began, moving closer to her. 'I'm thinking of organizing some amateur dramatics at my place. We'll put on a play with excellent parts for women. Eh? What do you think?'

They started discussing amateur dramatics. How violently this idle chatter clashed with the horror that had been written all over Olga's face when she had rushed weeping into the room only an hour before, her hair hanging loose. How cheap that horror, those tears!

Meanwhile, time passed. The clock struck twelve. At this respectable hour women usually go to bed. Olga should have already left, but half past struck, one o'clock and still she was sitting there chatting with the Count.

'Time for bed,' I said, looking at my watch. 'I'm off! May I see you home, Olga Nikolayevna?'

Olga glanced at me and then at the Count.

'Where can I go?' she whispered. 'I can't go back to *him*.'

'No, of course you can't go back to him,' the Count said. 'Who'll guarantee that he won't start beating you again? No, no!'

I walked up and down the room. All became silent. I paced from corner to corner, while my friend and my mistress followed my footsteps with their eyes. I felt that I understood both that silence and those looks – there was something impatient in them, something expectant. I put my hat down and sat on the couch.

'Well now,' mumbled the Count, impatiently rubbing his hands. 'Well now . . . that's what things have come to . . .'

Half-past one struck. The Count swiftly glanced at the clock, frowned and started walking up and down. From the looks he gave me it was obvious he wanted to tell me something important, but rather delicate and unpleasant.

'Listen, Seryozha,' he finally brought himself to say, seating himself next to me and whispering in my ear. 'My dear chap, don't take offence. Of course, you'll understand my position and my request won't strike you as strange or impudent.'

'Out with it! Don't beat about the bush!'

'Can't you see what's . . . going on? *Please* leave, my dear chap. You're cramping our style! She's staying here with me. Please forgive me for throwing you out but . . . you'll understand my impatience.'

'All right.'

My friend was loathsome. If I hadn't been so squeamish I might have squashed him like a beetle when, feverishly trembling, he asked me to leave him alone with Urbenin's wife. That sickly, effete anchorite, completely saturated with alcohol, wanted to take to himself that 'poetic' girl in red, who had been nurtured by forests and a turbulent lake, who had dreams of a dramatic death! No, she wasn't safe even within half a mile of him.

I went up to her and told her I was going. She nodded.

'Must I take my leave? Yes?' I asked, trying to read the truth on her pretty, flushed face. 'Yes?'

She turned away from me as one turns away from a tiresome wind. She didn't feel like talking. And why should she? It was impossible to reply in brief to such a prolix matter – and this was neither the time nor the place for long speeches.

I took my hat and left without saying goodbye. Subsequently, Olga told me that the moment I left, the moment the sound of my footsteps had mingled with the noise of the wind in the garden, the drunken Count was pressing her in his embrace. Closing her eyes and stopping her mouth and nostrils, she could barely stay on her feet from the revulsion she felt. There was even a moment when she very nearly broke loose from his clutches and ran into the lake. There were moments when she tore her hair and sobbed. Selling oneself is not easy!

When I left the house and went towards the stables where my Zorka was waiting, I had to pass the manager's house. I peered through the window. Pyotr Yegorych was sitting at a table in the dim light of a smoking lamp that had been turned up extremely high. I could not see his face, as it was buried in his hands, but his whole fat, clumsy figure betrayed so much grief, anguish and despair that there was no need to see his face in order to understand his state of mind. Two bottles were standing before him. One was empty, the other had only just been opened. Both were vodka bottles. The poor devil was seeking peace neither in himself nor in the company of others, but in alcohol.

Five minutes later I was riding home. It was terribly dark. The lake seethed angrily and seemed to be furious that a sinner like me, who had just witnessed a sinful deed, dared disturb its austere repose. It was too dark to see the lake and it was as if an invisible monster were roaring away and the enveloping darkness seemed to be roaring too. I reined in Zorka, closed my eyes and became lost in thought as I listened to the sound of the roaring monster.

What if I went back now and destroyed them? I thought. Terrible anger raged within me. That small measure of goodness and decency that remained within me after lifelong dissipation, all that had survived decay, all that I had cherished, nurtured, prided myself upon, had been outraged, spat upon, besmirched!

I had known earlier of venal women, I had bought them, studied them, but they did not possess that blush of innocence or those sincere blue eyes that I saw that May morning when I went through the forest to the fair at Tenevo. I, who was corrupt to the core, could forgive, preach tolerance for everything that was depraved, could be lenient towards frailty . . . I was convinced that one could never ask of filth that it should cease to be so, and I couldn't blame those gold coins that fall into filth by force of circumstance. But I hadn't known before that gold coins can dissolve in filth and merge with it into one single solid mass. That meant solid gold could dissolve too!

A strong gust of wind tore my hat off and bore it away into the surrounding gloom. As it flew through the air it brushed Zorka's muzzle and she took fright, reared and careered off down the familiar road.

When I was home I slumped onto the bed and when Polikarp suggested I take my clothes off he was called an old devil for no reason at all.

'Devil yourself,' growled Polikarp, stepping away from the bed.

'What did you say? *What* did you say?' I shouted, leaping up.

'There's none so deaf as those who won't hear!'

'Aaaah! How dare you be so impertinent again!' I cried, trembling as I vented my spleen on my poor lackey. 'Get out! Out of my sight, you scoundrel! Get out!'

Without waiting for my man to leave the room, I collapsed onto the bed and started sobbing like a child. My overtaxed nerves could take no more. My impotent rage, wounded feelings, jealousy – all this had to find some kind of outlet, one way or the other.

'A husband murdered his wife!' squawked my parrot, ruffling its thin feathers.

Prompted by this cry, the thought occurred to me that Urbenin might kill his wife . . .

When I fell asleep, I dreamt of that murder – it was an agonizing, suffocating nightmare. It seemed that my hands were stroking some cold object and that I only had to open my eyes to see a corpse. I dreamt that Urbenin was standing at the head of my bed and looking at me with pleading eyes.

After the night I have just described, a period of calm set in.

XVI

I settled down at home, allowing myself to leave the house and drive around on business only. A mass of work had accumulated, so there was no danger of my getting bored. From morning to night I sat at my desk, diligently scribbling away or cross-examining people who had fallen into my investigatory clutches. I had no inclination at all to go to Karneyevka, the Count's estate.

I dismissed Olga from my mind. What's lost is lost and she was precisely what I had lost – lost for ever, so it seemed. I thought no more about her, nor did I want to.

'Stupid, dissolute trash!' I invariably called her whenever she loomed in my imagination during my intensive labours.

But sometimes, when I went to bed and woke up the next

morning, I recalled different moments during my acquaintance and shortlived affair with Olga. I remembered Stone Grave, the cottage in the forest where the 'girl in red' lived, the road to Tenevo, the meeting in the grotto – and my heart began to pound. I felt a nagging pain . . . But none of this lasted very long. Those bright memories soon faded under the pressure of unpleasant ones. What poetry from the past could withstand the filth of the present? And now that I had finished with Olga I viewed that 'poetry' differently. Now I saw it as an optical illusion, as a lie, as hypocrisy – and in my eyes it lost half its charm.

The Count had now become utterly repulsive to me. I was glad that I wasn't seeing him and I always grew angry when his mustachioed face timidly appeared in my imagination.

Every day he sent me letters in which he implored me to stop moping and to visit someone who was no longer a 'solitary hermit'. Obeying his letters would have made things very unpleasant for myself.

'It's all over!' I thought. 'Thank God . . . I'm sick and tired of it.'

I decided to break off all relations with the Count and this determination didn't cost me the slightest effort. Now I was no longer the person of three weeks earlier who could barely stay at home after the quarrel over Pshekhotsky – there was nothing to entice me to the Count's any more.

After an unbroken spell at home I grew bored and wrote to Dr Pavel Ivanovich, asking him to come over for a chat. For some reason I received no reply, so I wrote again. But this second letter met with the same response as the first. Clearly, dear old Screwy was pretending to be angry. After being turned down by Nadezhda Nikolayevna the poor devil considered me the cause of his misfortune. He had every right to be furious and, if he'd never been angry before, it was because he didn't know how to be.

So, when did he manage to find out? I wondered, bewildered at the absence of any reply to my letters.

In the third week of my obstinate, continuous self-incarceration, the Count paid me a visit. After telling me off for not riding over or answering his letters, he stretched himself out on the couch and, before starting to snore, embarked on his favourite theme – women.

'I can understand,' he began, languidly screwing up his eyes and putting his hands under his head, 'your being touchy and difficult. You don't come and see me any more because you're afraid of spoiling our little duet, of being in the way. An unwanted guest is worse than a Tatar, as the saying goes. But a visitor during a honeymoon is worse than a horned devil! I do understand you. But you're forgetting, dear chap, that you're my friend and not simply a guest, that I like and respect you. Yes, your presence would only complete the harmony. And what harmony, old chap! Harmony that I can't find words to describe!'

The Count drew one hand from underneath his head and waved it.

'I just can't make out if living with her is good or lousy – the devil himself couldn't make head or tail of it! There really are moments when I would sacrifice half my life for an "encore". But then there are days when I pace the rooms like a madman and I'm ready to bawl my head off.'

'Because of what?'

'I can't make Olga out, old man. She's a type of fever, not a woman . . . with a fever you first get a temperature, then the shivers – that's exactly what it's like with her – she changes five times a day. Sometimes she feels cheerful, then she's so miserable she swallows her tears and prays. First she loves me, then she doesn't. There are times when she's very nice to me – nicer than any woman has ever been to me all my life. But sometimes it's like this: I wake up unexpectedly, open my eyes and I see a face staring at me . . . such a horrible, wild face, a face twisted with malice and revulsion! When you see things like that all the enchantment vanishes. And she often looks at me that way.'

'With revulsion?'

'Oh, yes, I just can't understand it. She swears she came to live with me only out of love, but not one night passes without my seeing a face like hers. What's the explanation for it? I'm beginning to think – of course, I don't want to believe it – that she can't stand me and that she's only given herself to me for the clothes I'm buying her now. She's mad about clothes! If she has a new frock, she's capable of standing in front of the mirror from morning to night. Because of a spoilt flounce she'll weep day and night. She's terribly vain! And what she likes most about me is the fact I'm a count. If I weren't a count she'd never have loved me. Not one dinner or supper goes by without her tearfully reproaching me for not surrounding myself with aristocratic society. She'd love to be queen of that society. Such a strange girl!'

The Count fixed his dull eyes on the ceiling and became lost in thought. To my amazement, I saw that on this occasion he was sober – unusually for him! This astonished and even touched me.

'You're perfectly normal today,' I said. 'You're not drunk and you haven't asked for vodka. What does this dream of mine signify?'

'Well now! I didn't have time to have a drink – I was always thinking . . . I have to tell you, Seryozha, that I'm head over heels in love, in real earnest. I like her enormously – and that's understandable too. She's a rare woman, quite exceptional – not to mention her appearance. She's not particularly bright, but what sensitivity, elegance, freshness! There's no comparison with all those earlier loves of mine – those Amalias, Angelicas and Grushas. She's a person from another world, a world that is unfamiliar to me.'

'You're getting philosophical!' I laughed.

'I was carried away, as if I'd fallen in love! But now I can see that I'm wasting my time trying to raise zero to the power of four. It was only a mask that aroused this false excitement in me. That bright flush of innocence turned out to be rouge, that loving kiss a request for a new dress. I took her into my house as a wife, but she behaved like a paid mistress. But enough of that! I'm trying to calm myself and beginning to see Olga as a mistress . . . And that's the long and short of it!'

'Well, what next? How's the husband?'

'The husband? Hm . . . how do you think he is?'

'I think that it would be hard to imagine an unhappier man at this moment.'

'Do you think so? That's where you're wrong . . . he's such a rogue, such a scoundrel that I don't feel sorry for him at all. Scoundrels can never be unhappy, they always find a way out.'

'But why are you running him down like this?'

'Because he's a swindler. You know that I respected him, trusted him as a friend. I myself – and even you – *everyone* considered him an honest, respectable man, incapable of deceit. But for all that he's been robbing me, fleecing me! Taking full advantage of his position as manager, he's been doing what he likes with my property. The only things he didn't steal were those that couldn't be moved.'

Since I'd always known Urbenin to be an extremely honest and unselfish person, I jumped up as if I'd been stung when I heard the Count's words and I went over to him.

'So, you've actually caught him stealing?'

'No, but I know about his thieving tricks from reliable sources.'

'*What* sources, may I ask?'

'Don't worry, I'm not going to accuse someone without good reason. Olga has told me everything about him. Even before she became his wife she saw with her own eyes the cart-loads of slaughtered chickens and geese that he was dispatching to town. More than once she saw my geese and chickens being sent as a present to certain benefactors with whom his schoolboy son was lodging. What's more, she saw him send flour, millet and lard there. I grant you, these are mere trifles, but surely these trifles don't belong to him? It's not a question of value, but of principles. Principles have been flouted. And there's more, my dear sir! She happened to see a bundle of banknotes in his cupboard. When she asked whose it was and where he'd got it he begged her not to let slip that he had money. You know that he's as poor as a church mouse, dear chap! His salary is barely large enough to pay for his board. So please explain to me where he got that money from?'

'And you're fool enough to believe that little reptile's words?' I shouted, disturbed to the very depths of my being. 'She's not satisfied with running away from him, blackening his name throughout the whole district – she had to go and deceive him! Such a small, puny body, but with so much vileness of every variety lurking in it! Fowls, geese, millet . . . oh, you're a fine landowner, you are! Your instinct for political economy, your agricultural obtuseness have been insulted by the fact that for church festivals he kept sending presents of slaughtered poultry that would have been eaten by foxes and polecats had the birds not been killed and given as presents. But have you checked even once those enormous accounts that Urbenin submits to you? Have you ever counted the thousands and tens of thousands? No! So what's the use of talking? You're stupid, just like an animal. You'd be pleased enough to have your mistress's husband locked up, but you've no idea how!'

'My affair with Olga has nothing to do with it. Whether he's her husband or not, once he's stolen I must openly declare him a thief. But let's leave this swindling to one side. Tell me: is it or isn't it dishonest to be paid a salary and lie around for days on end, constantly drunk? Every day he's drunk! Not one day passes without my seeing him reeling around. Respectable people don't behave like that!'

'He gets drunk because he's respectable.' I commented.

'You appear to have some sort of passion for standing up for gentlemen like him. But I've decided to show no mercy. Today I paid him off and asked him to clear out and make room for someone else. My patience is exhausted.'

I felt it was superfluous to try and convince the Count that he was being unfair, impractical and stupid: I had no intention of defending Urbenin against the Count.

Five days later I heard that Urbenin had gone to live in town with his schoolboy son and little daughter. They told me that he was dead drunk when they drove there and that he fell off the cart twice. The schoolboy and Sasha cried the whole way.

XVII

Soon after Urbenin's departure I was obliged to stay for a while – much against my wishes – on the Count's estate. One of the Count's stables had been broken into and thieves had made off with several valuable saddles. The investigating magistrate (that is, me) was informed and, *nolens volens*,[46] I had to go there.

I found the Count drunk and angry. He was marching through all the rooms, seeking refuge from his anguish, but to no avail.

'That Olga's more than I can take,' he said, waving his arm. 'She lost her temper with me this morning, threatened to drown herself, stormed out of the house – and as you can see, there's still no sign of her. I know she wouldn't drown herself, but it's a rotten business all the same. All yesterday she sulked and kept smashing crockery . . . The day before she gorged herself on chocolate. God only knows what kind of person she really is!'

I consoled the Count as best I could and sat down to dinner with him.

'No, it's time she stopped behaving like a child,' he muttered during dinner. 'It's high time – otherwise all this might turn into a stupid farce. Besides, I have to admit that she's already beginning to bore me with her sharp changes of mood. I need someone quiet and steady, modest – like Nadezhda Nikolayevna, you know. A splendid girl!'

When I was strolling in the garden after dinner I met the 'drowned girl'. When she saw me she turned crimson and – strange woman! – she laughed for happiness. The shame on her face mingled with joy, the grief with happiness. Giving me a sheepish look, she ran towards me and hung on my neck without a word.

'I love you,' she whispered, squeezing my neck. 'I've been pining for you so much that I would have died if you hadn't come.'

I embraced her and silently led her to one of the summer-houses. Ten minutes later, when I was saying goodbye, I took a twenty-five rouble note from my pocket and gave it to her.

'What's that for?'

'I'm paying you for today's love.'

Olga didn't understand and kept looking at me in amazement.

'You see, there are women,' I explained, 'who love for money. They're prostitutes. They have to be paid for with money. So take it! If you accept money from others, why don't you want to take it from me? I don't need any favours!'

However cynical this insult, Olga still didn't understand. As yet she had no knowledge of life and didn't understand the meaning of 'venal' women.

XVIII

It was a fine day in August. The sun shone with all the warmth of summer, the blue sky fondly beckoned one into the distance, but there was already a feeling of autumn in the air. Leaves that had come to the end of their lives were turning gold in the green foliage of the pensive forest, while the darkening fields had a wistful, melancholy look.

Presentiments of inescapable, oppressive autumn took hold of us too and it was not difficult to foresee that things would very soon come to a head. At some time the thunder had to rumble and the rain start pouring to freshen the humid air! It is usually close and sultry before a thunderstorm, when dark, leaden clouds approach, but we were already being stifled morally: this was evident in everything – in our movements, our smiles, in whatever we said.

I was riding in a light wagonette. Beside me sat Nadenka, the JP's daughter. She was as white as a sheet, her chin and lips trembling as if she were about to cry, her deep eyes were full of sorrow. But still she laughed the whole way, pretending that she was feeling extremely cheerful.

In front of us and behind us carriages of all kinds, ages and sizes were on the move. Gentlemen and ladies on horseback rode on either side. Count Karneyev, clad in a green shooting outfit that was more like a clown's than a huntsman's, leant forward and to one side as he mercilessly bounced up and down on his black horse. Looking at his bent body and the pained expression that constantly flitted across his haggard face you would think that he was riding a horse for the very first time. A new double-barrelled gun was slung across his back, while at his side hung a game bag, in which a wounded woodcock was writhing.

Olenka Urbenin was the shining jewel of the cavalcade. Seated on her black horse – a gift from the Count – and dressed in a black riding habit, with a white feather in her hat, she no longer resembled the 'girl in red', whom we had met in the forest only a few months before. Now there was something majestic about her, something of the *grande dame*. Every flourish of her whip, every smile – everything was calculated to appear aristocratic, magnificent. In her movements and smiles there was something provocative and inflammatory. She held her head high with snobbish affectation, and from the height of her horse she poured scorn on the whole company, as if she couldn't care less about the loud remarks directed at her by our local ladies of virtue. She was defiant, playing the coquette with her arrogance, with her position at the Count's – just as if she were unaware that the Count was sick and tired of her and that he was just waiting for the chance to get rid of her.

'The Count wants to throw me out,' she told me with a loud laugh after the cavalcade had ridden out of the courtyard. So, she must have known the position she was in – and she understood it.

But why that loud laughter? As I looked at her I was quite bewildered: where did that common forest dweller get so much energy from? When had she found time to learn to sit so gracefully in the saddle, to twitch her nostrils so proudly and to show off with such imperious gestures?

'A dissolute woman is the same as a pig,' Dr Pavel Ivanych told me. 'Seat her at the table and she'll plonk her legs on it.'

But this explanation was too simple. No one could have been more taken with Olga than I was, yet I would have been the first to throw stones at her. However, the vague voice of truth whispered to me that this was not the energy, nor the boastfulness, of a happy, contented woman, but despair, a presentiment of the imminent, inevitable denouement.

We were returning from the shoot, for which we had set off early that morning. It had been a failure. Just by the marshes, on which we had been pinning great hopes, we met a party of huntsmen who told us that all the game had been frightened off.

We managed to dispatch three woodcock and one duck to the next world – that was all that fell to the lot of ten huntsmen. Finally, one of the ladies developed toothache, so we had to hurry back. We took the beautiful path across the fields, where sheaves of newly harvested rye showed yellow against the dark background of the gloomy forest. On the horizon appeared the white church and the house on the Count's estate. To the right stretched the mirror-like surface of the lake, to the left loomed the dark mass of Stone Grave.

'What a terrible woman!' Nadezhda whispered to me every time Olga drew abreast of our wagonette. 'What a terrible woman! She's as evil as she's pretty. It's not long since you were best man at her wedding, is it? She'd barely time to wear out her wedding shoes[47] than she was already wearing someone else's silk and flaunting another's diamonds. This strange and swift metamorphosis is hardly credible. If these were her natural instincts it would have been at least tactful to have waited a year or two . . .'

'She's in a hurry to live![48] She's no time to wait!' I sighed.

'Do you know what's happening with her husband?'

'They say he's hit the bottle.'

'Yes, Papa was in town the day before yesterday and he saw him driving away from somewhere in a cab. His head was slumped to one side, he had no hat and there was mud all over his face. That man's finished! They say the family's terribly poor – they've nothing to eat, the rent's not paid. Poor little Sasha goes for days without food. Papa's described all this to the Count. But you know what the Count's like! He's honest and kind, but he doesn't like stopping to think and weigh things up. "I'll send him a hundred roubles," he says. So off he sends it. Without further ado. I don't think Urbenin could be more deeply insulted than to be sent that money . . . He'll take great offence at the Count's little sop and he'll only start drinking all the more.'

'Yes, the Count's stupid,' I said. 'He might at least have sent that money through me, and in my name.'

'He had no right to send him money! Do I have the right to feed you if I'm throttling the life out of you and if you hate me?'

'That's true.'

We became silent and pensive. The thought of Urbenin's fate had always been painful for me. But now, when the woman who had ruined him was caracoling before my very eyes, it gave rise to a whole series of mournful reflections. What would become of him and his children? What would become of *her*? In what moral cesspool would that feeble, pathetic Count end his days?

Next to me sat the only being who was decent and worthy of respect. I knew only two people in our district whom I was capable of liking and respecting, who alone had the right to snub me, because they stood higher than me – Nadezhda Nikolayevna and Dr Pavel Ivanych. What was in store for them?

'Nadezhda Nikolayevna,' I said. 'Without wishing to, I've caused you considerable grief and I'm less entitled than anyone to expect you to be frank with me. But I swear that no one will understand you as well as I do. Your sorrow is my sorrow, your happiness my happiness. If I'm asking you questions now, please don't suspect that it's merely out of idle curiosity. Tell me, my dear, why do you let this pygmy of a count go anywhere near you? What's stopping you from driving him away and ignoring his loathsome endearments? Surely his attentions do a respectable woman no honour! Why do you give these scandalmongers a reason for coupling your name with his?'

Nadezhda glanced at me with her limpid eyes and smiled cheerfully, just as though she could read the sincerity in my face.

'What are they saying?' she asked.

'That your Papa and yourself are trying to hook the Count and that in the end the Count will make fools of you.'

'They talk like that because they don't know the Count,' Nadezhda flared up. 'Those shameless, slandering women! They're used to seeing only the bad side of people. The good things are beyond their comprehension!'

'And did you find anything good in him?'

'Yes, I did! You're the first who should know that I would never have let him come anywhere near me if I hadn't been convinced of his honourable intentions.'

'So, things with you two have already come to "honourable

intentions",' I said in surprise. 'Soon . . . But why have you got "honourable intentions" into your head?'

'You'd like to know?' she asked – and her eyes sparkled. 'Those scandalmongers aren't lying. I do want to marry him! Now, don't look so surprised – and don't smile! You'll be telling me next that marrying without love is dishonest and all the rest of it . . . all that's been said a thousand times before but . . . what can I do? It's very hard, feeling that you're no more than a piece of unwanted furniture in this world. It's terrible living without any purpose. But when this man whom you dislike so much has made me his wife, I shall have a purpose in life. I shall reform him, make him stop drinking, teach him to work. Just take a look at him! He doesn't look anything like a man at the moment – but I shall make a man of him!'

'Etcetera, etcetera,' I said. 'You'll take care of his vast fortune, you'll do good deeds . . . The whole district will bless you and look upon you as an angel sent from on high to comfort the wretched. You'll be a mother, you'll bring up his children . . . Yes, it's a massive undertaking! You're an intelligent woman, but you reason like a schoolgirl!'

'Well, what if my idea *is* useless, what if it *is* ludicrous and naïve – the fact is, I live by it. Under its influence I've become healthier and more cheerful. Now, please don't disillusion me! Let me disillusion myself, but not now – some other time, later, in the distant future . . . Enough of this conversation!'

'Just one more indiscreet question – are you expecting a proposal?'

'Yes, judging from the note I received from him today my fate will be decided this evening. He writes that he has something very important to say. His whole future happiness will depend on my reply, he says.'

'Thanks for being so frank,' I replied.

The meaning of that note which Nadezhda received was quite clear to me. A vile proposal was awaiting that poor girl. I decided to free her from it.

'We've already reached my forest,' said the Count, drawing level with our wagonette. 'Would you like to stop for a while, Nadezhda Nikolayevna?'

Without waiting for an answer he clapped his hands.

'Sto-op!' he ordered in a loud, reverberant voice.

We settled ourselves along the edge of the forest. The sun had disappeared behind the trees, colouring with golden purple only the crowns of the loftiest alders and playing on the golden cross of the Count's church that was visible in the distance. Frightened merlins and orioles flew over our heads. One of the men fired his rifle and struck even more fear into that feathered kingdom, setting off an untiring avian concert. This kind of concert has its own peculiar charm in spring and summer, but when one senses the coming of chilly autumn in the air it irritates the nerves and hints at fast-approaching migration.

The freshness of evening wafted from the thick woods. The ladies' noses turned blue and the Count (who was sensitive to the cold) started rubbing his hands. Nothing could have been more appropriate than the smell of samovar charcoal and the clatter of crockery. One-eyed Kuzma, puffing and panting, and entangling himself in the long grass, brought out a case of brandy. We started warming ourselves.

A lengthy walk in cool, fresh air stimulates the appetite better than any artificial appetizer. After a long walk, cured sturgeon, caviare, roast partridge and other victuals delight the eye, like roses on an early spring morning.

'You're very clever today!' I told the Count, cutting myself a slice of sturgeon. 'Cleverer than ever before. You couldn't have arranged things better!'

'The Count and I arranged it together,' tittered Kalinin, winking at the coachmen who were carrying hampers of food, wine and crockery from the wagonettes. 'It's going to be a wonderful little picnic! And we're going to round it off with bubbly!'

The JP's face at this moment beamed with contentment as never before. Was he thinking that a proposal would be made to his Nadezhda that same evening? Wasn't that his reason for stocking up with champagne to toast the young couple? I stared at his face, but as usual all I could read in it was immeasurable contentment, repletion – and a dull pomposity that suffused his entire portly figure.

Cheerfully we attacked the savouries. Only two of the company were indifferent towards the sumptuous banquet that lay spread out before us on some rugs – Olga and Nadezhda Nikolayevna. The first stood to one side, leaning on the back of the wagonette without moving or saying a word as she gazed at the game bag that the Count had thrown to the ground; the wounded woodcock was tossing about in it. Olga was following the unfortunate bird's movements and seemed to be waiting for it to die. Nadezhda was sitting next to me, looking indifferently at the mouths of the picnickers who had been eating away so cheerfully.

'When will it all end?' her weary eyes said.

I offered her a caviare sandwich. She thanked me and put it to one side. Obviously she didn't feel like eating.

'Olga Nikolayevna! Why don't you sit down?' the Count shouted to her.

Olga didn't reply and continued standing there as still as a statue, watching the bird.

'What heartless people there are,' I said, going over to Olga. 'How can you, a woman, calmly watch the sufferings of that woodcock? Instead of observing its contortions you'd better give orders for it to be put out of its misery.'

'Others suffer, so let it suffer too,' Olga said, without looking at me and knitting her eyebrows.

'But who else is suffering?'

'Leave me in peace,' she said hoarsely. 'I don't feel like talking to you today – nor with that idiotic Count of yours! Now go away from me!'

She glanced at me with eyes that were full of anger and tears. Her face was pale, her lips were trembling.

'What a change!' I said, picking up the game bag and dispatching the woodcock. 'What a tone! I'm stunned, simply stunned!'

'Leave me in peace, I'm telling you. I'm in no mood for jokes!'

'What's the matter, my enchantress?'

Olga looked me up and down and turned her back on me.

'Only dissolute women, prostitutes, are spoken to in that tone of voice,' she said. 'You consider me one of them . . . well then, go back to your saintly women friends! In this place I'm worse, viler than anyone else. When you were riding with that virtuous Nadezhda you were too afraid to look at me. Well, go back to them, what are you waiting for? Go!'

'Yes, you're the worst, the lowest of the lot in this place,' I said, feeling that anger was gradually gaining the upper hand. 'Yes, you're dissolute and mercenary.'

'I remember when you offered me that damned money . . . I didn't understand what it meant at the time, but I do now.'

Anger gripped my whole being – and this anger was as strong as the love that had once begun to stir within me for the girl in red. After all, what person, what stone would have remained indifferent? Before me I saw beauty that had been cast by merciless fate into the mire. Neither youth, beauty nor grace had been spared. And now, when that woman struck me as more beautiful than ever, I felt what a great loss Nature had sustained in her – and an agonizing feeling of rage at the injustice of fate and the order of things filled my heart.

In moments of anger I am unable to control myself. I simply don't know what else Olga would have had to listen to had she not turned her back on me and walked off. She walked slowly towards the trees and soon disappeared behind them. She seemed to be crying.

'My dear ladies, my dear gentlemen!' I heard Kalinin say as he embarked on his speech. 'On this day, when we are all gathered here to . . . to unite together . . . Here we are, all assembled together, we all know one another, we are all enjoying ourselves and for this long-awaited union we are indebted to none other than our luminary, the shining star of our province . . . Now, please don't be embarrassed, Count! The ladies understand whom I'm talking about. Heeheehee! Well, to continue. Since we owe all of this to our enlightened, to our youthful . . . our youthful Count Karneyev, I propose a toast to . . . But who's that coming this way? Who is it?'

A carriage was bowling along from the direction of the Count's estate towards the clearing where we were sitting.

'Who can that be?' the Count said in amazement, training his field glasses on the carriage. 'Hm . . . strange . . . It must be some people passing by. Oh no! I can see Kaetan Kazimirovich's ugly mug. Who's that with him?'

Suddenly the Count leapt up as if he'd been stung. His face turned deathly pale, the field glasses fell from his hands, his eyes darted about like those of a trapped mouse and – as if pleading for help – came to rest, first on me, then on Nadezhda. Not everyone noticed his confusion, since most people's attention was distracted by the approaching carriage.

'Seryozha! Come over here for a moment!' he whispered, seizing my arm and leading me to one side. 'My dear chap, I beg you, as the best of friends, as the best of men . . . no questions, no inquiring looks, no surprise! I'll tell you everything later. I swear that not one iota of this will be kept a secret from you. There's been such a calamity in my life, such a terrible disaster, that I simply cannot describe it to you. You'll know everything later, but for the moment – no questions! Help me!'

Meanwhile the carriage came nearer and nearer . . . Finally it stopped and our Count's stupid secret became the property of the whole district. Out of the carriage stepped Pshekhotsky, puffing and smiling, and clad in a new light-brown tussore[49] silk suit. After him a young lady of about twenty-three nimbly sprang out. She was a tall, shapely blonde, with regular but unpleasant features and dark-blue eyes. All I can remember is those blue, expressionless eyes, that powdered nose, that heavy but sumptuous dress and several massive bracelets on each arm . . . I remember the smell of evening damp and spilt brandy yielding to the pungent odour of some kind of perfume.

'So many people here!' the strange lady said in broken Russian. 'You must all be having gay old time! Hullo, Aleksis!'

She went over to Aleksis and offered him her cheek. The Count quickly gave her a smacking kiss and anxiously surveyed his guests.

'May I introduce my wife,' he mumbled. 'And these, Sozya, are my good friends. Hm . . . I've a bad cough . . .'

'I've only just arrived, but Kaetan keeps telling me that I should rest. I ask you why should I rest if I slept whole way? I'd much rather go shooting! So I dressed myself and here I am! Kaetan, where's my cigarettes?'

Pshekhotsky sprang forward and handed the blonde his gold cigarette case.

'He's my brother-in-law,' the Count continued mumbling, pointing to Pshekhotsky. 'But *please* help me,' he went on, jogging my elbow. 'Help me out of this, for God's sake!'

They say that Kalinin suddenly came over bad and that Nadezhda wanted to help him but was unable to get up from her seat. They say that many people rushed to their carriages and drove off. I saw none of this. I do remember going into the forest, trying to find the path, not looking ahead and going where my legs took me.*

Bits of sticky clay hung from my legs and I was covered in mud when I emerged from the forest. Most probably I had to leap across a stream, but that's something I cannot remember. I felt so exhausted, so worn out, it was as if I'd been severely beaten with sticks. I should have gone straight back to the Count's estate, mounted Zorka and ridden off. But this I didn't do and I set off home on foot. I couldn't bear to see either the Count or his damned estate.†

My path lay along the banks of the lake. That watery monster had already begun to roar its evening song. Lofty, white-crested waves covered its entire, vast expanse. There was a rumbling and booming in the air. A cold, damp wind penetrated to my bones. To the left was the angry lake, while from the right came the monotonous noise of the grim forest. I felt that I was face to face with Nature, as if I were confronting someone in court. It seemed that all its anger, all those noises, all that bellowing, were intended for me alone. In any other circumstances I might have felt apprehensive, but now I barely noticed the giants that

* Here 140 lines of Kamyshev's manuscript are crossed through. A. C.

† At this point in the manuscript there's a pen and ink drawing of a pretty girl's head, her face distorted in horror. All that is written underneath has been meticulously blotted out. The upper half of the following page is also blotted out and through the dense ink blots only one word – 'temple' – is decipherable. A. C.

surrounded me. What was Nature's wrath in comparison with the storm that was raging within me?*

XIX

Back home I collapsed into bed without even undressing.

'At it again, you shameless man – swimming in the lake fully dressed!' growled Polikarp as he pulled off my wet and muddy clothes. 'Again I have to suffer! You think you're a gentleman, an educated man, but you're worse than any chimney sweep! I don't know what they taught you at university.'

Unable to stand either human voices or faces, I wanted to shout at Polikarp to leave me in peace, but my words stuck in my throat. My tongue was as weak and exhausted as the rest of my body. However agonizing the ordeal, I still had to let Polikarp pull all my clothes off – even down to my drenched underwear.

'You could at least turn over!' my servant grumbled, rolling me from side to side like a small doll. 'Tomorrow I'm handing in my notice! No, no – not for all the money in the world – I'll be damned if I stay here any longer. This old fool's had enough!'

Fresh, warm linen didn't warm up or relax me. I was trembling so violently with rage and fear that my teeth were chattering. But I could find no explanation for this fear. Neither apparitions nor ghosts had ever scared me – not even the portrait of my predecessor Pospelov hanging over my head: he never took his lifeless eyes off me and seemed to be winking. But I wasn't in the least ruffled when I looked at him. Although my future wasn't crystal clear, I could say with a high degree of probability that nothing was threatening me, that no black clouds were near. Death was still far off, I had no serious illnesses and I attached no significance to personal disasters. So, what was I afraid of and why were my teeth chattering?

Nor was I able to explain the reason for my anger. It couldn't have been the Count's 'secret' that infuriated me so much.

* This has also been blotted out. A. C.

Neither the Count nor his marriage, which he had concealed from me, was any concern of mine. All that remains is to explain my state of mind at the time as shattered nerves and exhaustion. Any other explanation is beyond me.

When Polikarp had left I covered myself up to the head with the intention of sleeping. It was dark and quiet. My parrot kept turning restlessly in its cage and I could hear the regular ticking of the wall clock in Polikarp's room. Everywhere else there reigned peace and quiet. Physical and moral exhaustion prevailed and I began to doze off. I felt that some great weight was gradually being lifted from me, that those hateful images were giving way in my consciousness to clouds of mist . . . I remember that I even began to have dreams. I dreamt that on one bright winter's morning I was walking along Nevsky Prospekt[50] in St Petersburg, looking into shop windows for want of something to do. I felt cheerful, gay at heart. I had no reason to hurry anywhere, I had nothing to do – complete freedom, in fact. The realization that I was far from my village, from the Count's estate and from that cold angry lake, put me in an even more relaxed and cheerful frame of mind. I stopped by the largest shop window and started inspecting women's hats. These hats were familiar to me. I had seen Olga wearing one of them, Nadezhda another; a third I had seen on the day of the shooting party on the fair head of Sozya, who had arrived so unexpectedly. Under these hats familiar faces began to smile at me. When I wanted to tell them something all three merged into one large, red face. This face rolled its eyes angrily and stuck its tongue out. Someone squeezed my neck from behind.

'A husband murdered his wife!' the red face shouted. I shuddered, cried out and jumped out of bed as if I had been stung. My heart beat violently and a cold sweat broke out on my forehead.

'A husband murdered his wife!' repeated the parrot. 'Now, give me some sugar! How stupid you are. You fool!'

'It's only the parrot,' I said, calming myself as I lay down again on my bed . . . Thank God . . .'

Then I heard a monotonous murmur – it was the rain pattering on the roof. The clouds that I had seen in the west when I was walking along the banks of the lake had now filled the whole sky. Faint flashes of lightning illuminated the portrait of the late Pospelov; thunder rumbled right over my head.

The last storm this summer, I thought.

I remember one of the first storms. Exactly the same kind of thunder had once rumbled in the forest when I had visited the forester's house for the first time. The girl in red and I had stood by the window then, watching the lightning illuminate the pine trees. Fear shone in the eyes of that beautiful creature. She told me that her mother had been struck by lightning and that she herself was thirsting for a dramatic death. She would have liked to dress just like the richest lady aristocrats in the district. Luxurious dresses went well with her beauty, she felt. Conscious and proud of her delusions of grandeur, she wanted to ascend Stone Grave – there to die a dramatic death!

Her dream came tr— although not on Sto—*

Having abandoned all hope of getting to sleep, I got up and sat on my bed. The gentle murmur of the rain gradually turned into the angry roar that I loved so dearly when my heart was free from fear and anger. But now that roar appeared menacing; one thunderclap followed the other.

'A husband murdered his wife!' squawked the parrot.

Those were its last words. Closing my eyes in abject fear, I groped in the darkness for the cage and hurled it into the corner.

'To hell with you!' I shouted, hearing the crash of the cage and the parrot's screeching.

That poor, noble bird! The flight into the corner had cost it dear. Next day its cage contained a cold corpse. Why had I killed it? If it was its favourite phrase about the husband who murdered his wife that rem . . . .
. . . .†

When she handed over the flat, my predecessor Pospelov's

* Here almost a whole page has been carefully crossed out. Only a few words that provide no clue to deciphering what's been crossed out have been spared. A. C.

† Unfortunately everything is crossed out here. It is clear that Kamyshev did not cross any words out at the time of writing, but afterwards. I shall pay *special* attention to these crossings-out towards the end of this story. A. C.

mother made me pay for all the furniture – even for the photographs of people I didn't know. But she wouldn't take one copeck for the valuable parrot. On the evening of her departure for Finland she spent the whole night bidding her noble bird farewell. I remember the sobbing and lamentations that accompanied this valediction. I remember her tears when she asked me to look after her friend until her return. I gave her my word of honour that her parrot would not regret making my acquaintance. And I had not kept my word: I had killed the bird. I can imagine what the old crone would have said if she had found out about the fate of her squawker!

XX

Someone tapped cautiously on my window. The little house where I lived stood on a road that was right on the edge of the village and I often used to hear tapping on my window, especially in bad weather when travellers were looking for somewhere to stay the night. This time it was no traveller tapping on the window. When I went over to it and waited until the lightning flashed, I saw the dark outline of some tall, thin man. He was standing in front of the window and seemed to be shivering from the cold. I opened the window.

'Who's there? What do you want?' I asked.

'It's me, Sergey Petrovich,' came that plaintive voice in which people who are chilled to the marrow and terribly frightened tend to speak. 'It's me. I've come to see you, old chap.'

That dark silhouette's plaintive voice I was amazed to recognize as that of my friend Dr Pavel Ivanovich. I was baffled by this visit from Screwy, who normally led a regular life and who always went to bed before midnight. What could have prompted him to break his rules and turn up at my place at two o'clock in the morning – and in such bad weather into the bargain!

'What do you want?' I asked, in my heart of hearts consigning that unexpected visitor to hell.

'I'm sorry, old chap. I wanted to knock on the door but your

Polikarp must surely be sleeping like a log now. So I decided to tap on the window.'

'Well, what do you want?'

Pavel Ivanovich came closer to the window and mumbled something incomprehensible. He was shaking and seemed to be drunk.

'I'm listening!' I said, losing patience.

'I can see you're getting angry, but . . . if you only knew everything that's happened you wouldn't lose your temper over such trifles as having your sleep disturbed and being visited at this unsociable hour. There's no time for sleeping now! Oh, my God! I've lived thirty years in this world and today is the first time I've been so dreadfully unhappy! I'm *so* unhappy, Sergey Petrovich!'

'Ah . . . but what on earth's happened? And what's it got to do with me? I can barely stand up . . . I don't feel like seeing anyone right now.'

'Sergey Petrovich,' Screwy said in a tearful voice, in the darkness holding out to my face a hand that was wet with rain. 'You're an honest man! You're my friend!'

And then I heard a man weeping: it was the doctor.

'Go home, Pavel Ivanovich!' I said after a short silence. 'I can't talk just now. My state of mind scares me – and yours as well. We won't understand each other . . .'

'My dear chap,' the doctor pleaded. 'Marry *her*!'

'You're out of your mind!' I said, slamming the window.

After the parrot the doctor was next to suffer from my tantrums: I hadn't invited him in and I'd shut the window in his face. These were two boorish outbursts for which I would have challenged even a woman to a duel.* But that meek, inoffensive Screwy had no idea about duels. He didn't even know the meaning of 'angry'.

Two minutes later there was a flash of lightning and as I looked through the window I could see the bent figure of my

* This last phrase is written over a crossed-out line, in which one can make out: 'I would have torn his head from his shoulders and broken all the windows.' A. C.

visitor. This time he was in a pleading posture, as expectant as a beggar seeking charity. No doubt he was waiting for me to forgive him and let him have his say.

Fortunately my conscience pricked me. I felt sorry for myself, sorry that Nature had implanted so much cruelty and vileness in me. My base soul was as hard as stone – just like my healthy body . . .* I went to the window and opened it.

'Come in!' I said.

'There's no time! Every moment is precious! Poor Nadya has poisoned herself, she has a doctor constantly at her bedside. We just managed to save the poor girl . . . Isn't that a calamity? And all you can do is ignore me and slam the window!'

'All the same . . . is she still alive?'

'"All the same"! That's no way to talk about unfortunate wretches, my good friend! Who would have thought that this clever, honest creature would want to depart this life because of a fellow like the Count? No, my friend, unfortunately for men, women cannot be perfect! However clever a woman may be, whatever imperfections she may be endowed with, there's still some immovable force within her that prevents both herself and others from living. Take Nadezhda for example . . . Why did she do it? Vanity, simply vanity! Morbid vanity! Just to wound you she thought she would marry the Count. She needed neither his money nor his position. She merely wanted to satisfy her monstrous vanity. And suddenly she met with failure! You know that *his* wife has arrived. That old roué turns out to be married! And they say women have more staying-power, that they can take things better than men! But where's *her* staying-power if she resorts to sulphur matches for such a pathetic reason? That's not staying-power – it's sheer vanity!'

'You'll catch cold!'

'What I've just witnessed is worse than any cold . . . Those eyes, that pallor . . . ah! Unsuccessful suicide has now been

* There follows a strikingly pretentious interpretation of the author's emotional resilience. The sight of human misery, blood, autopsies apparently left him completely unmoved. The whole of this passage is tinged with boastful naïveté, insincerity. It is startlingly crude and I have deleted it. As far as characterization of Kamyshev is concerned, it's of no importance. A. C.

added to unsuccessful love, to an unsuccessful attempt to spite you. It's difficult to imagine a greater misfortune! My dear chap, if you have one ounce of pity if . . . if you could see her . . . well, why *shouldn't* you go to her? You did love her! But even if you don't love her any more why not sacrifice some of your time for her? Human life is precious – one could give everything for it! Save her life!'

There was a violent bang on my door. I shuddered. My heart was bleeding . . . I don't believe in presentiments, but on this occasion I was not alarmed for nothing. Someone out in the street was knocking on my door.

'Who's there?' I shouted out of the window.

'I've come to see yer 'onner!'

'What do you want?'

'I've a letter from the Count, yer 'onner. Someone's bin murdered!'

A dark figure wrapped in a sheepskin coat came up to the window, cursing the weather as he handed me a letter. I quickly stepped away from the window, lit the candle and read the following:

'For God's sake drop everything and come *at once*! Olga's been murdered. I'm in a dead panic and now I go out of my mind.

Yours A. K.'

Olga murdered! That brief phrase made my head spin and I saw black. I sat on the bed and let my hands drop to my sides – I just didn't have the strength to think about it.

'Is that you, Pavel Ivanych?' I heard the messenger's voice.'I was just on my way to you. I've a letter for you too.'

XXI

Five minutes later Screwy and I were driving in a covered carriage to the Count's estate. The rain beat on the carriage roof, ahead there were constant, blinding flashes of lightning. We could hear the roar of the lake . . .

The last act of the drama was beginning and two of its characters were driving off to witness a heart-rending spectacle.

'Well, what do you think is in store for us?' I asked Pavel Ivanych on the way.

'I just can't imagine . . . I simply don't know . . .'

'I don't know either . . .'

'As Hamlet once regretted that the Lord of heaven and earth had forbidden the sin of suicide,[51] so I regret now that fate made me a doctor. I deeply regret it!'

'And I fear that *my* turn might come to regret that I'm an investigating magistrate,' I said. 'If the Count hasn't confused murder with suicide and Olga has actually been *murdered*, then my poor nerves really will suffer!'

'You could refuse the case . . .'

I looked questioningly at Pavel Ivanych, but I could of course detect nothing, because it was so dark. How did he know that I *could* refuse the case? I was Olga's lover, but who knew about it except Olga herself – yes, and perhaps Pshekhotsky, who had once accorded me his applause?

'Why do you think I can refuse?' I asked Screwy.

'Well, you might become ill, or retire . . . None of that would be dishonourable – not by a long chalk – because there's someone to take your place. But a doctor's position is quite different.'

'Is that all?' I wondered.

After a long, killing journey over clayey soil the carriage finally came to a halt at the entrance. Directly above it there were brightly lit windows and through the last one on the right, in Olga's bedroom, a light faintly glimmered; but all the others were like dark patches. On the stairs we were met by Owlet. She peered at me with her tiny, piercing eyes and her wrinkled face creased into an evil, mocking smile.

'There's a nice little surprise in store for you!' her eyes said. She was probably thinking that we had come on a drinking spree and didn't know that the house had been struck by disaster.

'Let me recommend this woman for your attention,' I told Pavel Ivanych, pulling off the old crone's bonnet to reveal a completely bald head. 'This old witch is ninety, dear chap. If you and I had to perform an autopsy on this specimen one day we'd reach very different conclusions. You would find senile atrophy of the brain, whereas I'd convince you that she's the cleverest, craftiest creature in the whole district. A devil in petticoats!'

I was stunned when I entered the room. The scene that met me was completely unexpected. All the chairs and sofas were occupied. Groups were standing in the corners and by the windows too. Where could they have come from? If someone had told me earlier that I'd meet these people here I would have laughed my head off. Their presence was so improbable, so out of place in the Count's house at the very time when, perhaps, the dead or dying Olga was lying in one of the rooms. It was the head gipsy Karpov's choir from the London restaurant – the same choir with which the reader will be familiar from one of the earlier chapters. When I entered, my old friend Tina detached herself from one of the groups and on recognizing me she cried out for joy. A smile spread over her pale, dark-complexioned face when I gave her my hand and tears flowed from her eyes – she wanted to tell me something. But she couldn't speak for tears and I didn't manage to extract one word from her. I turned to the other gipsies and they explained their presence as follows. That morning the Count had sent a telegram to town with instructions for the whole choir – in its full complement – to be at the Count's house by nine o'clock that same evening without fail. They had obeyed these 'instructions', caught the train and by eight o'clock they were already in the ballroom. 'And we had visions of bringing pleasure to His Excellency and his gentlemen guests. We know so many new songs! And suddenly . . .'

And suddenly a peasant had come tearing up on horseback with the news that a brutal murder had been committed at the shooting party and with orders to prepare a bed for Olga. They hadn't believed this peasant, as he was as drunk as a pig. But when noises were heard on the stairs and a dark body was carried across the ballroom, there was no further room for doubt.

'And now we don't know what to do . . . We can't stay here . . . when there's a priest around it's time for cheerful people to clear off. Besides, all the girls are upset and crying. They can't stay in a house where there's a corpse! We want to leave, but they won't give us any horses. Mr Count is ill in bed and won't see anyone and the servants just laugh at us when we ask for horses. We can't walk in this weather, on such a dark night! And generally speaking the servants are terribly rude! When we asked for a samovar for the ladies they told us to go to hell.'

All these complaints culminated in a tearful appeal to my magnanimity. Couldn't *I* see that they were given carriages, so that they could get out of that damned house?

'If the horses haven't been stabled and if the coachmen haven't been sent out somewhere else, you'll be able to get away,' I said. 'I'll give instructions.'

For those poor devils in buffoons' costumes, who were used to swaggering about with great panache and bravado, those glum faces and hesitant poses were quite out of character. My promise to arrange for them to be taken to the station roused their spirits somewhat. Male whispers turned into loud talk and the women stopped crying.

And then, as I made my way to the Count's study through a whole series of dark, unlit rooms, I peeped through one of the numerous doorways and a deeply moving sight met my eyes. At a table, by the hissing samovar, sat Sozya and her brother Pshekhotsky. Dressed in a light blouse, but still wearing those same bracelets and rings, Sozya was sniffing a scent bottle and languidly, delicately, sipping from a cup. Her eyes were red from weeping. Probably the incident at the shooting party had completely shattered her nerves and ruined her state of mind for some time to come. As wooden-faced as ever, Pshekhotsky was drinking his tea in large gulps from the saucer and telling his sister something. Judging from his mentor-like expression and gestures, he was trying to calm her and persuade her to stop crying.

Needless to say, I found the Count emotionally in tatters. That flabby, feeble man had grown thinner and more pinched-looking than ever. He was pale and his lips trembled feverishly; his head was bound with a white handkerchief, whose sharp vinegary smell filled the whole room. When I entered he leapt up from the sofa where he was lying and dashed towards me, the folds of his dressing-gown wrapped tightly around him.

'Ah? Ah?' he began, trembling and in a choking voice. 'Well?'

After emitting several vague sounds he pulled me by the sleeve over to the sofa and after waiting for me to sit down pressed against me like a small, frightened dog and began pouring out his troubles.

'Who would have expected it, eh? . . . Just a moment, dear chap, I want to wrap myself in this rug, I feel feverish . . . The poor girl's been murdered. And how barbarously! She's still alive, but the local doctor says she'll die tonight. A terrible day! Then my wife suddenly turns up out of the blue, damn and blast her – *that* was my most unfortunate mistake! I was drunk when I got married in St Petersburg, Seryozha. I hid this from you, as I felt ashamed. But now she's here – and you can see what she's like. I just take one look and I blame myself! Oh, that damned weakness of mine! Under the influence of the moment and vodka I'm capable of doing anything you like! My wife's arrival is the first little present, the scandal with Olga is the second. Now I'm waiting for the third . . . I know that something else will happen . . . I know! I shall go out of my mind!'

After a good cry, three glasses of vodka and calling himself an ass, layabout and drunkard the Count described the drama that had taken place at the shooting party, his tongue faltering from emotion. What he told me was roughly as follows:

About twenty or thirty minutes after I'd left, when my astonishment at Sozya's arrival had somewhat subsided and when, after meeting all the assembled company, Sozya started acting like a true madam, suddenly everyone heard a piercing, heart-rending shriek. It came from the direction of the forest and was echoed four times. It was so unusual that those who heard it leapt to their feet, dogs barked and horses pricked up their ears. It was an unnatural cry, but the Count managed to detect in it a woman's voice. It was resonant with despair and horror. Women who see a ghost or witness the sudden death of a child must surely shriek like that. The alarmed guests looked at the Count and the Count at them. For three minutes, deathly silence reigned.

While the guests were surveying each other without a word, the coachmen and lackeys ran towards the place where the shriek had come from. The first messenger of woe was the old footman Ilya. He came running out of the forest to the clearing, his face pale, his pupils dilated: he wanted to tell us something but he was so breathless and agitated it was some time before he could utter a word. Finally, taking a grip and crossing himself he said:

'The young lady's been murdered!'

What young lady? Who murdered her? But Ilya gave no reply to these questions. The role of second messenger fell to someone whom they had not been expecting and whose appearance stunned them completely. The sudden appearance and the look of this man were truly startling. When the Count saw him and remembered that Olga had been wandering around in the forest, his heart sank and his legs gave way from some terrible foreboding.

It was Pyotr Yegorych Urbenin, the Count's former manager and Olga's husband. At first the company had heard heavy footsteps and the crackle of brushwood. It was as if a bear were making its way to the forest edge. But then the massive bulk of the unfortunate Pyotr Urbenin appeared. As he came out into the clearing and saw the company, he took one step back and stood as if rooted to the spot. For about two minutes he said nothing and did not budge, thus giving everyone the chance to take a good look at him. He was wearing his everyday grey waistcoat and trousers that were already pretty threadbare. He was hatless and his tousled hair clung to his sweaty forehead and temples. On this occasion his face – normally crimson and often deep purple – was pale. His eyes looked around dementedly, with an unnaturally wide stare, and his lips and hands were trembling.

But most striking of all, and what captured the stunned onlookers' attention more than anything else, were his bloodstained hands: his hands and cuffs were soaked as if they had been washed in a bath of blood.

After standing there in a stupor for a further three minutes, Urbenin squatted on the grass as if waking from a dream and started groaning . . . The dogs, scenting something unusual, surrounded him and began to bark. Surveying the company with his dull eyes, Urbenin covered his face with both hands and sank into another stupor.

'Olga, Olga! What have you done?' he groaned.

Dull sobs came from his chest and his powerful shoulders started shaking. When he removed his hands from his face the company could see the blood left by his hands on his cheeks and forehead.

At this point the Count waved his arm and feverishly downed a glass of vodka.

'After that my memory becomes confused,' he continued. 'As you can imagine, all these events shocked me so much that I lost all capacity for thought. I don't remember anything after that! All I remember is that some men carried a body in a torn, bloodstained dress out of the forest. I couldn't bring myself to look at it. They put it into a carriage and drove off. I heard neither groans nor weeping. They say she'd been stabbed in the side with the little dagger she always carried with her. Do you remember it? I gave it her as a present. It was a blunt dagger, blunter than the edge of this glass. Imagine the strength it must have taken to thrust it into her! I used to be fond of Caucasian weapons, dear chap, but to hell with them now! Tomorrow I'll give orders for them to be thrown out!'

The Count drank another glass of vodka.

'What a disgrace!' he continued. 'What an abomination! We brought her back to the house . . . you know, everyone was in despair, horrified. And suddenly – to hell with those gipsies! – we heard wild singing . . . They were drawn up in rows and then those devils let rip. You see, they wanted to greet her in style, but it was completely misplaced. It was rather like that Ivan the Fool who went into raptures on meeting a funeral and yelled: "Keep carrying, but don't carry it off." Yes, my friend, I wanted to entertain my guests, that's why I sent for the gipsies. But it all turned out a dreadful mess. I should have invited doctors and priests instead of gipsies! And now I don't know what to do! What *shall* I do? I'm not familiar with all the formalities, the correct procedure, whom to call in, whom to send for . . . Perhaps the police should be here, the investigating magistrate? Damned if I know, for the life of me! Thank heaven Father Jeremiah came to perform the last rites when he heard of the scandal – I'd never have thought of sending for him myself. I beg you, old boy, *please* take all this off my hands! God, I'm going out of my mind! My wife turning up . . . the murder . . . brrr! Where's my wife now? Have you seen her?'

'Yes I have. She's having tea with Pshekhotsky.'

'With her brother, that is . . . Pshekhotsky. What a bastard! When I slipped secretly out of St Petersburg he got wind of my flight and now I can't shake him off. The mind cannot comprehend how much money he swindled me out of during all that time!'

I had no time for lengthy conversations with the Count, so I stood up and went towards the door.

'Listen,' the Count said, stopping me. 'That Urbenin won't stab me, will he?'

'Surely it wasn't *he* who stabbed Olga?'

'Of course it was. Only, I don't know where he turned up from . . . what the hell brought him to the forest? And why *that* particular forest? Let's assume he hid there and waited for us: then how did he know I'd want to make a halt just there and not somewhere else?'

'You don't understand a thing,' I said. 'By the way, I'm asking you for the very last time . . . If I take this case on I'd rather you didn't give me your opinion on the matter. You must try and simply answer my questions, nothing more.'

XXII

After leaving the Count I went to the room where Olga was lying.* A small blue lamp was burning in the room, faintly illuminating people's faces. It was impossible to read or write

* Here two lines are crossed out. A. C.

by its light. Olga was lying on her bed, her head bandaged. All I could make out was her extraordinarily pale, sharp nose and her closed eyelids. At the moment I entered, her breast was bare; they were putting an ice bag on it.* That meant Olga was still alive. Two doctors were fussing around her. When I entered, Pavel Ivanych, huffing and puffing non-stop and screwing up his eyes, was listening to her heart.

The district doctor, who looked extremely weary and by all appearances was a sick man, sat pensively in an armchair by the bed, apparently taking her pulse. Father Jeremiah, who had just finished what he had to do, was wrapping his crucifix in his stole and preparing to leave.

'Don't grieve, Pyotr Yegorych!' he said, sighing and looking into one corner. 'Everything is as God wills it. You must turn to God for help.'

Urbenin was sitting on a stool in a corner of the room. He had changed so dramatically that I barely recognized him. His recent idleness and drunkenness were as evident in his clothes as in his general appearance. These clothes were as worn out as his face. The poor devil sat motionless, rested his head on his fists and didn't take his eyes off the bed. His face and hands were still covered with bloodstains . . . he had forgotten all about washing them off.

Oh, that prophecy of my soul and my poor bird! Whenever that noble bird of mine, that I had killed, squawked that phrase about the husband who murdered his wife, Urbenin invariably made his appearance in my imagination. Why? I knew that jealous husbands often kill unfaithful wives – and at the same time, that men like Urbenin don't go around murdering people. And I dismissed any possibility of Olga having been murdered by her husband as preposterous.

'Was it him or wasn't it?' I asked myself as I looked at his wretched face.

* I draw the reader's attention to one circumstance. Although Kamyshev is so fond of holding forth to all and sundry about the state of his soul, even when he's describing his clashes with Polikarp, he says nothing about the impression the dying Olga made on him. I think that this omission is deliberate. A. C.

To be honest, I didn't answer myself in the affirmative, in spite of the Count's story and the blood I had seen on his hands and face.

'If he had done it he would have washed the blood from his hands and face long ago,' I thought, recalling the theory of an investigating magistrate I once knew: murderers cannot stomach the blood of their victims.

If I'd been inclined to stir my grey matter I could have thought of many similar situations, but it was no good anticipating and stuffing my head with premature conclusions.

'My compliments!' the district doctor said. 'I'm delighted that you've at last done us the honour of coming. Now, please tell me who's master of this house.'

'There's no master here . . . here reigneth chaos,' I replied.

'A charming little phrase, but it doesn't help me in the least,' said the doctor with an irritable cough. 'I've been asking for three hours now, simply *begging* for a bottle of port or champagne to be brought to me and not one person has seen fit to grant my request! They're all as deaf as doorposts here. They've only *just* brought me some ice, although I asked for it three hours ago. What's going on here? Someone is dying of thirst and all they can do is laugh! It's all very well for the Count to swig liqueurs in his study, but they can't even bring me a glass! When I wanted to send someone to the chemist in town they told me that the horses were exhausted and that no one was in a fit state to go because they were all drunk. I wanted to send for medicine and bandages from my hospital and they do me a favour – they give me some drunkard who can barely stand up. It's about two hours since I told him to go – and what happens? They say he's only just left! Isn't that a disgrace? They're nothing but drunken oafs, the whole lot of them – one way or the other they're all idiots! I swear by God it's the first time in my life I've come across such heartless people!'

The doctor's indignation was justified. He was not exaggerating in the least – on the contrary. A whole night wouldn't have sufficed for him to vent his spleen on all the goings-on and scandals that had occurred on the Count's estate. Demoralized by idleness and lawlessness, the servants were perfectly loathsome. There wasn't one footman who couldn't have served as the very model of someone who had outstayed his time – and grown fat in the process.

I went off to get some wine. After distributing two or three clouts on the head I managed to obtain both champagne and Valerian drops, to the doctor's ineffable delight. An hour later* a male nurse arrived from the hospital, bringing all that was necessary.

Pavel Ivanovich succeeded in pouring a tablespoonful of champagne into Olga's mouth. She tried hard to swallow and groaned. Then they injected her with something that looked like Hofman drops.[52]

'Olga Nikolayevna!' the district doctor shouted, leaning towards her ear. 'Olga Ni-ko-la-yevna!'

'It's too much to expect her to regain consciousness,' sighed Pavel Ivanych. 'A great deal of blood has been lost. Besides, the blow on the head with some blunt instrument must have caused concussion.'

It was not for me to decide whether it was concussion or not, but Olga opened her eyes and asked for a drink. The stimulants had worked.

'Now you can ask her anything you like,' Pavel Ivanych said, nudging my elbow. 'Go ahead.'

I went over to the bed . . . Olga's eyes were turned on me.

'Where am I?' she asked.

'Olga Nikolayevna!' I began. 'Don't you recognize me?'

For a few seconds Olga looked at me and then she closed her eyes. 'Yes,' she groaned. 'Yes!'

'I'm Zinovyev, the investigating magistrate,' I went on. 'I had

* I must direct the reader's attention to yet another very important circumstance. For two or three hours all Mr Kamyshev does is pass from room to room, becomes exasperated (together with the doctors) at the servants, and liberally bestows clouts on the ear, etc. Would you recognize this person as an investigating magistrate? Evidently he's in no hurry and is only trying to kill time somehow. Obviously he knew who the murderer was. What's more, that needless search of Owlet's room, the questioning of the gipsies (described a little further on) – more like mockery than cross-examination – could only have been carried out as a delaying tactic. A. C.

the honour of knowing you and – if you remember – I was even best man at your wedding.'

'Is it you?' Olga whispered, holding her left arm out. 'Sit down.'

'She's delirious,' sighed Screwy.

'I'm Zinovyev, the investigating magistrate,' I repeated. 'Do you remember? I was at the shooting party. How do you feel?'

'Please restrict yourself to essential questions,' the doctor whispered. 'I can't guarantee that she'll remain conscious for much longer.'

'I must ask you to stop lecturing me!' I retorted, taking offence. 'I don't know what to say, Olga Nikolayevna,' I continued, turning to her. 'Please try and recall the events of the past day. I'll help you. At one o'clock you mounted your horse and rode off with the shooting party. The shoot lasted about four hours. Then a halt was made at the edge of the forest . . . Do you remember?'

'And you . . . *you* killed . . .'

'The woodcock? After I finished off the wounded woodcock you frowned and left the main party. You went into the forest.* Now, please try to summon all your strength and stir your memory. While you were walking in the forest you were attacked by some person unknown. I'm asking you as an investigating magistrate – who was it?'

Olga opened her eyes and looked at me.

'Tell us the name of that man! There are three others here besides me.'

Olga negatively shook her head.

'You must name him,' I continued. 'He will be severely punished. The law will make him pay for his barbarity. He'll be sent to Siberia† . . . I'm waiting.'

* This evasion of a question of the first importance could have had only one objective: to drag the time out and await loss of consciousness, when Olga would no longer be able to name the murderer. A trick that's quite in character and it's amazing that the doctors didn't see through it. A. C.

† All this seems naïve only at first glance. Evidently, Kamyshev had to make Olga aware of the serious consequences any declaration on her part would have for the murderer. If the murderer was dear to her, *ergo*, she had to keep quiet. A. C.

Olga smiled and negatively shook her head. Further questions led to nothing. I failed to elicit one more word, one more movement from Olga. At a quarter to five she passed away.

XXIII

At about six o'clock in the morning the elder and the witnesses I had requested arrived from the village. To drive out to the scene of the crime was impossible: the rain that had started during the night was still bucketing down. Small puddles had turned into lakes. The leaden sky looked bleak and promised no sun. The soaked trees with their dejectedly drooping branches scattered great showers of heavy spray with every gust of wind. Riding there was out of the question – and perhaps there would have been no point in it anyway: the traces of the crime – bloodstains, human footprints, etc. – had probably been washed away by the rain during the night. But the formalities demanded that the scene of the crime be inspected and I postponed the visit until the police arrived. In the meantime I busied myself with making out a rough report and cross-examining the witnesses. I questioned the gipsies first. Those poor singers had been sitting all night long in the Count's rooms waiting for horses to take them to the station. But they were not given any horses. The servants sent them to the Count, warning them at the same time that His Excellency had forbidden anyone to be 'admitted'. They were not even given the samovar they had asked for that morning. Their more than odd, uncertain position in a strange house, where a dead woman was lying, their not knowing when they would be able to leave, the wet, miserable weather – all this reduced those wretched male and female gipsies to such despair that they grew pale and thin in the course of a single night. They wandered from one room to the other, as if scared out of their lives and expecting some stern judgement upon their heads. My questioning only lowered their spirits all the more. In the first place, my lengthy cross-examination delayed their departure from that damned house for ages; secondly, it frightened the lives out of them. When those simple folk concluded that they were strongly suspected of murder they tearfully started assuring me that they weren't guilty, that they knew nothing at all about it. When Tina saw that I was there in my official capacity she completely forgot our previous relationship, trembled and grew numb with fear when she spoke to me – just like a girl who has been whipped. In reply to my request not to panic and my assurances that I saw them solely as witnesses, assistants of justice, the gipsies announced in one voice that they had never witnessed a thing, that they knew absolutely nothing and that they hoped in future God would free them from any close acquaintance with the legal fraternity.

I asked them which way they had driven from the station, whether they had passed through the forest where the murder had been committed, whether someone had broken off from the main party – even for a short while – and whether they had heard Olga's heart-rending shriek.* This line of questioning led nowhere. Alarmed by it, the gipsies detailed two young men from the choir and sent them off to the village to hire carts. Those poor devils dearly wanted to get away. Unfortunately for them, there was already much talk in the village about the murder in the forest and those swarthy envoys were looked upon with suspicion, apprehended and brought to me.

Only that evening did the exhausted choir escape from the nightmare and was it able to breathe freely: having hired five peasant carts at three times the proper price they rode away from the Count's house. Later on they were paid for their visit, but no one paid them for the moral torments they had suffered in the Count's mansion . . .

After questioning them I carried out a search in Owlet's room.†

In her trunks I found piles of every imaginable kind of old woman's junk, but after sorting through all those shabby bon-

* If Mr Kamyshev found all this necessary, wouldn't it have been easier to question the coachmen who had driven the gipsies? A. C.

† Why? Assuming all this was done by the investigating magistrate when he was drunk or half-asleep then why write about it? Wouldn't it have been better to conceal these gross errors from the reader? A. C.

nets and darned stockings, I found neither money nor valuables that the old crone might have stolen from the Count and his guests. Nor did I find the items that were stolen at some time from Tina. Obviously the old witch had another hiding place, known only to herself.

I shall not give my report here – the preliminary evidence from my inspection. It's very long – what's more, I've forgotten most of it. I shall give it in brief only, just the main details. First of all I described the condition in which I found Olga and my cross-examination of her, down to the very last detail. From this examination it was obvious that Olga had been fully conscious when she answered me and had deliberately concealed the murderer's name. *She did not want* the murderer to be punished and this inevitably leads one to suppose that the criminal was near and dear to her.

The inspection of the clothes that I had carried out with the district police officer (who soon turned up) provided a great deal of evidence. The jacket of her riding habit (of velvet with silk lining) was still damp. The right side, with the hole made by the dagger, was soaked in blood and in places was covered with clotted blood. The bleeding had been severe and it was a wonder that Olga hadn't died on the spot. The left side was also bloodstained. The left sleeve was torn at the shoulder and wrist. The two top buttons had been torn off and we didn't find them during the inspection. The black kashmir skirt of the riding habit was found in a dreadfully crumpled state – this had happened when Olga was carried from the forest to the carriage and from there to her bed. Then it had been pulled off, bundled up anyhow and shoved under the bed. It was torn at the belt. This lengthwise tear, which was about six inches long, had probably occurred when the body was being conveyed and pulled along. It could also have been made when she was alive. Olga disliked mending, didn't know to whom to give the skirt for repair and might have concealed the tear under her coat. I think that there was no evidence here of the work of a frenzied, maniacal criminal, as the deputy prosecutor later stressed in his speech. The right section of the belt and the right pocket were soaked in blood. The handkerchief and glove that were lying in this pocket resembled two shapeless, rust-coloured lumps. The whole skirt, from belt to hem, was spattered with bloodstains of varying shapes and sizes. Most of them were the imprints of the bloodstained fingers and palms (as it later transpired at the examination) of the coachmen and footmen who had conveyed Olga. The chemise was covered in blood, chiefly on the right side, where there was a hole produced by a sharp instrument. And similarly, as with the jacket, there were tears along the left shoulder and near the wrist. The cuff was half torn off.

The items that Olga had been wearing – a gold watch, a long gold chain, a diamond brooch, earrings, rings and a purse with silver coins – were found with the clothes. Clearly the criminal had not been governed by mercenary motives.

The results of the post-mortem, carried out in my presence by Screwy and the district doctor the day after Olga's death, culminated in an extremely lengthy report, the gist of which I give here. On external examination the following injuries were found by the doctors. On the left side of the head, at the suture of the temporal and parietal bones, was a one-and-a-half inch wound that extended to the bone. The edges of the wound were neither smooth nor straight . . . it had been inflicted by a blunt instrument, most probably, as we later decided, by the haft of the dagger. Extending across the rear half of the neck, level with the cervical vertebrae, was a red line in the form of a circle. On the entire length of this stripe there were found lesions to the skin and slight bruising. On the left arm, about an inch above the wrist, were four blue patches: one on the back and three on the palmar side. They had been caused by pressure, most likely from fingers. This last fact was further confirmed by the discovery of a small scratch made by a fingernail in one of the patches. Corresponding to the area where these patches were found (the reader will remember), the left sleeve of the jacket had been torn off and the left sleeve of her chemise was half torn off . . . Between the fourth and fifth ribs, on an imaginary vertical line drawn downwards, from the middle of the armpit, there was a gaping wound, about an inch long. Its edges were smooth, as if they had been cut, and were steeped in both thin and coagulated blood. It was a deep wound and had been made by a sharp weapon. As was evident from the preliminary data that had been gathered, it was made by a dagger whose width corresponded exactly to the size of the wound. The internal examination revealed injuries to the right lung and pleura, inflammation of the lung and haemorrhage of the pleural cavity.

As far as I can remember, the doctors came to the following approximate conclusions: a) death was caused by anaemia following significant blood loss. The blood loss was explained by the presence of a gaping wound on the right side of the chest; b) the head wound must be considered a serious injury, but the chest wound was undoubtedly fatal; this latter must be taken as the immediate cause of death; c) the head wound had been inflicted by a blunt instrument, but the chest wound by a sharp and most probably two-edged blade; d) none of the above described wounds could have been self-inflicted; e) there was no apparent attempt at rape.

In order not to shelve matters and later repeat myself, I shall immediately convey to the reader the picture I formed of the crime, created from my first impressions after the inspection, two or three cross-examinations and the reading of the post-mortem report.

When Olga parted from the main company, she went for a stroll in the forest. Either day-dreaming or surrendering herself to melancholy thoughts (the reader will recall her mood that fateful evening), she strayed into the depths of the forest. There she met her murderer. When she was standing under the trees, deep in thought, a man came up to her and started talking to her. There was nothing suspicious about him, otherwise she would have cried out for help – but her cries wouldn't have been of the heart-rending variety. After a few words with her, the murderer seized her left arm – so violently, that he tore the sleeves of her jacket and blouse and left marks in the form of those four patches. At this point it is possible that she produced the shriek heard by the company – she shrieked from pain – and evidently after she had read the murderer's intentions from his face. Whether he wanted to stop her screaming again, or perhaps under the influence of evil feelings, he grabbed her by the front of her dress, near the collar, to which the two torn-off top buttons and the red stripe found by the doctors bear witness. Grasping at her chest and shaking her, the murderer pulled off the golden chain she had been wearing around her neck. The stripe was caused by friction and the tightening of the chain. Then the murderer struck her on the head with some blunt instrument – a stick, for example, or perhaps even the haft of the dagger that was hanging on Olga's belt. Then, in a fit of frenzy, or finding that one wound wasn't enough, he bared the dagger and plunged it into her right side with great force: I say with great force, since the dagger was blunt.

Such was the sombre aspect of the picture that I was able to paint on the basis of the above-mentioned data. The question – who was the murderer? – was clearly not difficult and solved itself. Firstly, the murderer was not ruled by mercenary motives but by something else. Therefore there was no need to suspect some stray tramp or ruffians who had been fishing on the lake. The victim's shriek couldn't have frightened off a robber: removing the brooch and watch would have been the work of a second. Secondly, Olga intentionally didn't reveal the murderer's name – this she would never have done had the murderer been a common thief. Evidently the murderer was dear to her and she didn't want him to suffer severe punishment on her account. It might have been her crazy father or the husband she didn't love but before whom she probably felt guilty; or the Count, to whom in her heart of hearts she possibly felt an obligation. On the eve of the murder, as the servants subsequently testified, her crazy father was sitting in his cottage in the forest and he spent the whole evening writing a letter to the chief of police, asking him to keep under strict control those imaginary thieves who were apparently surrounding the lunatic's home day and night. The Count didn't leave his guests before or at the time of the murder. It only remained to bring the whole weight of suspicion to bear on that unfortunate Urbenin – no one else. His unexpected appearance on the scene, the very look of him, etc. could only serve as substantial evidence.

Thirdly, Olga's life of late had been one uninterrupted affair. This particular affair had been the kind that usually ends in a capital crime. An old, doting husband, betrayal, jealousy, blows, flight to the lover-Count a month or two after the wedding . . .

If the beautiful heroine of a novel like this happens to be murdered, don't look for thieves and crooks, but go in pursuit of the heroes. Regarding this third point, the most likely hero-murderer was that same Urbenin.

XXIV

I held the preliminary inquiry in the 'mosaic' room, where once I loved to loll on the soft couches and flirt with the gipsy girls. First to be examined by me was Urbenin. He was brought to me from Olga's room, where he still continued to sit on a stool in the corner without taking his eyes off the empty bed for one moment. For a minute he stood before me in silence, looked at me indifferently and then, probably guessing that I intended addressing him in the manner of an investigating magistrate, spoke as one who was weary, broken by grief and anguish.

'Please question the other witnesses first, Sergey Petrovich, but me afterwards . . . I just can't . . .'

Urbenin considered himself a witness – or thought that he was considered one.

'No, I must question you here and now,' I said. 'Please be seated.'

Urbenin sat down opposite me and lowered his head. He was ill and exhausted, replied reluctantly and it took a great effort to extract a statement from him.

He testified that he was Pyotr Yegorych Urbenin, gentleman, aged fifty, member of the Orthodox faith; that he had owned a property in the neighbouring district of K— where he had worked during the elections and for two periods of three years, and had been an honorary JP. After going bankrupt, he mortgaged his estate and thought he should get a job. He had become the Count's manager about six years previously. With a great love of agriculture, he wasn't above working for a private person and thought that only fools were ashamed of hard work. The Count always paid him his salary on the dot and he had nothing to complain about. He had a son and daughter from his first marriage, etc. etc.

He had married Olga out of passionate love: after a long and painful struggle with his feelings, neither common sense nor the logic of a practical, mature mind prevailed. He had to bow to his feelings and get married. He knew that Olga wasn't marrying him for love, but since he thought her highly virtuous, he decided to content himself with her faithfulness and friendship, which he hoped to earn. When he reached the point where disenchantment and the insult of grey hair begins, Urbenin asked permission not to talk of 'the past, for which God will forgive her' – or at least to postpone any talk of this until a later date.

'I can't . . . it's very hard for me . . . you can see that for yourself.'

'All right, let's leave it for another time. Just tell me now: is it true that you beat your wife? They say that on one occasion, when you found she had a note from the Count, you struck her.'

'That's not true. I only grabbed her arm, but she burst into tears and that same evening she ran off to complain about it.'

'Did you know of her relationship with the Count?'

'I did ask if this conversation could be postponed. And what's the point of it?'

'Please just answer this one question, which is extremely important. Did you know of your wife's relationship with the Count?'

'Of course I did.'

'Right. I'll make a note of that, but we'll leave everything else that concerns your wife's adultery for another time. Now let's turn to another question – can you please explain how you came to be in the forest?'

'Well, sir, I've been living in town with my female cousin since I lost my job. I kept myself busy trying to find work and drank to drown my sorrows. I've been drinking particularly heavily this month. For example, I can't remember a thing about last week, as I drank round the clock. The day before yesterday I got drunk too. In short, I'm finished! Finished for good!'

'You wanted to tell me how you came to be in the forest yesterday.'

'Yes, sir. Yesterday I woke up early, at about four o'clock. I had a hangover from the day before, aches and pains all over, as if I were feverish. As I lay on my bed and looked through the window at the sunrise I remembered all kinds of different things. I felt really low. Suddenly I had the urge to see her, to see her once more, possibly for the last time. And I was gripped by anger and despair. I took out of my pocket the hundred roubles the Count had sent me, looked at them and started trampling them underfoot. I stamped and stamped, after which I decided to go and throw his charity in his face.

'I may be hungry and down at heel, but I cannot sell my honour and I consider every attempt to buy it a personal insult. Well, sir, I wanted to have a look at Olga and fling the money right in that seducer's ugly mug. And I was so overcome by this longing that I nearly went out of my mind. I had no money for the journey here – I couldn't bring myself to spend *his* hundred roubles on myself. So I set off on foot. Fortunately, on the way, I met a peasant I knew and he took me ten miles for ten copecks, otherwise I'd still be slogging it. The peasant set me down at Tenevo. From there I made my way on foot and so I arrived at about ten o'clock.'

'Did anyone see you at the time?'

'Yes, sir. Nikolay the watchman was sitting by the gate and he told me that the master wasn't at home and had gone shooting. I was almost dying from exhaustion, but my desire to see my wife was stronger than any pain. I had to walk to the place where they were shooting without resting for a single moment. I didn't take the road, but set off through the forest. I know every single tree and it would be as hard for me to get lost in the Count's forest as it would be in my own room.'

'But by going through the forest and not by the road you might have got separated from the shooting party.'

'No, sir. I kept to the road the whole time and I was so close that I could hear not only the shooting but the conversation as well.'

'So, you didn't expect to meet your wife in the forest?'

Urbenin glanced at me in amazement and replied after a pause for thought:

'If you don't mind my saying so, that's a strange question. You wouldn't expect to meet a wolf, but meeting with a terrible disaster is all the more unlikely. God sends misfortunes without warning. Take this dreadful incident . . . There I was, walking through Olkhovsk woods, not expecting any trouble, since I had enough trouble as it was, when I suddenly heard a terrible shriek. It was so piercing that I thought someone had cut my ear with a knife . . . I ran towards the place where the shriek came from . . .'

Urbenin's mouth twisted to one side, his chin quivered. Then he blinked and burst into sobs.

'I ran towards the shriek and suddenly I saw Olga lying there. Her hair and forehead were covered in blood, her face looked terrible. I started shouting, calling her by name. She didn't move. I kissed her and lifted her up.'

Urbenin choked and covered his face with his sleeve. A minute later he continued:

'I didn't see the villain . . . but when I was running towards her I heard someone's hurried footsteps. It was probably him running away.'

'That's all very neatly thought out, Pyotr Yegorych,' I said. 'But are you aware that investigating magistrates are usually very sceptical about such rare events as the murder coinciding with that chance stroll of yours, etc. Quite cleverly invented, but it explains very little.'

'What do you mean *invented*?' Urbenin exclaimed, opening his eyes wide. 'I wasn't inventing anything, sir.'

Urbenin suddenly went red and stood up.

'It seems as if you suspect me,' he muttered. 'It's possible to suspect anyone, but you, Sergey Petrovich, have known me a long time . . . It's a sin branding me with such suspicions. After all, you know me very well.'

'Of course I know you . . . but my personal opinions are irrelevant here. The law allows only juries to have personal opinions, but an investigating magistrate deals purely with the evidence . . . And there's a great deal of evidence, Pyotr Yegorych.'

Urbenin looked at me in alarm and shrugged his shoulders.

'But whatever the evidence,' he said, 'you must understand

... Well, do you really think *I* would have been capable of murder ... ? *Me?* And of murdering *her?* I could easily kill a quail or a woodcock, but a human being, someone dearer to me than life itself, dearer than my own salvation, the very thought of whom used to brighten my miserable existence like the sun! And suddenly you suspect *me*!'

Urbenin made a despairing gesture and sat down.

'As it is, all I want to do is die – and yet you have to insult me into the bargain! It would be bad enough if some civil servant. I didn't know was insulting me, but it's *you*, Sergey Petrovich!! Please let me go!'

'You may ... I'll examine you again tomorrow, but in the meantime, Pyotr Yegorych, I must place you under house arrest ... I hope that by tomorrow's examination you'll have come to appreciate all the importance of the evidence we have against you, that you won't start dragging things out for nothing and that you'll confess. I'm convinced Olga was murdered by you. That's all I have to say today. You may go.'

This said, I bent over my papers. Urbenin looked at me in bewilderment, stood up and stretched his fingers out somewhat peculiarly.

'Are you joking ... or are you serious?' he asked.

'This is beyond a joke,' I said. 'You can go.'

Urbenin still remained standing. He was pale and he looked at my papers in dismay.

'Why are your hands bloodstained, Pyotr Yegorych?' I asked.

He looked down at his hands, on which there were still traces of blood, and twitched his fingers.

'Why is there *blood*? Hm ... if you think this is evidence then it's very poor evidence. When I was lifting bloodstained Olga I couldn't avoid getting my hands bloodied. I wasn't wearing any gloves.'

'You just told me that when you saw your wife you shouted for help. How is it no one heard your shouts?'

'I don't know. I was so stunned at the sight of Olga that I couldn't shout out loud ... But I don't know anything. I don't have to defend myself. Besides, it's not my policy ...'

'But you could hardly have shouted ... After killing your

wife you ran off and were absolutely stunned to see those people at the edge of the forest.'

'I didn't notice those people of yours either. I had no time for people.'

With this my examination of Urbenin was over for the time being. Urbenin was then put under house arrest and locked up in one of the Count's outbuildings.

XXV

On the second or third day Polugradov, the deputy prosecutor, a man whom I cannot recall without spoiling my mood, came bowling in from town. Imagine a tall, thin man of about thirty, dressed like a fop, smoothly shaven, with hair as curly as a lamb's. He had fine features, but they were so dry and insipid that it wasn't difficult to deduce that individual's shallowness and pomposity from them. His voice was soft, sugary and sickeningly polite.

He arrived early in the morning, in a hired carriage, with two suitcases. Wearing an extremely worried expression and complaining of 'fatigue' with great affectation, he first of all inquired whether there was a room for him in the Count's house. On my instructions a small but very comfortable and bright room had been set aside, where everything was provided, from a marble washstand to a box of matches.

'Listen to what I say, my good man! Bring me some hot water,' he began, making himself comfortable and squeamishly sniffing the air. 'My deah fellow! I'm talking to *you*! Hot water, if you don't mind!'

And before getting down to business he spent ages dressing, washing and preening himself. He even cleaned his teeth with red powder and took three minutes to clip his sharp, pink nails.

'Well, sir!' he said, at last getting down to business and leafing through our reports. 'What's it all about?'

I told him the facts of the case without omitting a single detail.

'Have you been to the scene of the crime?'

'No, not yet.'

The deputy prosecutor frowned, ran his white womanish hands across his freshly washed forehead and strode up and down the room.

'I simply don't understand why on earth you haven't been there!' he muttered. 'That's the very first thing you should have done, I assume! Did you forget – or didn't you think it necessary?'

'Neither: yesterday I was waiting for the police. But I shall go today.'

'There's nothing left there now. It's been raining every day and you gave the criminal time to cover his tracks. You could have at least stationed a guard there. No? I don't un-der-stand!'

And the fop imperiously shrugged his shoulders.

'Drink your tea, it's getting cold,' I said in an indifferent tone.

'I like it cold.'

The deputy prosecutor leant over the papers. Filling the whole room with his heavy breathing he started reading in an undertone, occasionally making his own notes and corrections. Twice his mouth twisted into a sarcastic smile. For some reason that cunning devil* was pleased neither with my report nor the doctors'. It was only too easy to see in that sleek, freshly washed civil servant a pedant, stuffed with self-importance and the consciousness of his own worth.

At noon we were at the scene of the crime. It was pouring with rain. Of course, we found neither stains nor tracks. Everything had been washed away by the rain. Somehow I managed to find one of the missing buttons from the murdered Olga's riding habit; and the deputy prosecutor picked up some kind of red pulp that later turned out to be a tobacco packet. At first we came across a bush with two of its branches broken off along one side. The deputy prosecutor was delighted at this discovery: they could have been broken off by the criminal and would therefore indicate the direction he took after murdering Olga.

* Kamyshev had no reason to abuse the deputy prosecutor. All the prosecutor was guilty of was the fact that Mr Kamyshev didn't like his face. It would have been more honest to admit either to inexperience or deliberate mistakes. A. C.

But his joy was unfounded: we soon found several bushes with broken-off branches and nibbled leaves. It turned out that a herd of cattle had wandered over the scene of the crime.

Having sketched out a plan of the locality and questioned the coachmen we had taken with us about the position in which Olga had been found, we returned empty-handed. When we were inspecting the scene an outside observer would have detected apathy and sluggishness in our movements. Perhaps we were partly inhibited by the fact that the criminal was already in our hands and that there was therefore no need to embark on an analysis *à la* Le Coq.[53]

After he returned from the forest Polugradov once again took ages to wash and dress himself, and once again he demanded hot water. After completing his toilet he expressed a wish to question Urbenin once again. Poor Pyotr Yegorych said nothing new at this cross-examination – as before, he denied his guilt and didn't give a damn for our evidence.

'I'm amazed you can even suspect me,' he said, shrugging his shoulders. 'Very strange!'

'Don't play the innocent, old bean!' Polugradov told him. 'No one's going to suspect you without good reason, and if they do then they *must* have reasons!'

'But whatever the reasons, however strong the evidence, you must be humane in your reasoning. I'm *incapable* of murder . . . do you understand? I simply couldn't . . . So, how much is your evidence worth?'

'Well, well!' exclaimed the deputy prosecutor with a wave of the arm. 'These educated criminals are a real pain in the neck: you can din things into a peasant's head, but you just try and talk to these fellows! – "I'm *incapable*", "humane" – they're all going in for psychology these days!'

'I'm not a criminal,' Urbenin said, 'and I must ask you to be more careful in your choice of words!'

'Oh, do shut up, old bean! We've no time to apologize to the likes of you or listen to your complaints! If you don't want to confess, then don't, only please permit us to consider you a liar.'

'As you wish,' Urbenin growled. 'You can do what you like with me . . . you're in charge . . .' He waved his arm apathetically and looked out of the window. 'It's all the same to me anyway,' he continued, 'my life's ruined . . .'

'Listen, Pyotr Yegorych,' I said. 'Yesterday and the day before you were so grief-stricken that you could barely keep on your feet, you could hardly answer briefly and to the point. Today, on the other hand, you seem to be positively *flourishing* – relatively speaking, of course – and you're even indulging in resounding phrases. In fact, grief-stricken people aren't usually very talkative, but not only are you being terribly long-winded, you're even airing your petty grievances now. How do you explain such a sharp turnaround?'

'How would *you* explain it?' Urbenin asked, sarcastically screwing up his eyes at me.

'I explain it by the fact that you've forgotten your part. After all, it's difficult to keep up play-acting for long: either one forgets one's part or one gets bored with it . . .'

'That's a typical lawyer's invention!' laughed Urbenin. 'And it does honour to your resourcefulness. Yes, you're right. I've undergone a big change.'

'Can you explain it?'

'Of course I can, I've no reason to conceal the fact. Yesterday I was so shattered and overwhelmed by grief that I thought I might take my own life . . . or that I'd go mad. But last night I thought better of it. It struck me that death had freed Olga from a life of debauchery, that it had wrested her from the filthy hands of the idle rake who's ruined me. I'm not jealous of death, as long as Olga is better off in death's clutches than the Count's. This thought cheered me up and gave me strength. Now I'm not so heavy at heart.'

'Neatly thought out,' Polugradov said through his teeth and swinging one leg. 'He's not short of a reply!'

'I feel I'm speaking sincerely and I'm amazed that educated men like yourselves can't distinguish between sincerity and pretence! Besides, prejudice is all too powerful an emotion – it's difficult not to err under its influence. I understand your position, I can imagine what will happen when they start trying me after they've accepted your evidence. I can imagine them taking my brutish face and my drunkenness into consideration. Well, I don't have a brutish appearance, but prejudice will have its way . . .'

'Fine, fine, that's enough,' said Polugradov, leaning over his papers. 'Off with you now.'

When Urbenin had left we began questioning the Count. His Excellency attended the examination in his dressing-gown and with a vinegar compress on his head. After making Polugradov's acquaintance he sprawled in an armchair and began his statement.

'I'm going to tell you *everything*, right from the start. By the way, what's that president of yours, Lionsky, up to these days? Hasn't he divorced his wife yet? I bumped into him when I was in St Petersburg. Gentlemen, why don't you order yourselves something? A drop of brandy always adds a little cheer to a conversation . . . yes, I've no doubts at all that Urbenin is guilty of this murder.'

And the Count told us everything that the reader already knows. At the prosecutor's request he told of his life with Olga down to the very last detail and in describing the charms of life with a pretty woman he became so carried away that several times he smacked his lips and winked. From his statement I learnt one very important detail that the reader doesn't know about. I discovered that when Urbenin was living in town he perpetually bombarded the Count with letters. In some of them he cursed him, in others he begged for his wife to be returned, promising to forget all the insults and infamy. The poor devil grasped at these letters like straws.

After questioning two or three coachmen, the deputy prosecutor ate a hearty dinner, reeled off a whole list of instructions for me and departed. Before driving off he went to the outbuilding where Urbenin was being detained and told him that our suspicions as to his guilt had become a certainty. Urbenin waved his arm despairingly and asked permission to attend his wife's funeral: this was granted.

Polugradov had not been lying to Urbenin. Yes, our suspicions had become certainties, we were convinced that we knew who the murderer was and that he was already in our hands. But this certainty didn't stay with us for long!

XXVI

One fine morning, just as I was sealing a parcel for Urbenin to take with him to the town prison, I heard a dreadful noise. When I looked out of the window an engaging spectacle greeted my eyes: a dozen brawny youths were dragging one-eyed Kuzma out of the servants' kitchen. Pale and dishevelled, his feet firmly planted on the ground and unable to defend himself with his hands, Kuzma was butting his assailants with his large head.

'Yer 'onner, please go and sort it out, 'e don't wanner go,' the panic-stricken Ilya told me.

'Who doesn't want to go?'

'The murderer.'

'Which murderer?'

'Kuzma . . . it's 'im what done the murder, yer 'onner. Pyotr Yegorych's suffering for what 'e ain't done. I swear it, sir!'

I went outside and made my way to the servants' kitchen, where Kuzma, having detached himself from those robust hands, was distributing clouts right and left.

'What's all this about?' I asked, going over to the crowd.

I was told something strange and unexpected.

'Yer 'onner, it's Kuzma what murdered 'er!'

'They're lying!' howled Kuzma. 'God strike me down if they're not lying!'

'Then why did you – you son of the devil – wash away the blood if yer conscience is clear? You wait, 'is 'onner'll sort it all out!'

When he was passing the river, Trifon the horse dealer happened to notice that Kuzma was hard at work washing something. At first Trifon thought that he was washing linen, but on closer inspection he saw that it was a tight-fitting coat and a waistcoat. This struck him as strange: cloth garments are never washed.

'What are you doing?' shouted Trifon.

Kuzma was taken aback. After an even closer look Trifon noticed reddish-brown spots on the coat.

'I guessed immediately that it must be blood . . . I went into the kitchen and told 'em all there. They kept watch and that night they sees 'im hanging out the coat to dry in the garden. Well, 'e were scared stiff, 'e were. Why should 'e go and wash it if 'e were innersent? Must be crooked if 'e were trying to 'ide it. Racked our brains we did and in the end we hauls 'im off to yer 'onner. As we dragged 'im along he jibbed, like, and spat in our eyes. Why should 'e jib if 'e weren't guilty?'

After further questioning it transpired that just before the murder, when the Count was sitting at the forest edge drinking tea with his guests, Kuzma went off into the forest. He hadn't helped carry Olga, therefore he couldn't have got any blood on himself.

When he was brought into my room Kuzma was at first so agitated that he couldn't say a word. Rolling the white of his single eye, he crossed himself and muttered an oath under his breath.

'Now calm down,' I said. 'Just tell me what you know and I'll let you go.'

Kuzma fell at my feet, stuttered and started swearing.

'May I rot in hell if 'twere me. May neither me father nor me mother . . . Yer 'onner . . . May God destroy my soul if . . .'

'Did you walk off into the forest?'

'That I did, sir. I walks away from them – I'd bin serving the guests brandy and – begging yer pardon – I took a little swig meself. Went straight to me 'ead it did and all I wanted was to lie down. So I goes and lies down and I falls fast asleep. But as to who did the murder – I ain't got a clue, that I ain't. I'm telling you the truth!'

'But why did you wash the blood off?'

'I were scared they might think things . . . that they might take me as a witness . . .'

'But how did there come to be blood on your jacket?'

'Can't rightly say, yer 'onner.'

'But why can't you say? Surely it was your coat?'

'Oh yes, it were mine all right, but I just can't say – I saw the blood there after I was already woken up.'

'That means you must have soiled your coat in your sleep.'

'That's right!'

'Well, off with you my friend. Go and think it over. What

you're telling me is complete nonsense. Think about it and come and tell me tomorrow. Now go!'

Next day when I woke up I was informed that Kuzma wanted a word with me. I gave instructions for him to be brought in.

'Well, have you had a good think about it?'

'Yes – that I 'ave!'

'So, how did the blood get on your coat?'

'Yer 'onner, I remembers it as if 'twere a dream. I remembers things as if they was all in a fog, can't say for sure whether they're true or not.'

'And what do you remember?'

Kuzma raised his one eye, reflected and replied:

'It were amazing, just like in a dream or in a fog. There I be lying there drunk on the grass and dozing – neither really dozing nor dreaming, like. All I hears is someone passing by and stamping 'eavily with 'is feet. I opens me eyes and I sees – just like I were unconscious or dreaming – some gent coming up to me. 'E bends down and wipes 'is 'ands on the flaps of me jacket. Wiped them on me coat, 'e did, then 'e dabbed me waistcoat. That's what 'appened.'

'Who was that gentleman?'

'That I can't rightly say. All I remembers is that 'e weren't no peasant, but a gent . . . in gent's clothes. But who 'e was, what 'is face was like – that I can't remember, for the life of me.'

'What colour was his suit?'

'How should I know? Might 'ave bin white, or might 'ave bin black . . . all I remembers is that 'e were a gent – and I don't remember nothing more. Oh yes, I remembers now! When he bent down 'e wiped 'is 'ands and said "drunken swine!"'

'Did you dream it?'

'Can't say . . . perhaps I did. But where did that blood come from?'

'That gentleman you saw . . . was he like Pyotr Yegorych?'

'I don't think 'twere 'e . . . but perhaps it were. Only 'e shouldn't 'ave called me a swine.'

'Now try and remember . . . go on, sit down there and try to remember. Perhaps it will all come back to you.'

'Yes, sir.'

XXVII

This unexpected irruption of one-eyed Kuzma into an almost completed novel created an impenetrable muddle. I was at a loss and just didn't know what to make of Kuzma: he denied his guilt categorically and the preliminary investigation argued against any such guilt. Olga had not been murdered for mercenary motives and any attempt at rape had 'probably not occurred' – according to the doctors. Could one really assume that Kuzma had committed the murder and had not taken advantage of a single one of these objectives, simply because he was terribly drunk and incapable? Or was he afraid that none of this tallied with the circumstances of the murder?

But if Kuzma wasn't guilty, then why had he been unable to explain the blood on his jacket and invented those dreams and hallucinations? Why had he dragged in that gentleman whom he had seen and heard, but whom he remembered so vaguely that he had even forgotten the colour of his clothes?

Polugradov breezed in again.

'So there you are, my deah sir!' he said. 'If you had taken the trouble to inspect the scene of the crime right away – then, believe me, everything would be as clear as daylight now! Had you questioned all the servants immediately we would have known who carried Olga's body and who did not. But now we cannot even determine at what distance from the scene of the crime this drunkard was lying.'

For two hours he struggled with Kuzma, but he could get nothing new out of him. All Kuzma said was that he was half-asleep when he saw the gentleman, that the gentleman had wiped his hands on the flaps of his jacket and called him 'drunken swine'. But who this gentleman was, what his face and clothes were like he couldn't say.

'And how much brandy did you drink?'

'Polished off arf a bottle.'

'Well, perhaps it wasn't really brandy?'

'Oh yes it was sir, real fine shompagner . . .'

'Ah, so you even know the names of spirits!' laughed the deputy prosecutor.

'And why shouldn't I? Thank God, I've waited on gents for thirty year now . . . I've 'ad time to learn.'

For some reason the deputy prosecutor suddenly felt that Kuzma needed to be confronted with Urbenin. Kuzma took a long look at Urbenin, shook his head and said:

'No, I don't remember. Perhaps it *were* Pyotr Yegorych and perhaps it weren't. God knows!'

Polugradov waved his arm helplessly and drove off, leaving me to find the real murderer out of these two.

The investigation dragged on and on. Urbenin and Kuzma were incarcerated in cells in the same village where I lived. Poor Pyotr Yegorych completely lost heart, grew thin and grey, and fell into a religious frame of mind. Twice he sent me a request to let him see the penal code. Evidently he was interested in the severity of the punishment in store for him.

'What will become of my children?' he asked me at one of the examinations. 'If I were all on my own your mistake wouldn't cause me any distress, but I have to live . . . live for my children! They'll perish without me . . . and I'm in no state to part with them! What are you doing to me!?'

When the guard started talking down to him and when they made him walk a couple of times from the village to town and back, under armed guard, in full view of people he knew, he was plunged into despair and became highly irritable.

'They're not lawyers!' he shouted, loud enough for everyone in the prison to hear. 'They're cruel, heartless oafs who spare neither people nor the truth. I know why I'm locked up here, I know! By pinning the blame on me they want to cover up for the real culprit! The Count committed the murder. And if it wasn't him it was one of his hirelings.'

When he found out about Kuzma's arrest he was absolutely delighted at first.

'Now you've found the hireling!' he told me. 'Now you've got him!'

But before long, when he saw that he wasn't going to be

released and when he was told of Kuzma's statement, he once again became depressed.

'Now I'm finished . . . well and truly finished,' he said. 'To get out of prison that one-eyed devil Kuzma will sooner or later name me and say that *I* . . . wiped my hands on his jacket. But you saw for yourself that my hands hadn't been wiped.'

Sooner or later our suspicions were bound to be resolved.

That same year, at the end of November, when snowflakes were circling before my windows and the lake resembled a boundless white desert, Kuzma expressed a wish to see me. He sent the guard to tell me that he'd had a 'good think'. I gave instructions for him to be brought to me.

'I'm delighted that you've finally had a "good think",' I said, greeting him. 'It's high time you stopped being so secretive and trying to make fools of us, as if we were little children. So, what have you had a good think about?'

Kuzma didn't reply. He stood in the middle of my room, looking at me without blinking or saying a word. And he really did have the look of someone scared out of his wits. He was pale and trembling and a cold sweat streamed down his face.

'Well, tell me what you've had a good think about,' I repeated.

'About things more weird and wonderful than you could ever imagine,' he said. 'Yesterday I remembers the colours of tie that gent was wearing and last night I thinks 'ard about it and I remembers 'is face.'

'So, who was it?'

Kuzma produced a sickly smile and wiped the sweat from his forehead.

'It's too terrible to tell, yer 'onner, please allow me not to say. It was all so weird and wonderful that I thinks I must 'ave been dreaming – or I imagined it all!'

'Well, who did you imagine you saw?'

'Please allow me not to say! If I do you'll convict me. Let me 'ave a good think and I'll tell you tomorrow. Cor, I'm scared stiff!'

'Pah!' I exclaimed, getting angry. 'Why are you bothering me like this if you don't want to tell me? Why did you come here?'

'I thought of telling you, like, but now I'm afraid. No, yer 'onner, please let me go now. I'd better tell you tomorrow . . . You'd get so mad if I told you, I'd be better off in Siberia . . . you'd convict me.'

I lost my temper and ordered Kuzma to be taken away.*

That same evening, in order not to waste time and to have done once and for all with that tiresome murder case, I went to the cells and fooled Urbenin by telling him that Kuzma had named him as the murderer.

'I was expecting that,' Urbenin said, waving his hand. 'It's all the same to me now . . .'

Solitary confinement had had a terrible effect on Urbenin's robust health. He had turned yellowish and lost almost half his weight. I promised him that I would instruct the warders to let him walk up and down the corridors during the day – and even at night.

'We're not worried that you might try and escape,' I said.

Urbenin thanked me and after I had gone he was already strolling down the corridor. His door was no longer kept locked.

After leaving him I knocked at the door of Kuzma's cell.

'Well, have you had a good think?'

'No, sir,' a feeble voice replied. 'Let Mr Prosecutor come – I'll tell 'im. But I'm not telling *you*!'

'Please yourself.'

Next morning everything was decided.

Warder Yegor came running to tell me that one-eyed Kuzma had been found *dead* in his bed. I went off to the prison and convinced myself that this was the case. That sturdy, strapping peasant, who only the day before had radiated health and had invented various fairy tales to obtain his release, was as still and cold as a stone. I shall not begin to describe the warder's and my own horror: the reader will understand. Kuzma was valuable to me as defendant or witness, but for the warders he was a prisoner, for whose death or escape they would have to pay

* A fine investigating magistrate! Instead of continuing his questioning and extracting useful evidence, he lost his temper – behaviour that forms no part of a civil servant's duties! Moreover, I place little trust in all of this . . . If Mr Kamyshev couldn't give a damn about his duties, then plain human curiosity should have compelled him to continue with the questioning. A. C.

dearly. Our horror was all the greater when the subsequent autopsy confirmed a violent death. Kuzma died from asphyxiation. Convinced that he had been strangled, I started searching for the culprit and it did not take me long to find him . . . he was close at hand.

I went to Urbenin's cell. Unable to restrain myself, and forgetting that I was an investigator, I named him as the murderer, in the harshest possible terms.

'You scoundrel! You weren't satisfied with killing your poor wife,' I said. 'On top of that you had to kill someone who had discovered your guilt. And still you persist with your filthy, villainous play-acting!'

Urbenin turned terribly pale and staggered.

'You're lying!' he shouted, beating his breast with his fist.

'It's not me who's lying! You shed crocodile tears at our evidence, you mocked it. There were moments when I wanted to believe you rather than the evidence itself . . . Oh, you're such a fine actor! But now I wouldn't believe you even if blood flowed from your eyes instead of those false, theatrical tears. Tell me – you did kill Kuzma, didn't you?'

'You're either drunk or making fun of me, Sergey Petrovich. There are limits to a man's patience and subservience. I can't take any more of this!'

With flashing eyes Urbenin banged his fist on the table.

'Yesterday I was rash enough to allow you some freedom,' I continued. 'I allowed you what no other inmate is allowed – to walk down the corridors. And now, as a token of gratitude, you went to that unfortunate Kuzma's cell during the night and strangled a sleeping man. Do you realize it's not only Kuzma whom you've destroyed – because of you, all the warders will be ruined.'

'But what in heaven's name have I done?' Urbenin asked, clutching his head.

'Do you want me to prove it? Let me explain. On my orders your door was left unlocked. Those idiotic warders opened the door and forgot to hide the padlock – all the cells are locked with the same key. During the night you took the key, went out into the corridor and unlocked your neighbour's door. After strangling him you locked the door and put the key back in the lock.'

'But why should *I* want to strangle him? Why?'

'Because he named you as the murderer. If I hadn't told you this yesterday he'd still be alive. It's sinful and shameful, Pyotr Yegorych!'

'Sergey Petrovich! You're a young man!' the murderer suddenly said in a soft and gentle voice, grasping my hand. 'You're an honest, respectable person . . . don't ruin me and don't sully yourself with unfounded suspicions and over-hasty accusations. You've no idea how cruelly and painfully you've insulted me by foisting a new accusation on my soul, which is guilty of absolutely nothing! I'm a martyr, Sergey Petrovich! You should be ashamed of wronging a martyr! The time will come when you'll have to apologize to me – and that time's not far off. I haven't been formally charged yet, but my defence will not satisfy you. Rather than attacking and insulting me so horribly, you'd do better if you questioned me humanely – I won't say as a friend – you've already washed your hands of our friendship! I would have been more useful to you in the cause of justice as witness and assistant than in the role of accused. Take for example this new accusation – I could have told you a great deal: last night I didn't sleep and I could hear everything that was going on.'

'What did you hear?'

'Last night, at about two o'clock, it was very dark . . . I heard someone walking ever so quietly down the corridor and constantly trying my door. He kept walking and walking – and then he opened my door and came in.'

'Who was it?'

'I don't know – it was too dark to see. He stood for about a minute in my cell, then he left. And just as you said, he took the key out of my door and unlocked the door to the next cell. For about two minutes I heard hoarse breathing, then a scuffle. I thought that it was the warder fussing about and I took the noise to be nothing else than snoring, otherwise I would have raised the alarm.'

'Fairy tales!' I said. 'There was no one here except you who could have killed Kuzma. The duty warders were asleep. One of their wives, who didn't sleep all night, testified that all three warders had slept like logs the whole night and never left their beds for one minute. The poor devils didn't know that such brutes could be knocking around in this wretched prison. They've been employed here for more than twenty years and all that time there hasn't been one escape, not to mention such abominations as murder. Now, thanks to you, their lives have been turned upside down. And I'll catch it too for not sending you to the main prison and for giving you freedom to stroll down the corridors. Thank you very much!'

That was my last conversation with Urbenin. I never had occasion to talk to him again – apart from replying to two or three questions he put to me, as if I were a witness being questioned in the dock.

XXVIII

I have called my novel the story of a crime and now, when 'The Case of Olga Urbenin's Murder' has become complicated by yet another murder – hard to comprehend and mysterious in many respects – the reader is entitled to expect the novel to enter its most interesting and lively phase. The discovery of the criminal and his motives offers a wide field for a display of mental agility and acumen. Here an evil will and cunning wage war with forensic knowledge and skill – a war that is fascinating in every aspect.

I waged war – and the reader is entitled to expect me to describe the way victory became mine: he will surely expect all manner of investigatory subtleties, such as those that lend sparkle to the thrillers of Gaboriau and our own Shklyarevsky,[54] and I'm ready to justify the reader's expectations. However, one of the main characters leaves the battlefield without waiting for the end of the conflict – he's not allowed to enjoy victory. All that he has done so far comes to naught and he joins the ranks of the spectators. This particular character in the drama is 'Yours Truly'. The day after the above conversation with Urbenin I received an invitation – an order, rather – to resign. The tittle-tattle and idle gossip of our local scandalmongers had done their work. The murder in the prison, statements taken from the servants without my knowledge by the deputy prosecutor, and – if the reader still remembers – the blow I had dealt that peasant on the head with an oar during a nocturnal orgy of the past – all this made a substantial contribution to my dismissal. That peasant really set the ball rolling: there was a massive shake-up. After about two days I was ordered to hand over the murder case to the investigator of serious crimes.

Thanks to rumours and newspaper reports, the entire Directorate of Public Prosecutions was stirred into action. Every other day the prosecutor himself rode over to the Count's estate and took part in the questioning. Our doctors' official reports were sent to the Medical Board – even higher up. There was even talk of exhuming the bodies and holding fresh post-mortems, which, incidentally, would have led nowhere.

Twice Urbenin was dragged off to the county town to have his mental faculties examined and on both occasions he was found to be normal. I began to figure as witness.* The new investigators became so carried away that even my Polikarp was called upon to testify.

A year after my retirement, when I was living in Moscow, I received a summons to attend the Urbenin trial. I was glad of the opportunity to see once more those places to which I was drawn by habit – and off I went. The Count, who was living in St Petersburg at the time, did not attend and sent in a doctor's certificate instead.

The case was tried in our county town, at the local assizes. The public prosecutor was Polugradov, that same individual who cleaned his teeth four times a day with red powder. Acting for the defence was a certain Smirnyaev, a tall, thin, fair-haired man with a sentimental expression and long, straight hair. The jury consisted entirely of shopkeepers and peasants, only four of whom were literate, and the rest, when they were given

* A role certainly more suited to Kamyshev than that of investigator: he could not have been an investigating magistrate in the Urbenin case. A. C.

Urbenin's letters to his wife to read, broke into a sweat and became confused. The foreman of the jury was the shopkeeper Ivan Demyanych, the same person from whom my late parrot got its name.

When I entered the courtroom I didn't recognize Urbenin: he had gone completely grey and had aged about twenty years. I had expected to read on his face indifference to his fate, and apathy, but I was wrong: Urbenin took a passionate interest in the proceedings. He challenged three of the jurors, embarked on lengthy explanations and questioned witnesses. He categorically denied his guilt and spent ages questioning every witness who did not testify in his favour.

The witness Pshekhotsky testified that I had been living with the late Olga.

'That's a lie!' Urbenin shouted. 'He's a liar! I don't trust my own wife, but I do trust *him*!'

When I was giving evidence the counsel for the defence questioned me as to my relationship with Olga and acquainted me with evidence given by Pshekhotsky, who had once applauded me. To have told the truth would have amounted to testifying in favour of the accused. The more depraved a wife, the more lenient juries tend to be towards an Othello-husband – that I understood very well. On the other hand, my telling the truth would have deeply wounded Urbenin – on hearing it he would have suffered incurable pain. I thought it best to tell a lie.

'No!' I said.

Describing Olga's murder in the most lurid colours, the public prosecutor paid particular attention in his speech to the murderer's brutality, his wickedness. 'An old roué sees a pretty, young girl. Aware of the whole horror of her situation in her insane father's house, he tempts her with food, lodgings and brightly decorated rooms. She agrees: an elderly husband of means is easier to bear than a mad father and poverty. But she was young – and youth, gentlemen of the jury, has its own inalienable rights. A girl who has been weaned on novels, brought up in the midst of Nature, is bound to fall in love sooner or later ...' The upshot of all this was:

'He, having given her nothing but his age and brightly

coloured dresses and seeing his booty slipping away from him, became as frenzied as an animal that has had a red-hot iron applied to its snout. He loved like an animal, therefore he must have hated like one', and so on.

When he accused Urbenin of Kuzma's murder, Polugradov singled out 'those villainous tricks, so cleverly devised and calculated, that accompanied the murder of a sleeping man who had been imprudent enough the day before to testify against him. I assume that there is no doubt in your minds that Kuzma wanted to tell the prosecutor something that directly concerned him.'

Smirnyaev, counsel for the defence, did not deny Urbenin's guilt: he only asked that the fact that Urbenin had acted under the influence of temporary insanity should be taken into account and that therefore they should be lenient. Describing how painful feelings of jealousy can be, he alluded to Shakespeare's Othello as evidence for his deposition. He examined this 'universal type' from all aspects, quoting from various critics, and he got himself in such a muddle that the presiding judge was obliged to stop him by remarking that 'a knowledge of foreign literature was not obligatory for jurors'.

Taking advantage of this last statement, Urbenin called on God to witness that he was guilty in neither word nor deed.

'Personally, it's all the same where I end up – in this district where everything reminds me of my undeserved disgrace and my wife, or in a penal colony. But I'm deeply concerned about my children's fate.'

Turning to the public he burst into tears and begged for his children to be taken into care:

'Take them! Of course, the Count won't miss the opportunity of flaunting his magnanimity. But I've already warned the children and they won't accept one crumb from him.'

When he noticed me among the public he glanced at me imploringly. 'Please protect my children from the Count's good deeds,' he said.

Evidently he had forgotten all about the impending verdict and his thoughts were completely taken up with his children. He kept talking about them until he was stopped by the presiding judge.

The jury did not take long to reach a verdict. Urbenin was found guilty unconditionally and was not recommended for leniency on a single count. He was sentenced to loss of all civil rights and fifteen years' hard labour.

So dearly did that meeting on a May morning with the romantic 'girl in red' cost him.

More than eight years have passed since the events described above. Some of the actors in the drama have departed this world and have already rotted away, others are suffering punishment for their sins, others are dragging out their lives, struggling with the tedium of a pedestrian existence and expecting death from day to day.

Much has changed during eight years. Count Karneyev, who never stopped entertaining the most sincere friendship for me, has finally become a hopeless drunkard. His estate – the scene of the crime – has passed from his hands into those of his wife and Pshekhotsky. He's poor now and I support him. Some evenings, when he's lying on the sofa in my flat, he loves to reminisce about the old times.

'It would be nice to listen to the gipsies now,' he mutters. 'Send for some brandy, Seryozha!'

I too have changed. My strength is gradually deserting me and I feel that my health and youth are abandoning my body. No longer do I have the physical strength, the agility, the stamina that I took so much pride in flaunting at one time, when I didn't go to bed for several nights running and drank quantities of alcohol that I could barely cope with now.

One after the other, wrinkles are appearing, my hair is going thin, my voice is growing coarser and weaker . . . Life is over . . .

I remember the past as if it were yesterday. I see places and have visions of people as if they were in a mist. I do not have the strength to view them impartially: I love and hate them as violently, as intensely as before, and not a day passes without my clutching my head in a fit of indignation or hatred. For me, the Count is as loathsome as ever, Olga revolting, Kalinin plain ridiculous with his stupid conceit. Evil I consider evil, sin I consider sin.

Yet there are often moments when I stare at the portrait that stands on my writing table and I feel an irresistible urge to go walking with the 'girl in red' in the forest, to the murmur of lofty pines, and to press her to my breast, despite everything. At these moments I forgive both her lies and that decline into the murky abyss: I am ready in forgive everything – if only a tiny fragment of the past could be repeated. Wearied by the boredom of the town, I would like to listen once more to the roar of the giant lake and gallop along its banks on my Zorka. I would forgive and forget everything if I could once again stroll along the road to Tenevo and meet Franz the gardener with his vodka barrel and jockey cap. There are moments when I'm even ready to shake that hand which is crimson with blood, discuss religion, the harvest, popular education with that good-natured Pyotr Yegorych. I would like to meet Screwy and his Nadenka again.

Life is as frantic, dissolute and as restless as that lake on an August night. Many victims have vanished beneath its dark waves for ever . . . A thick sediment lies at the bottom. But why are there times when I love life? Why do I forgive it and rush towards it with all my heart, like a loving son, like a bird released from its cage?

The life that I see now through the window of my hotel room reminds me of a grey circle – totally grey, with no shades, no glimmer of light.

But if I close my eyes and recall the past I see a rainbow formed by the sun's spectrum. Yes, it's stormy there – yet there it's brighter . . .

S. Zinovyev.

Conclusion

Under the manuscript is written:

> Dear Mr Editor,
> I would request you to print the novel (or novella if you prefer) that I am offering without any abridgements, cuts or additions – as far as possible. However, any changes can be made with the author's agreement. In the event of this novel being unsuitable I request you to return the manuscript safely. My temporary Moscow address is the England Rooms in Tversky Street c/o Ivan Petrovich Kamyshev.
> PS Fees: at the editors' discretion.
> Year and date

And now that I have acquainted the reader with Kamyshev's novel, I shall continue my interrupted conversation with him. Above all, I must warn the reader that the promise I gave him at the beginning of the story has not been kept: Kamyshev's novel has not been printed without omissions, not *in toto*, as I had promised, but with substantial cuts. The fact is, *The Shooting Party* could not be printed in the newspaper mentioned in the first chapter of this story: that newspaper had ceased to exist when the manuscript went to press. The present editorial board, having taken Kamyshev's novel under their wing, have found it impossible to print without cuts. Throughout the printing they kept sending me proofs of individual chapters, with requests for amendments. As I did not wish to be guilty of the sin of tampering with someone else's work, I found it more expedient and prudent to omit entire passages rather than amend unsuitable ones. With my agreement, the editors omitted many passages that were striking in their cynicism, longueurs and slovenly style. These omissions and cuts called for care and time, which is the reason why many chapters were late. Among other things we have omitted two descriptions of nocturnal orgies. One of these took place in the Count's house, the other on the lake. The description of Polikarp's library and his original manner of reading have also been omitted. This passage was found to be far too drawn out and exaggerated.

The chapter that I defended above all others – and which the editorial office disliked most – was that which described the desperate card games that used to rage among the Count's servants. The most fanatical players were Franz the gardener and the old crone called Owlet. They played mainly *stukolka* and *three leaves*.[55] At the time of the investigation, when Kamyshev happened to be walking past one of the summer-houses and took a look inside, he saw a crazy game of cards in progress – the players were Owlet and Pshekhotsky. They were playing *blind stukolka*, with stakes of ninety copecks and forfeits of as much as thirty roubles. Kamyshev joined them and 'plucked them clean', like partridges. Having lost all his money, Franz wanted to carry on and went to the lake where his money was hidden. Kamyshev followed his tracks, took note of the hiding place and cleaned him out, not leaving him with one copeck. He gave the stolen money to Mikhey the fisherman. This peculiar benevolence provides an excellent character sketch of that hare-brained investigator, but it is described so carelessly and the card players' conversation glitters with such pearls of obscenity that the editors would not even agree to changes.

Several descriptions of Olga's meetings with Kamyshev have been omitted. One of his intimate conversations with Nadenka Kalinin has also been left out, and so on . . . But I think that what *has* been printed sums up my hero pretty well. *Sapienti sat.*[56]

Exactly three months later the janitor at the editorial offices announced the arrival of the 'gentleman with the badge'.

'Ask him to come in,' I said.

In came Kamyshev, just as rosy-cheeked, healthy and handsome as three months before. His footsteps were just as silent.

He placed his hat so carefully on the windowsill that you might have thought he was depositing something very weighty. As before, there shone something childlike and infinitely good-natured in his blue eyes.

'I'm disturbing you again!' he began, smiling and gingerly sitting down. 'For heaven's sake, forgive me! Well? What's the verdict on my manuscript?'

'Guilty, but recommended for mercy,' I said.

Kamyshev burst out laughing and blew his nose on a scented handkerchief. 'So that means banishment to the flames of the fireplace?' he asked.

'No, why so severe? It does not deserve any punitive measures – we shall employ *corrective* ones.'

'So, it needs correcting?' he asked.

'Yes, there's one or two things . . . by mutual consent.'

We said nothing for a quarter of an hour. My heart was pounding and my temples throbbed. But it wasn't part of my strategy to show alarm.

'By mutual consent,' I repeated. 'Last time you told me that you took a real event for the plot of your novel.'

'Yes – and now I'm ready to say it again. If you had read my novel . . . then . . . I have the honour to introduce myself: Zinovyev.'

'So, you were best man at Olga Nikolayevna's wedding?'

'Best man and friend of the family. Don't I appear in a good light in this novel?' Kamyshev laughed, stroking his knee and blushing. 'A really nice chap, eh? I should have been flogged, but there was no one to do it.'

'Exactly . . . Well, I like your story. It's better and more interesting than the vast majority of crime novels these days. However, you and I, by mutual consent, will need to make some substantial changes in it.'

'That's possible. What do you think needs changing, for example?'

'The very *habitus*[57] of the novel, its physiognomy. In common with most crime novels it has everything: a crime, evidence, investigations – even fifteen years' hard labour as a titbit. But the most essential thing's missing.'

'And what precisely is that?'

'There's no real villain in it.'

Kamyshev opened his eyes wide and stood up.

'Frankly, I don't understand you,' he said after a brief pause. 'If you don't consider the man who did the stabbing and strangling the true culprit then ... I really don't know who should be considered guilty. Of course, criminals are products of society – and society is guilty. But if you take a more elevated point of view, one should give up writing novels and compile reports.'

'What have "elevated points of view" to do with it? It wasn't Urbenin who committed the murder!!'

'What did you say?' Kamyshev asked, moving closer to me.

'It wasn't Urbenin!'

'That may well be ... *humanum est errare*[58] – and investigators aren't perfect. Judicial errors are quite common under the moon. So, you think I was mistaken?'

'No, you were not mistaken, but you wanted to be.'

'I'm sorry, but again I don't follow,' Kamyshev laughed. 'If you find that the investigation led to an error and even an intentional mistake – if I understand you right – it would be interesting to have your views on the matter. In your opinion, who was the murderer?'

'You!!'

Kamyshev looked at me in astonishment, almost in terror, flushed and took a step backwards. Then he turned away, went to the window and started laughing.

'Now, here's a pretty kettle of fish!' he muttered, breathing on the window pane and nervously tracing patterns on it.

I watched his hand as he drew and I seemed to recognize in it that same iron, muscular hand that alone could have throttled the sleeping Kuzma or lacerated Olga's frail body at one attempt. The thought that I was looking at the murderer filled me with an unusual feeling of horror and dread – not for myself – no! but for *him*, for that handsome and graceful giant ... for mankind in general.

'*You* were the murderer!' I repeated.

'If this isn't a joke, then I congratulate you on the discovery!'

laughed Kamyshev, still not looking at me. 'However, judging from your trembling voice and your pale face, it's difficult to conclude that you're joking. Heavens, you're so jumpy!'

Kamyshev turned his burning face to me and tried to force a smile.

'I'm curious to know,' he continued, 'how such ideas could have entered your head. Did I write anything of the sort in my novel? By God, this is really interesting! Please tell me! Once in a lifetime it's worth experiencing the sensation of being looked upon as a murderer . . .'

'*You're* the murderer,' I said, 'and you can't even conceal the fact. In your novel you gave yourself away and now you're putting on a pathetic act.'

'That's really quite fascinating – I'd be interested to hear – word of honour!'

'If it's interesting, then listen!'

I jumped up and walked excitedly around the room. Kamyshev looked behind the door and made sure it was properly shut. By this precaution he gave himself away.

'What are you afraid of?' I asked.

Kamyshev gave an embarrassed cough and waved his arm.

'I'm not afraid of anything, I was just looking around the door. What do you want from me now? Come on, tell me.'

'Allow me to question you.'

'As much as you like.'

'I'm warning you that I'm no investigating magistrate and no expert in cross-examination. Don't expect any method or system, but please don't try and confuse and muddle me. Firstly, please tell me where you disappeared to after you left the edge of the forest, where you were boozing after the shoot.'

'It says in the story – I went home.'

'In the story the description of the path you took is carefully crossed out. Didn't you go through the forest?'

'Yes, I did.'

'Therefore you could have met Olga there?'

'Yes, I could,' Kamyshev laughed.

'And you *did* meet her.'

'No, I didn't meet her.'

'At the inquiry you forgot to mention one very important witness, namely yourself. Did you hear the victim's shrieks?'

'No . . . now look here, old chap, you haven't a clue about cross-examining.'

This overfamiliar 'old chap' really jarred on me. It was quite out of keeping with the apologies and embarrassment with which the conversation had begun. I soon noticed that Kamyshev was looking at me condescendingly, arrogantly and was almost revelling in my inability to disentangle myself from the mass of questions that were plaguing me.

'Let's assume that you didn't meet Olga in the forest,' I continued, 'although in fact it was harder for Urbenin to meet Olga than for you, since Urbenin didn't know she was in the forest. Therefore he wasn't looking for her. But since you were drunk and in a mad frenzy, you couldn't fail to look for her. And look for her you certainly did, otherwise why did you have to go home through the forest and not along the main road? But let's suppose you didn't see her. In that case how can one explain your grim, almost demented state of mind on the evening of that fateful day? What prompted you to kill the parrot that kept squawking about the husband who murdered his wife? I think that it reminded you of your evil deed. That night you were summoned to the Count's house and instead of getting down to business right away, you delayed things until the police arrived almost a whole twenty-four hours later and you probably weren't even aware of it. Only investigators who already know the identity of the criminal delay like that. He was known to you . . . Further, Olga didn't reveal the murderer's name because he was dear to her. If her *husband* had been the murderer she would have named him. Had she been in a position to denounce him to her lover-Count, then she would have lost nothing by accusing him of murder. She did not love him and he wasn't in the least dear to her. She loved you, it was *you* who were dear to her. Also, permit me to ask why you took your time asking her questions that were to the point when she momentarily regained consciousness? Why did you ask her completely irrelevant questions? Let's suppose that you did all this as a delaying tactic, to prevent her from naming you. Meanwhile Olga was dying. In your novel you haven't written one word about the effect of her death on you. There I can detect caution: you don't forget to mention the number of glasses you managed to empty, but an important event such as the death of the "girl in red" vanishes without trace in the novel. Why?'

'Go on, go on.'

'And you conducted the investigation in the most disgracefully slapdash way. It's difficult to accept the fact that a clever and extremely cunning person like yourself didn't do this on purpose. Your entire investigation reminds one of a letter written with deliberate grammatical mistakes . . . all this exaggeration gives you away. Why didn't you inspect the scene of the crime? It wasn't because you forgot to or considered it unimportant, but because you waited for the rain to wash away your tracks. You say little about the servants' cross-examination. Therefore Kuzma wasn't cross-examined by you until you caught him washing that coat. Obviously there was no need for you to involve him. Why didn't you question the guests who had been carousing with you on the forest's edge? They had seen the bloodstained Urbenin and heard Olga's shrieks – so you should have questioned them. But this you did not do, in case one of them remembered during the inquiry that shortly before the murder you had disappeared into the forest. They were probably questioned later, but by then this circumstance had already been forgotten by them.'

'Very clever!' Kamyshev said, rubbing his hands. 'Please do go on!'

'Surely all that's been said is enough for you? To establish beyond all doubt that Olga was murdered by you, I must again remind you that you were her lover, a lover who was replaced by a man you detested! A husband can kill from jealousy and I assume a lover can do likewise. Now, let's turn to Kuzma. Judging from the last cross-examination that took place on the eve of his death, he had *you* in mind. You wiped your hands on his coat and called him "drunken swine". If it wasn't you, then why did you conclude the interrogation at the most interesting point? Why didn't you inquire about the colour of the murderer's tie when Kuzma told you that he remembered what colour it was? Why did you give Urbenin his freedom at the precise moment when Kuzma remembered the name of the murderer? Why not earlier? Why not later? It was obvious you needed a scapegoat, someone to wander down the corridor at night. Therefore you murdered Kuzma because you were afraid he might testify against you.'

'That's enough!' laughed Kamyshev. 'Enough! You've got yourself so worked up and you've turned so pale, you look as if you're about to faint any minute. Please stop now. In fact you're right. *I* was the murderer.'

There was silence. I paced from corner to corner. Kamyshev did the same.

'I committed the murders,' Kamyshev went on. 'You've scored a bull's eye! Congratulations! Not many people could manage that – more than half your readers will be damning old Urbenin and be dazzled by my investigatory brilliance!'

Just then one of my colleagues came into the office and interrupted our conversation. Noticing that I was very preoccupied and excited, he hovered around my table, looked quizzically at Kamyshev and went out. After he had gone Kamyshev stepped over to the window and started breathing on the glass.

'Eight years have passed since then,' he resumed after a brief silence, 'and for eight years I've been carrying this secret around with me. But secrets and living blood cannot coexist in the same organism. One cannot know what the rest of humanity does *not* know without suffering for it. Throughout these eight years I've felt like a martyr. It was not my conscience that tormented me – no! Conscience is something apart and I don't take any notice of it. It can be easily stifled by arguing how accommodating it can be. When reason doesn't function I deaden my conscience with wine and women. With women I am as successful as ever, but that's by the by. However, something else was tormenting me: all that time I thought it strange that people should look upon me as an ordinary individual. Throughout those entire eight years not once has a single soul ever given me a questioning look. I thought it strange that I didn't need to hide away. There was a terrible secret lurking within me – and suddenly there I was, walking down the street, attending dinners, parties, flirting with women! For one guilty of a crime such a situation is unnatural and distressing. I wouldn't have suffered so much if I'd simply had to hide and dissemble. Mine is a psychosis, old man! Finally, I was gripped by a kind of passion . . . I suddenly wanted to unburden myself somehow – to sneeze on everyone's head, to blurt out my secret to everyone, to do something of that sort, something *special*. And so I wrote this story, a document in which only a fool would have difficulty in seeing that I'm a man with a secret. There isn't one page that doesn't give a clue to the solution. Isn't that so? I dare say you realized that at once. When I was writing it I took the average reader's level of intelligence into consideration.'

Once again we were interrupted. Andrey entered with two glasses of tea on a tray. I hastily sent him away.

'And now everything seems easier,' Kamyshev laughed. 'You look at me now as if I'm someone out of the ordinary, as if I'm a man with a secret – and *I* feel my situation is perfectly normal! But it's already three o'clock and they're waiting for me in the cab.'

'Stop . . . put your hat down . . . You told me what prompted you to become an author. Now tell me how you came to commit the murder.'

'Would you like to know that, as a supplement to what you've read? All right . . . I murdered in a mad fit of passion. Nowadays people smoke and drink tea under the influence of fits of passion. Just now you got so worked up you picked up my glass instead of yours – and you're smoking more than you did before. Life is one continuous aberration – that's how it strikes me. When I went into the forest thoughts of murder were far from my mind. I was going there with only one purpose: to find Olga and carry on hurting her. When I'm drunk I always feel the need to hurt people. I met her about two hundred paces from the forest edge. She was standing under a tree, gazing pensively at the sky. I called out to her . . . when she saw me she smiled and stretched her arms out. "Don't be hard on me," she said. "I'm so unhappy."

That evening she looked so lovely that, drunk as I was, I forgot everything in the world and firmly embraced her. She vowed that she had never loved anyone but me – and that was true: she *did* love me. And at the height of her vows she suddenly took it into her head to utter the hateful phrase: "I'm so unhappy! If I hadn't married Urbenin I could marry the Count right now!" For me this phrase was like a bucket of cold water. All that had been seething within me suddenly erupted. Seized by a feeling of revulsion and despair, I grasped that small, loathsome creature by the shoulder and threw her to the ground as if she were a ball. My anger had reached boiling point. Well, I finished her . . . I just went and finished her . . . Now you'll understand what happened with Kuzma.'

I glanced at Kamyshev. On his face I could detect neither remorse nor regret. 'I just went and finished her' was said as nonchalantly as 'I just smoked a cigarette'. And I in turn was gripped by a feeling of anger and revulsion. I turned away.

'And is this Urbenin doing hard labour in Siberia now?' I quickly asked.

'Well, they say he died on the way, but it hasn't been confirmed yet. What of it?'

'I'll tell you what. An innocent man has suffered and all you can say is "What of it?" '

'But what should I do? Go and confess?'

'I suppose so.'

'Well, let's suppose so! I'm not averse to taking Urbenin's place, but I won't give in without a struggle. Let them come and take me if they want, but I shan't go and give myself up. Why didn't they take me when I was in their hands? I howled so loudly at Olga's funeral, I became so hysterical that even a blind man must have spotted the truth . . . It's not my fault that they're so stupid.'

'I find you perfectly loathsome,' I said.

'That's only natural . . . I'm loathsome to myself.'

Silence followed. I opened the cash ledger and mechanically started totting up some figures. Kamyshev reached for his hat.

'I see you find it stuffy in here with me,' he said. 'By the way, would you care to see Count Karneyev? He's outside sitting in the cab.'

I went to the window and looked out. With his back towards us there he sat, a small, hunched figure in a shabby hat and faded collar. It was hard to recognize him as one of the leading characters in the drama!

'I've heard that Urbenin's son is living here in Moscow, in Andreyev's Chambers,' Kamyshev said. 'I want to arrange for the Count to receive a little "offering" from him . . . Let at least one of them be punished! However, I must bid you *adieu*!'

Kamyshev nodded and hurried out of the room. I sat at the table and gave myself up to bitter thoughts.

I felt suffocated.

Notes

1. *Spencer*: Herbert Spencer (1820–1903), English sociologist and biologist. In his *Education: Intellectual, Moral, Physical* (1861), he championed the many-sided development of man, giving special emphasis to physical education. Chekhov mentions him often and in a letter to Aleksandr Chekhov (17/18 April 1883) praises the chapter dealing with moral education.
2. '*sweet sounds*' in words: Periphrasis of last words of Pushkin's famous *Poet and the Crowd* (1829):

   We are born for inspiration
   For sweet sounds and prayers.

3. *Gaboriau*: Emile Gaboriau (1832–73), originator of crime novel (*roman policier*) in France, whose detective Monsieur Lecoq was a forerunner of Sherlock Holmes. His thrillers – they first appeared as feuilletons – include *Monsieur Lecoq* (1869): extremely popular in Russia, it appeared in Russian translation in the year of its publication. His other main detective novels are *L'Affaire Lerouge* (1865–6); *Le Crime d'Orcival* (1867); and *Le Dossier no. 113* (1867). The young Maxim Gorky was acquainted with the French writer, whom he avidly read – along with others such as Dumas *père* (*My Apprenticeship*, Harmondsworth, 1974).
4. *Shklyarevsky*: A. A. Shklyarevsky (1837–83), Russian author of detective novels and known as the 'Russian Gaboriau'. His main novels are: *Tales of an Investigating Magistrate* (1872) and *The Unsolved Crime* (1878). For details of the current vogue for detective novels see A Note on the Text, p. xx.
5. *sui generis*: Unique.
6. *Lecoq*: See note 3.

7. *The Count of Monte Cristo*: By Alexandre Dumas (Dumas *père*, 1802–70), highly popular novel (1844–5) of betrayal and vengeance. In a letter of 28 May 1892 to Suvorin, Chekhov writes: 'What shall I do with Monte Cristo? I've abridged it until it resembles someone suffering from typhus. The first part – until the Count becomes rich – is very interesting and well written, but the second (with few exceptions) is unbearable, since Monte-Christo performs and speaks inflated nonsense. But on the whole the novel is quite effective.' In 1892 Suvorin intended publishing an abridged version of the novel, on which Chekhov worked May/June that year.
8. *Auguste Comte*: French mathematician and philosopher (1798–1857), founder of Positivism. His *Cours de philosophie positive* (1830–42) expounds a religion of humanity.
9. *you*: Actually the familiar form in Russian = 'thou'.
10. *Riga balsam*: A kind of brandy, usually black, distilled with herbs.
11. *Eynem's*: famous Moscow shop selling biscuits and preserves.
12. *Leporello*: Faithful servant and confidant of Don Juan, hero of Pushkin's *Stone Guest* (1830).
13. *stukolka*: A popular card game of the time.
14. *The Cornfield* (*Niva*): A popular illustrated family magazine published in St Petersburg (1870–1918).
15. '*I lo-ove the storms of early Ma-ay*': The first line of the poem *Spring Storm* (1829) by Fyodor Tyutchev (1803–73). It was set to music by many composers.
16. *one of Born's books*: Pseudonym of Georg Fülleborn (1837–1902), highly prolific German novelist, author of cheap 'boulevard' novels. His *Eugene, or Secrets of the French Court* was published in Russian translation in 1882.
17. *Yevtushevsky's Mathematics Problem Book*: A collection of arithmetical problems by A. A. Yevtushevsky (1836–88).
18. *The Task*: Literary-political journal, published in St Petersburg (1866–88).
19. *Miscellany*: A literary miscellany published in St Petersburg in 1874 for the benefit of famine sufferers in Samara district. It comprised minor works by Turgenev, Dostoyevsky, Ostrovsky, Goncharov and others.
20. '*pitcher-snouts*': Reference to Gogol's clerk Ivan Antonovich in *Dead Souls* (1848), whose face appeared to have turned into one enormous nose: '. . . the whole of the middle of his face stuck out and looked like a nose – briefly, it was the kind of face commonly called pitcher-snout' (chap. 7).

21. *Mount Athos*: Athos – a Greek peninsula in Chalcidice (Macedonia), with numerous monasteries and churches, the object of pilgrimages since the eleventh century.
22. *English bitters*: Liquor with bitter flavour used for mixing with cocktails.
23. *Depré's*: Well-known wine shop in Moscow.
24. '*Ah, Moscow, Moscow . . . stone walls*': From the well-known folk song.
25. '*Down Mo-other Volga . . . Vo-olga*': Famous folk song.
26. '*Oh burn, oh speak . . . speak!*': Refrain from folk dance song, 'See the young dandy strutting down the street.'
27. '*Nights of madness, nights of gladness*': Inaccurate quotation from the poem *Nights of madness, sleepless nights* (1886) by A. N. Apukhtin (1841–93). It was set to music by Tchaikovsky and others. In the 1880s it became a very popular gipsy romance, with various musical settings. The second line runs: 'Wild words, tired glances . . .'
28. *Shandor candle*: A heavy candlestick.
29. *ad patres*: (Lat.) to his forefathers – i.e. he died.
30. *terra incognita*: (Lat.) unknown territory. Latin and French tags occur frequently in Chekhov's earlier stories.
31. *Themis*: Greek goddess of justice and law.
32. *casus belli*: (Lat.) an act or situation provoking war.
33. *beau monde*: Fashionable society.
34. *sinister old crones*: Words spoken by Chatsky, hero of A. S. Griboyedov's comedy *Woe from Wit* (1822–4).
35. *A kind of Onegin*: Reference to the disenchanted hero of Pushkin's *Eugene Onegin* (1831). One of the first exemplars of the Superfluous Man in Russian literature, disillusioned and at odds with society.
36. *Homo sum*: (Lat.) possible reference to the Roman playwright Terence: *Homo sum; humani nil a me alienum puto* (I am a man, I count nothing human indifferent to me).
37. *Pukirev's picture*: The painting referred to is *Misalliance* (1862), by V. V. Pukirev (1832–90), a savage denunciation of women's lack of rights and of the treatment of marriage as a commercial transaction. The painting had far-reaching social repercussions.
38. *bon vivant*: Person indulging in good living.
39. *He was as impressive as forty thousand best men put together*: A humorous periphrasis of Hamlet's words after Ophelia's death:

I lov'd Ophelia. Forty thousand brothers
Could not with all their quantity of love
Make up my sum.
Hamlet, Act V, Scene 1

. In his early stories Chekhov liked to refer to this 'forty thousand' in a humorous context, for example in 'Night in a Cemetery' (1886) where he writes: '... I got as drunk as forty thousand brothers.'

40. *Like Risler Senior in Alphonse Daudet's novel*: The novel is *Fromont jeune et Risler Aîné* (1874), which tells of a senile, wealthy proprietor of a Paris wallpaper factory marrying a young girl.
41. *Krylov's fable*: Reference to *Hermit and Bear* (1804) by I. A. Krylov (1769–1844). In this fable a bear befriends a hermit, who when sleeping is pestered by a fly. When all other efforts to drive it away have failed, the despairing bear hurls a rock at it, thus smashing his friend's skull. Chekhov frequently refers to Krylov's fables.
42. *infusoria*: A class of Protozoa, so called because they are found in infusions of decaying animal or vegetable matter.
43. *jeune premier*: Leading man/character.
44. *like Pushkin's Tatyana*: The heroine of *Eugene Onegin* who thrusts her love upon the uninterested, blasé hero.
45. '*your hand in mine*': Line from aria in Act 4 of Borodin's opera, *Prince Igor*.
46. *nolens volens*: (Lat.) willy-nilly, perforce.
47. *barely time to wear out her wedding shoes*: Periphrasis of words spoken by Hamlet, in A. Kroneberg's Russian translation. The actual lines are:

... or ere those shoes were old
With which she follow'd my poor father's body
Like Niobe, all tears.
Hamlet, Act I, Scene 2

48. *She's in a hurry to live!*: Possibly a reference to *First Snow* (1819), by Pushkin's close friend Prince P. A. Vyazemsky (1792–1878). The epigraph to Chapter 1 of *Eugene Onegin* runs: 'He hurries to live and hastens to feel.'
49. *tussore*: A strong, coarse silk made in India.
50. *Nevsky Prospekt*: Famous thoroughfare in St Petersburg, running

for about two and a half miles from the Admiralty to the Aleksandr Nevsky Monastery.

51. *'As Hamlet . . . the sin of suicide'*: The actual lines are:

> Or that the Everlasting had not fix'd
> His canon 'gainst self-slaughter!
>
> *Hamlet*, Act I, Scene 2

Chekhov often quotes from *Hamlet* in his stories.

52. *Hofman drops*: In a letter of 20 June 1891 to Lidiya Mizinova (who was not well) Chekhov writes (after giving dietary advice): 'Take something bitter before food: Hofman's elixir (*Elixir visceralis Hofmani*) or tincture of quinine.' And in a letter to his sister Masha of 23/24 July 1897 he writes: 'Tell Mother if she has dizzy spells to take 15 Hofman drops at a time.'
53. *à la Le Coq*: See note 3.
54. *of Gaboriau and our own Shklyarevsky*: See notes 3 and 4.
55. *three leaves*: Like *stukolka* (see note 13), a popular card game.
56. *Sapienti sat*: (Lat.) enough for a wise man.
57. *habitus*: (Lat.) general aspect.
58. *humanum est errare*: (Lat.) to err is human.